The Earl's Bargain...

The impossibly young, stunningly beautiful widow Louisa
Phillips finds herself penniless upon the death of her no-good
husband. What's a man-hating bluestocking to do?

Enter the Earl of Wycliff, who offers her financial security
for life. All she has to do is travel across England posing as
his wife. They're both hiding secrets – not the least of which
is their budding love for each other.

Some of the praise for Cheryl Bolen's writing:

"One of the best authors in the Regency romance field today." – *Huntress Reviews*

"Bolen's writing has a certain elegance that lends itself to the era and creates the perfect atmosphere for her enchanting romances." – *RT Book Reviews*

The Earl's Bargain
Finalist, Best Historical Novel, International Digital Awards, 2012.

My Lord Wicked
Winner, Best Historical Novel, International Digital Awards, 2012.

The Bride Wore Blue (Brides of Bath, Book 1)
Cheryl Bolen returns to the Regency England she knows so well. . .If you love a steamy Regency with a fast pace, be sure to pick up *The Bride Wore Blue*. – *Happily Ever After*

With His Ring (Brides of Bath, Book 2)
"Cheryl Bolen does it again! There is laughter, and the interaction of the characters pulls you right into the book. I look forward to the next in this series." – *RT Book Reviews*

The Bride's Secret (Brides of Bath, Book 3)
"*W*hat we all want from a love story...Don't miss it!"
– *In Print*

To Take This Lord (Brides of Bath, Book 4)
"Bolen does a wonderful job building simmering sexual tension between her opinionated, outspoken heroine and deliciously tortured, conflicted hero." – *Booklist of the American Library Association*

Also by Cheryl Bolen

Regency Romance

The Brides of Bath Series:
The Bride Wore Blue
With His Ring
The Bride's Secret
To Take This Lord
Love In The Library

The Regent Mysteries Series:
With His Lady's Assistance (Book 1)
A Most Discreet Inquiry (Book 2)
The Theft Before Christmas (Book 3)

The Earl's Bargain
My Lord Wicked
A Lady by Chance
His Lordship's Vow
A Duke Deceived
One Golden Ring
Counterfeit Countess

Novellas:
Lady Sophia's Rescue
Christmas Brides (3 Regency Novellas)

Inspirational Regency Romance

Marriage of Inconvenience

Romantic Suspense

Texas Heroines in Peril Series:
    Protecting Britannia
    Capitol Offense
    A Cry in the Night
    Murder at Veranda House

Falling for Frederick

American Historical Romance

A Summer to Remember (3 American Historical Romances)

World War II Romance

It Had to be You

THE EARL'S BARGAIN

CHERYL BOLEN

Harper & Appleton

$\mathscr{P}$rologue
London, 1818

An austere butler with sunken eyes and hollow cheeks let Godwin Phillips into Tremaine House and silently led him through a darkened hallway to the morning room. This chamber was only dimly lit through a gap in the faded velvet draping a tall window which gave on to Queen Street. Never would Godwin understand the ways of the nobility. Lord Tremaine had money to burn, yet he kept his town house completely shut up most of the year and on the rare occasions when he was in residence was too miserly to light fires. Godwin was most appreciative the butler had not asked to take his coat for he was rather glad to keep it on in the dank, musty house.

Lord Tremaine did not trouble himself to stand when Phillips entered the room, nor did Godwin expect such courtesy. He was, after all, merely a hireling of sorts to the eccentric peer.

From behind the French writing desk, Tremaine appraised his caller a moment before addressing him. "I see you continue to prosper. Weston?"

Godwin nodded. Only the best tailor would do. He had developed exceptional taste since he had begun his association with Lord Tremaine, who had honed the occupational skills for which Godwin already showed an aptitude. And now, at age fifty, Godwin was finally on the cusp of living the life he had always sought.

"Well, well," Tremaine said, leaning his own frail body back in his once-luxurious tufted velvet chair, not removing his gaze from Godwin. "I understand you have been admitted to Waiters?"

"Why, yes," Godwin said, peering suspiciously at Tremaine from beneath lowered brows.

"Did it not strike you as being exceedingly simple to be accorded membership?"

His eyes widened. "You used your influence?"

"Surely you did not hope to gain membership into one of London's most exclusive clubs on your own questionable merit?" Tremaine smiled. Not a smile of mirth, but a smug, conspiratorial grin. "As it happens, membership in that establishment is also enjoyed by your next . . .how shall I say it? Lamb?"

"Indeed?"

The gray-haired baron nodded as he watched Godwin. "The Earl of Wycliff."

"I see." Godwin's mouth was a taut line.

"Already I have *adjusted* his stocks. Lord Wycliff has lost Cartmore Hall in Sussex." Tremaine's mouth tweaked into a sinister smile as he spoke of destroying another man.

What had Wycliff done to ignite Tremaine's hatred? Godwin would take care to never earn Tremaine's wrath. "Anything else, your lordship?" He was particularly anxious to know what would be his reward for causing a man's ruin.

"If you are successful, we will gain Wycliff House in Grosvenor Square. How would you and the young lady you're about to wed enjoy living in one of the finest houses in London?"

How had he learned about Louisa? "I should like it very much, my lord."

"Then you know what to do." Tremaine put his elbows on the dusty desk, a smile curving his lips. "Shall it be pasteboards or dice?"

"I think the pasteboards."

$\mathcal{C}$hapter 1
London, 1826

The scalloped rows of brilliant diamonds and emeralds laced through the long, manly fingers of Harold Blassingame, the seventh Earl of Wycliff. A lump balled in his throat as he remembered how the necklace had looked on his mother, whose beauty stilled eight years previously. Oddly, recovering the Wycliff Jewels did not bring the triumph he had expected. Even the recovery of Cartmore Hall from nearly a decade in a usurper's possession had left Harry wanting. Vindication of the Wycliffs would not be complete until he regained Wycliff House in Grosvenor Square.

Edward Coke, the cousin who was as close to Harry as a brother, planted one booted foot on the Jacobean desk that separated the two young men. "How many quid to persuade Livingston to part with Aunt Isobel's jewels?"

Harry eyed Edward, a somber look in his black eyes. "Twice what Rundel & Bridge would have valued them."

His cousin winced. "Daresay Livingston knew you'd have come up with ten times the amount, though I bloody well don't know how he learned of your fat purse. 'Twas common knowledge when you left England eight years ago that Uncle

Robert had left you penniless."

"The fact that I did not balk at Kindale's asking price for Cartmore Hall has no doubt carried through London like leaves scattering on the wind," Harry said.

"The Hall I can understand. Deuced fine stables you've got there, but to spend such blunt on some bloody stones?" Edward shook his closely cropped head of blond hair before leaning forward to pluck the Wycliff wedding ring from a heap of sparkling jewels on the desk. "Think you to find a suitable young lady to wear this, Harry?" He slid the emerald encrusted band on his pinky finger, but it stopped well short of his bony knuckle.

Harry shrugged. How could he tell Edward his reasons for returning to England? How could anyone else understand the magnetic pull of the land that had been in his family for three-hundred years? How could he explain his need to restore the family's good name or his need for a family? And a wife.

But as his tracks to redemption grew steadier, Harry's conscience burdened him. What decent and noble woman would have him if she knew what he had been doing these last eight years? Oh, he could avoid the truth. His title and fortune alone could likely snare any woman of his choice.

The problem was he did not desire a marriage based on deception. What he sought was a loving match. The kind his parents had enjoyed. His stomach twisted at the memory of his father's perfidy. Yet his mother had never lost her love for the man she had wed when she was twenty. The two shared everything. It was almost as if their hearts beat in the same rhythm. And when his

father's heart stopped, his countess followed him
to the grave not a month later.

"Think you a woman would have me if she
knew by what means I achieved my wealth?"
Harry asked.

Edward's eyes rounded. "Surely you don't have
to tell a wife *everything*. Take my father. He
bloody well shields my mother from any manner
of his, er, activities."

A flicker of annoyance flashed across Harry's
face. "You mean from the facts about his
mistresses?"

Edward swallowed and did not meet his
cousin's gaze. "Well, of course. Simply isn't done."

"Despite his grave faults, my father was ever
honest with — and faithful to — my mother,
admirable qualities in a marriage, I think." Harry
drew his attention from Edward and looked at the
tall casements that gave onto Upper Brook Street.
"I doubt I'll ever have a wife with whom I can be
completely honest."

"Enough talk about wives!" Edward shuddered.
"Let us make up for the lost years of debauchery."
A broad smile lighted his youthful face.

Harry could not repress his grin as he got to
his feet. "I would prefer to see Wycliff House. I
plan to make Mr. Godwin Phillips's widow an offer
that cannot be refused."

Edward's slender torso rose to its full height,
which was several inches shorter than his elder
cousin's. "Hope she's not as unscrupulous as her
husband was. By the way, I've learned who now
possesses your father's diamond snuff box. What
say you we also pay a call on Lord Cleveland?"

Harry whirled to face his cousin. "Whoever told
you I wanted *his* snuff box?"

"I. . .I just thought you were going to great pains to reclaim everything--"

"I want nothing of *his*," Harry sneered.

* * *

As they rounded the corner to Grosvenor Square, Harry's heartbeat began to roar. He had not gazed upon Wycliff House in nearly a decade. Outwardly, the three-story edifice of creamy brick had not changed. It made up for in grandeur what it lacked in size. Lavish iron balusters lined the street level, save for the arched entry portico. Rows of tall, pedimented casements distinguished the upper floors that already stood out from neighboring houses because graceful Corinthian columns framed each window. A chiseled frieze of Grecian athletes banded the top of the building.

No other modes of transportation waited in front of the house where he and Edward tethered their horses. Harry could barely remember a time when a variety of conveyances had not lined this street. The old earl had taken seriously his role as a Member of Parliament and had entertained often when Lords was in session.

The front door was opened by a middle-aged butler to whom Harry presented his card. "It is a matter of a somewhat personal nature that I wish to discuss with Mrs. Phillips."

The butler's brows elevated slightly when he read the card. "Won't you come to the morning room, my lord?"

They strode across the broad entry hall's marbled floor and settled in a small room his mother had called the morning room. "My mistress is presently engaged." The butler lowered his voice. "'Tis Tuesday, you know. Her meeting day. I shall inform her of your presence."

That the morning room looked remarkably as it had nearly ten years earlier pleased Harry. Elegant draperies of light blue moire hung beneath gilded cornices on the windows facing Grosvenor Square. Blue silk damask sofas and chairs scattered about the room on a patterned carpet of gold and royal blue. A large crystal chandelier suspended from a ceiling bordered in ivory molding. *Thank God the scoundrel Godwin Phillips had the good sense to change nothing.*

A moment later the butler reappeared. "Mrs. Phillips said her meeting's almost over, that it would do an aristocrat good to sit in on the remainder of it."

Harry exchanged puzzled glances with Edward. What did the widow mean *it would do an aristocrat good?*

With a strange mix of emotions, Harry entered the drawing room at the back of the first floor. Like the morning room, it had changed little. Its walls were still the same asparagus green, as were many of the silk brocade sofas. However, the room's occupants had changed considerably. Harry could not remember ever seeing a more somberly dressed assemblage. And the drably attired consisted entirely of women. Good heavens! Had he wandered into a gaggle of bloody bluestockings?

From amidst the sea of gray and brown woolens rose one of the prettiest young women Harry had ever seen. Though she wore a dreary graphite colored morning gown of serge, the lovely blonde sparkled like a diamond in a bed of coal. Of rather small bones, her body curved gently in the right places, but it was her face that drew his attention, for it was flawless: a perfect oval with a perfectly chiseled nose and full mouth revealing even white teeth. She took two steps forward, looking at Harry, her expression inscrutable.

When she spoke, he realized her voice, too, was lovely. Smooth and clear and youthful without being flippant. "Which of you is Lord Wycliff?"

He moved toward her and bowed. "At your service, madam."

She barely inclined her head, then indicated extra chairs. "You may sit until we're finished."

"There must be some mistake," Harry said. "I particularly wanted to speak with *Mrs.* Phillips." He could not remove his gaze from the young woman's extraordinary eyes. They were lighter blue than a robin's egg.

"I am Mrs. Phillips," she said impatiently.

"But---"

"You expected an older woman." Her careless response indicated a pattern grown tediously routine.

"You are the widow of Godwin Phillips?" It seemed incredulous this youthful beauty could have been married to Phillips. The man had been the age of Harry's father, and Harry estimated his own age of two and thirty to be a decade older than the slim blonde who stood before him all defiance and arrogance.

"I am." Indicating the dozen or so women who sat primly around the room, she said, "I will not bother you with introductions, *my lord*. If you and your companion will be kind enough to sit down--"

"Yes, of course," Harry said, taking a seat on a satin brocaded sofa beside Edward, who already had displayed the good sense to be seated and escape Mrs. Phillip's scathing gaze. For the first time in his life, Harry sensed rebuke at being called *my lord*.

He paid little heed to the words bandied about among the prudish gathering, so moved was he at once again sitting in the room which enfolded him in memories of the loving family he had been part of. He could almost see his mother sitting in the very chair Mrs. Phillips used, her golden head bent over her ever-present embroidery. With his brows lowering, Harry remembered, too, sitting at the walnut game table happily playing backgammon or chess with his father.

"What is fair about every peer of the realm having a vote when other men — men who are far harder working than the idle lords — have no vote at all?"

Hearing peers so maligned cut into Harry's reverie, and he looked up to see that the speaker was a matron whose age exceeded his own. She wore spectacles and heavy merino so shapeless it completely concealed any hint of feminine roundness.

A second speaker rose. "Certainly no consideration given to *the greatest good for the greatest number*. And something is inherently wrong with a franchise that extends only to freeholders."

Aghast, Harry watched this second speaker, a young woman who wore a three-cornered hat much like his father used to wear, and epaulets clung to her well-covered shoulders. *A man-hating bluestocking, to be sure.*

"Since we have digressed from the topic of injustices in the penal system," said the lovely hostess, "I would suggest we discuss Mr. Bentham's principles of utility at next Tuesday's meeting."

While the ladies stood up and began to exit the room, Harry stood, as any proper gentleman would do. None of them acknowledged his presence or that of Edward, who stood silently beside him. The men watched as Mrs. Phillips followed her guests from the room, chatting merrily.

When all the women were gone, Harry turned to his cousin and spoke in a low voice. "Bloody bluestockings."

"A good thing they've no guillotine," Edward said.

Harry shook his head. "Violence, I should think, holds no appeal for these do-gooders."

A woman's voice responded. "That is absolutely correct, Lord Wycliff."

Peering at the angelic face of Mrs. Phillips, Harry could well believe violence was as alien to her as pock marks to her smooth, creamy skin. "I perceive you are a follower of Jeremy Bentham."

"I admire him greatly but am not a utilitarian purist," she answered.

"How gratifying," Harry murmured. "Tell me, in what way do your views differ from Mr. Bentham's?"

She perused him through narrowed eyes. "Whereas Jeremy Bentham promulgates the greatest good for the greatest number of people — a belief that has much merit — I think that ignores the worth of the individual."

Harry nodded. "Then you're more of a Rousseau disciple?"

"If I were forced to choose between the two important thinkers, then, yes, I would prefer Rousseau."

She looked skeptically at him and began to

move from the room. "I suppose you would like to see your former residence?"

"Very much. In fact, I should like to make you an offer for the house."

She spun around to face him, her eyes flashing. "That you cannot do. I found out only this morning that I am not the owner."

"Then I beg that you direct me to the owner."

"That I cannot do."

Harry stopped in front of a massive painting of the Spanish Armada, a painting that had been commissioned by his great-great-grandfather. "And why can't you, Mrs. Phillips?" Despite his efforts to conceal it, anger crept into his voice.

"Because I do not know who the owner is. My communication came through the owner's solicitor."

"Then if you will give me the solicitor's direction--"

"I will not."

She stood in the doorway to the ivory dining room, framed in a golden radiance from the wall of uncovered windows.

Harry seethed. "May I ask why?"

She nodded, her manner haughty. "I dislike nobles."

Harry only barely resisted the urge to clasp his hands upon her shoulders and shake her. "Surely your study of equality has taught you that every man is an individual. Cannot I be given the opportunity to earn your respect before being dismissed as an *idle* noble?"

Edward pushed past Harry to confront Mrs. Phillips. "I'll have you know, my cousin here was left without two farthings to rub together, and by his own cunning has rebuilt his family fortune."

Harry watched the youthful beauty for a reaction, and when she turned her attention on him, he found himself reading her face as one reads Shakespeare, finding still another facet to admire.

"I hope you use your fortune," she said, "to improve the living of the cottagers who've toiled generations for Wycliffs." Presenting her back to him, Mrs. Phillips strolled toward the dining room.

"I say, Mrs. Phillips, that's beastly unfair of you," Edward said. "My cousin took care of all the Wycliff servants and cottagers before ever spending a tuppence on himself."

The fair one looked contrite. "Forgive me, my lord. How rude you must think me."

Harry stared her down until those pale blue eyes of hers blinked. "On the contrary, Mrs. Phillips, I think nothing of you. It's my habit to reserve judgment until I've had the opportunity to get to know someone."

Her lips pursed, and he detected a glint of humor. "Then as I've not had the opportunity to get to know you, I shall reserve my opinion as to whether you've just maligned me."

He tossed his head back and laughed.

Which had the effect of cracking through his icy reception.

"I think you'll find the dining room unchanged," she said as she swept open its door.

Indeed, it was. Powerful emotions swamped him as he moved into the eerily silent room. These walls now so quiet had once echoed the lively conversations of prime ministers and heads of state, as much of England's business had been conducted at the very table Harry now surveyed.

He could picture his father seated at the head of the gleaming mahogany table, surrounded by other members of the House of Lords and leaders of Commons. At the other end, his elegant mother would have sat, softly conversing.

His heart caught at the sight of the baroque family silver, the Wycliff crest etched on the footed teapot. His need to reclaim these possessions was as strong as his obsession to see them again.

A lump in his throat, he had to look away. Sunlight poured into the room from windows draped in faded gold silk. His gaze flicked to the ceiling where a pair of glistening chandeliers suspended from cream colored plaster medallions.

When he looked back at the wall behind the head of the table, disappointment crashed over him. A Flemish tapestry hung where the Gainsborough portrait of his mother had been displayed for as long as he could remember. He wheeled around to Mrs. Phillips. "Where, may I ask, is the portrait of my mother which hung where the tapestry is now?"

She gave him a blank look. "I remember no portrait. What did it look like?"

"A typical Gainsborough. My mother was. . ." His voice gentled. "Very beautiful. She had golden hair and large, honey-colored eyes. In the painting she wore a gown the color of - - -" He pointed to a bowl of pale pink camellias. "Those."

Mrs. Phillips shook her head. "I have seen no such painting in the eight years I've lived here."

Eight years? She would have been but a girl. He almost commented on it, but his need to see his mother's portrait was stronger than his curiosity about the youthful widow. "You're sure? It's not in another room?"

Her features softened as she shook her head.

"Daresay it's in the attic?" Edward offered.

Harry cast a hopeful glance at Mrs. Phillips. "With your permission, I should like to have a look in the attic."

"Certainly, my lord. You know the way, I presume."

"Of course." He and Edward began to mount the stairs.

* * *

Louisa Phillips stood at the bottom of the stairs and watched the back of the handsome nobleman whose censure she had drawn. She bit her lip. His reprimand had been well deserved, given the unfairness of her blanket dismissal of him, based on nothing more than the circumstances of his birth. Why, it was no better than throwing out the baby with the bath water! Erroneous preconceptions had been the very topic of one of her well-received essays recently. Except the preconceptions cited in that tract dealt with lumping all cockneys in the batch with unsavory cutthroats because of their misfortune of birth.

Birth! She frowned as she retraced her steps to the drawing room. Lord Wycliff might not be an idle noble, but he was still an aristocrat. She bristled at the thought of them. They not only held all the land and wealth, they also hoarded legislative power, neglecting to write laws favorable to the individuals they repressed.

She had no admiration for those who sat back counting money earned by long-dead ancestors. Even though she was a woman who had been a dependent wife since the age of fifteen, she was capable of earning money by her own wits to put food on the table. She had managed to tuck away one hundred and fifty pounds from her essay writing. The money — as well as her authorship — had been hidden from Godwin. She had never willingly shared anything with her husband, much less her radical views which were so opposed to his Tory tastes. Never had he guessed the essayist Philip Lewis was his complacent young wife, Louisa Phillips.

Now she felt a tinge of remorse. Had she been saving the money from her writing so she could run away from Godwin? She had not allowed the intrusion of such thoughts while Godwin had been alive. And now it no longer mattered. She was free.

She felt wretchedly guilty over her lack of grief, but Godwin was not a nice man.

Her chest tightened. One hundred and fifty pounds would not go far if Godwin had not provided for her. She had always assumed this house would be hers. She was still reeling from the news that someone else owned the house she thought would come to her. Would all of Godwin's wealth also be taken from her?

What would she do? And how could she possibly make a home for her and Ellie if she were indeed penniless? Perhaps she should not have sent for her younger sister, Louisa thought, a sickening feeling in the pit of her stomach. It was too late now to withdraw the invitation. Ellie should arrive in London the next day.

She thought again of Godwin, and her hands curled into fists. Once more he had let her down. She strode angrily from the hallway, forcing her irritation onto Lord Wycliff. Even if he had soiled his noble hands making a fortune, Lord Wycliff was still born to the title, still confident he could swagger into his old home, make an exorbitant offer and once again possess the town house for which he held such an affinity.

She called for Williams. "You must put the chairs back as they were before the meeting," she told the butler.

"As you say, madam. A pity you must forever be telling me how to perform my duties. I should know that without having to be told."

Louisa looked kindly at him. "In time you will learn, my dear Mr. Williams. Remember, just a few months ago you were a gentleman's valet. You've learned much about being a butler, but it takes time."

With a mahogany chair in each hand, he strode across the room and replaced them at either side of the game table. "It's grateful I am that you've given me a chance."

"It's me," she reassured, "who is fortunate. You were a fine valet to Mr. Phillips, and you'll be an excellent replacement for Banbury, may God rest his soul." A sickening feeling surged through her. Surely Godwin had made provisions for Williams.

By the time she had instructed Williams in the drawing room, Louisa heard Lord Wycliff and his cousin coming down the stairs, and she hurried to greet them.

From the hollow expression in Lord Wycliff's dark eyes, she knew his search had yielded nothing but disappointment. "Any luck, my lord?"

"Unfortunately, no." He met her gaze, and she was taken aback by the grief she saw in his eyes.

"If I learn anything about the painting," she offered, "I will contact you."

He looked down at her. And she grew

uncomfortable. The dark lord was exceedingly handsome. She had put away dreams of handsome lords when she abandoned dolls, already having been pledged to a well-to-do man who was older than her father. And in the nine years since, her eyes had never appreciatively swept across the figure of a good-looking man. Of course, she's had no opportunity to do so — and of course, she loathed men.

With his sun-burnished face and well defined muscles, Lord Wycliff seemed out of place in a cut-away coat, freshly pressed cravat with silken vest, and pantaloons. She could imagine his muscled torso and generous shoulders rippling beneath the fine lawn of an unadorned shirt as he lunged booted feet and swished his saber in the defense of damsels. She could even picture him hammering at a blacksmith's anvil, sweat sheening his strong-boned face. Yet, despite the power and blatant masculinity he exuded, there was also touching tenderness.

"That would be most considerate of you," he said as he walked to the front door.

She wanted to do something that could balm the man's hurt. She almost offered the name of the solicitor, but that she refused to do.

After all, Lord Wycliff was an aristocrat.

* * *

The cousins settled in the carriage, then Edward turned to Harry. "I say, Mrs. Phillips could not have been much more than a babe when she wed that vile Godwin Phillips."

"I daresay you're correct." Harry spoke with no emotion, his thoughts low.

"Did you not think the widow's good looks rather extraordinary?" Edward asked.

Harry thought of the slim young woman who was such a paradox. Barely more than a girl, she bespoke the determination of a well seasoned dowager. "I did. A pity she's a bluestocking."

"I thought you admired women who had a head on their shoulders."

"True, but there must be a compromise between stupid women and the bloody do-gooder bluestockings."

"Think I'd rather have a slow-witted wife," Edward said.

Harry's dark eyes sparkled. "But I thought the idea of marriage was repugnant to you."

"So it is. Never saw a girl more dazzling than a set of perfectly matched bays."

A smile crept across Harry's face. "Tomorrow, my dear cousin, we shall call on Mrs. Phillips for enlightenment."

Edward shot him a questioning glance.

$\mathcal{C}$hapter 2

Louisa beamed at her younger sister, her eyes glistening. When she had last beheld her eight years ago, the ten-year-old Ellie had been all legs with uneven teeth too big for her dainty face. Now her legs were in perfect proportion to her woman's body. Her hair -- once the same pale blond as Louisa's -- was now the color of summer hay. Still lightly freckled, Ellie's face had grown into her teeth—teeth that were now smooth edged, pleasantly even, and bright white. She had blossomed into a lovely young woman, Louisa thought with pride.

Though Louisa had successfully guided her sister, through her letters, in most matters of taste, she had failed to dissuade Ellie from wearing utterly feminine clothing. While her sister's frilly pink dress was perfectly acceptable, it was far too fussy for Louisa's taste.

"I cannot tell you how very good it is to see you," Louisa said, taking her sister's slim hand within her own. "Why, you're as tall as me!" She divested herself of her bonnet and moved into the foyer. "But very selfish I'd be to have you sit and chat with me when I know you must be weary from the journey."

"Not at all!" Ellie protested. "'Tis wonderfully good to be safe with you." She began to stroll carelessly throughout the first floor, unconsciously studying the opulent displays of wealth. "I declare, I had not a minute's peace during the whole of the trip. I kept remembering Miss Grimm's warnings about all the men having designs on my virtue."

Her older sister suppressed a chuckle. "You mustn't take Miss Grimm's advice too seriously, my pet." Taking her sister's hand again, Louisa led her to the drawing room and rang for tea.

"How blessed it will be to have tea in your lovely home." Ellie's gaze traveled the length of his sister. "London has been good to you. You're as lovely as when you left Kerseymeade."

Louisa shrugged and sat across from Ellie in a French chair upholstered in silk damask.

"I've missed you so," Ellie continued. "Why did you never return to Chewton Manor? Not even at yuletide?"

Louisa's lips thinned, her eyes flashing. "You know what I told Papa when I left. I shall never forgive him."

"And you'll never again speak to him?"

Her eyes were cold. "Never."

"I must say, I, too, was glad to leave. I only hope London is not as wicked as Miss Grimm says for I shall never set foot out your door."

"I assure you, you'll be quite safe with me." Louisa's voice softened. "Oh, Ellie, I have lived for the day you would turn eighteen and I could have you with me." Her gaze traveled to the window. "I vowed eight years ago I would get you away before he sold you, too."

"So, here I am," Ellie said, spreading her arms

like an opera singer. "Shall I really get to meet Mr. Bentham?"

"Most assuredly," Louisa said.

"Papa would have apoplexy if he knew the contents of our letters, of our admiration for Mr. Bentham and the free thinkers."

Louisa's eyes twinkled, and she let out a little laugh. "Especially if he knew his eldest daughter was actually Philip Lewis."

"I must confess, Louisa, I did not at all like your last essay in the *Edinburgh Review*, though I have decidedly agreed with all your previous writing."

"The one against marriage?"

Ellie nodded as Louisa poured tea into two dainty porcelain cups and handed one to Ellie. "Just as one apple does not spoil the whole bunch, I think your bad marriage should not poison you completely against matrimony."

"It's not just my own unsatisfactory marriage," Louisa defended, "but the system. Classes marrying within classes. Women forced into matrimony--"

"But you advocated *free love*!" Ellie shrieked. "Have you actually taken lovers?"

That hard look came back on Louisa's face when she shook her head. "I have yet to meet the man upon whom I could freely bestow so intimate an offering."

Folding her arms, Ellie shot her sister a reproachful look. "I believe you dislike men."

Louisa bit her lip and did not respond for a moment. "I will own my only experiences with men -- with Papa and with Godwin -- have not shown their sex in a favorable manner. I do not believe there is such a thing as an honorable man."

A dreamy look came over Ellie's face. "I believe I shall find an honorable man."

A faint knock sounded at the door, then it opened. "Lord Wycliff to see you, madam," Williams said.

"Ask him to join us here."

* * *

A moment later Harry and his cousin filed into the sunlit room. Harry's eyes flashed over the room before settling on the beautiful widow.

She met his gaze. "Lord Wycliff, I should like to make you known to my sister, Ellie Sinclair. She's only just arrived from Warwickshire." The beautiful widow paused and looked at Edward. "And this, my dear Ellie, is Lord Wycliff's cousin. Pray, sir, I remember not your name."

He smiled appreciatively at the lovely little sister. "Edward Coke, at your service."

Harry decided to be his most charming self, moving to the girl's chair and taking her hand while not removing his eyes from hers. "May I hope your journey was pleasant?"

Color rose up the girl's pale, lightly freckled cheeks. "Yes very," she answered in a shaky voice.

Never to be outdone by his cousin, Edward marched up to the maiden, likewise taking her hand into his and pressing his lips to it. "I would be honored, Miss Sinclair, if you would allow my cousin and me to show you the sights of London."

Ellie's gaze darted to Louisa.

"Pray, please be seated," Mrs. Phillips coolly instructed her guests. "Allow me to ring for more cups so you can partake of tea with us."

The cousins sat on a silk brocade sofa. "No need," Harry replied. "We won't be here long." He needed Louisa Phillips as he had needed his daily bread eight years earlier. Only through her would he learn who now owned the house he cared for as a some men care for a woman. And only through her would he reclaim the portrait of his mother. He must not fail. "You may wonder why I'm here," he said to Mrs. Phillips.

Her brows arched, but she said nothing.

"I have been unable to shake your words from my thoughts. I spent the whole night troubled over the injustices of our society, and I have come to you for help directing me on the path to enlightenment." His Tory father would most certainly be spinning in his grave were his only child to start promulgating civil liberties.

He watched her anxiously, wondering if he had achieved his aim. He detected a slight softening in her expression, a glow in her spectacular blue eyes.

"What our movement needs, Lord Wycliff, is men like yourself -- men who are in Parliament -- who have the authority to do something about the deplorable conditions of our fellow countrymen."

"Then I shall be at your disposal, Mrs. Phillips, though I have never sat in Parliament. If I can ever reclaim Wycliff House, I will reclaim my father's seat in the House of Lords. I do know many lords and would be able to speak on behalf of the great masses if you could but guide me. I read the *Edinburgh Review,* but would like you to guide me in reading Jeremy Bentham's work."

Miss Sinclair straightened, her face alive, her flashing eyes darting toward her elder sister. "Oh, do you know Mr. Philip Lewis?" the girl asked.

"Of course," Harry answered. "That is, I've never met the chap, but I've read all of his works."

"And what do you think of him?" Mrs. Phillips asked warily.

"No question, the man is brilliant -- if a bit too mean spirited at times," Harry said.

Louisa's brows lifted. "How so?"

"Take his latest piece--"

"The one where he blasts the practice of marriage?" a now eager Edward asked.

Harry's face was grim. "The very one. While I'm not a religious man, I found it far too radical, undermining the sacred foundation of our society. Without family and commitment to family, man would be no better than animals."

"Then you're of the opinion sex, love, and marriage go hand in hand, my lord?" Mrs. Phillips challenged.

"In an ideal society, yes. And is not an ideal society what you seek most heartily, Mrs. Phillips?"

Louisa swallowed. "Yes, of course it is."

Harry got to his feet. "Enough serious talk for now." He glanced at Ellie. "I am sure Miss Sinclair would enjoy seeing the pleasures of London, and it is my fondest hope to be able to show them to her." He directed his attention to Ellie Sinclair. "Is there something you have particularly been wanting to see?"

The girl cast a quick glance at her sister, then back to Harry. "Oh, yes! I should ever so much wish to see the British Museum."

"Upon my word," Edward said, "'tis the most utterly fascinating thing I've ever beheld. Whenever it would be convenient for you, I would be honored to escort you there. I am at your service, Miss Sinclair." The young man effected a bow.

"Oh, Louisa, could we please go today?" Ellie asked.

"I'm sure the gentlemen must have other plans this afternoon."

Harry stepped toward Mrs. Phillips and held her in his gaze. "Nothing would give me greater pleasure than escorting two such lovely ladies to the museum."

* * *

The foursome rode to Bloomsbury in Lord Wycliff's sumptuous carriage. For reasons Louisa was unable to understand, Mr. Coke sat next to Ellie while the earl sat next to her. She could not remember any time in her life when she had sat beside a man who was not her father or her husband. She had especially not sat beside such a handsome man before. Of course, Louisa was *not* interested in men. She did not even like them.

As they came upon the museum, the earl slapped his head. "How stupid of me not to have remembered! They're demolishing Montegue House to make way for the fine new museum which will be built on the site."

Louisa peered from the window and was saddened over the demolition. She'd always loved Montague House.

"I know it's not as novel as the museum," Lord Wycliff said, "but a drive through Hyde Park would be somewhat interesting – and I could introduce you to some Members of Parliament." This he addressed to Louisa, who agreed.

As they rode along, the cousins frequently shot each other amused glances over Ellie's queries. She was most eager to see a thief since her governess, Miss Grimm, had told her they could be found on every corner in London. Mr. Coke even began to tease her good naturedly.

Louisa was glad that his lordship had not sat next to Ellie, for she had observed an uneasiness in Ellie when the earl talked to her sister. With the younger Mr. Coke, though, Ellie was relaxed -- even mildly flirtatious.

It must be the age, Louisa thought with irony. How anyone could prefer the insipid cousin over the earl she could not understand. If one were given to frippery like admiring appearances, anyone would have to admit the earl was far more handsome, more manly. She looked into her lap, willing herself not to think about his unsettling presence beside her, but she found her eyes riveted to his muscled legs, perfectly parallel to her own, yet so much longer.

For the second time in as many days, Louisa was struck by the impression that he was as out of place in frock coat and fine coach as a fish from water.

Unsettling, too, was the earl's sudden interest in the less fortunate. Just yesterday he was throwing around his wealth, vowing to reclaim Wycliff House, one of the finest homes in London. How could a man change so in just one day?

Harry turned to Louisa. "I believe your sister harbors many unfounded fears."

"How perceptive you are," she said facetiously.

She suddenly felt very shabby in her dark gray serge. For the first time in years, she actually desired to wear fine clothing, to look lovely. She told herself that then she would be in a better position to make a good impression on the lords who enacted laws. Her desire to look attractive had nothing whatsoever to do with the man sitting beside her.

By the time his carriage had reached Mayfair, she said, "I am hardly dressed for the grand promenade. I shouldn't wish to embarrass you, my lord."

"It would never be embarrassing to be seen with one as lovely as you."

She went unaccountably mushy inside and could not meet his lordship's probing gaze. "You're very gallant."

"Not at all. Only honest."

She swallowed. "Perhaps tomorrow we could go to the park with you. Then Ellie and I could dress more suitably -- that is, if it would not interfere with your plans."

"I have no plans that do not include you and your charming sister," Lord Wycliff said.

Chapter 3

Mrs. Phillips's perceptions about appropriate appearances had been bullseye correct, Harry admitted as they rode through Hyde Park the following afternoon, the men of his acquaintance fairly throwing themselves in his path while clamoring for an introduction to his lovely companion. Such popularity probably would have eluded her in the drab clothes she had worn the day before.

When he had called for her, Harry had nearly lost his breath when he gazed up the marble staircase to see the extraordinary blonde gracefully moving down the steps. Since she was still in mourning, she wore lavender, a thin muslin that draped over the gentle curves of her body. Stirred by powerful emotions, he was almost glad a woman once again inhabited Wycliff House.

Almost. He must not lose sight of his aim in befriending this unusual woman.

Louisa had to be well pleased with their outing today, Harry mused. Lord Seymour himself had chatted with her and invited her to a ball at his home Thursday night. A coup, indeed, since Lord Seymour's power in Parliament was legendary, despite that he proclaimed himself to be a Whig.

It was actually quite remarkable meeting him since a man as powerful as Seymour had no time for idle jaunts in the park. On this particular day, though, Seymour chose to flaunt his notoriety in an effort to introduce his niece to a variety of Eligibles.

The older man had run his eyes over the exquisite Mrs. Phillips, then tipped his hat to Harry. "Wycliff," he had said, drawing his phaeton to a halt.

Harry drew his carriage alongside of the noted Whig.

"I should like to make you known to my niece, who has just arrived in London from Middlesex," Lord Seymour said. Though he appeared to be speaking to Harry, the man's attention was clearly fixed on the woman sitting beside him.

Introductions behind them, Louisa said, "I cannot tell you how very pleased I am to finally meet you, Lord Seymour."

The man's eyes sparkled, but before he could reply, Harry explained, "Mrs. Phillips is a bluestocking who's desirous of expounding her ideas to powerful men in Parliament. Some might consider her ideas radical."

"Then you must come to a ball my house Thursday night," Lord Seymour said to her. "And you, too, Wycliff. I give you my word, Mrs. Phillips, you shall have my ear then." Taking up his crop, Lord Seymour bid them farewell.

Harry took great pains not to drive in the vicinity of his recently settled mistress, Lady Davenwood, though he was powerless to keep the flamboyant woman from drawing the attention of the two young ladies who shared his conveyance.

"Who, pray tell, is that. . .buxom blond lady in

purple?" Miss Sinclair had asked.

Harry obliged her by imparting the information that the woman was Lady Davenwood, then he directed the coachman to drive in the opposite direction.

"I declare," Ellie shrieked, "I cannot believe Lady Davenwood is not blushing scarlet! How can a woman parade about so scantily clad?"

Harry was unable to suppress an amused grin. Indeed, Fanny left little to the imagination. Her low-cut gown only barely concealed her generous bosom -- hardly a sight one was likely to have seen in broad daylight in Kerseymeade.

Mrs. Phillips met his gaze, a bemused expression on her beautiful face. "Be careful, pet, or Lord Wycliff will think you are a Methodist."

"You're not?" Harry teased, directing his comments to Louisa.

She gave him a quizzing look. "A Methodist?"

"I would have thought a reformer like you would embrace Mr. Wesley's faith," he said.

"I admit there was a time I examined Methodism closely, but I decided it was not for me," the widow said.

Harry wanted to give the appearance of being eager to understand her views. "And why would that be?"

She thought for a moment before answering. Harry found himself watching her intent profile and thinking of her classical perfection. Something about her touched him in a place no woman had ever ventured, in a way he could not begin to explain. She was lovely, intelligent, and totally resistant to his charms. In fact, she was the only woman he had ever known who was unimpressed by his title. When she finally answered, he was struck by the soothing pitch of her melodious voice.

"I am not nearly pious enough. Also, I believe the Bible is literature, that it was never intended to be picked apart and taken literally."

Harry lifted a single brow. "Then you *do* read the Bible?"

She nodded. "And poetry, and Shakespeare, and political treatises."

"And which political tracts do you find most enlightening, Mrs. Phillips?" Harry asked.

"Though it is nothing new, I find Thomas Paine's *Rights of Man* exciting, and it has undoubtedly influenced thinkers for the past thirty years. Mr. Wesley, too, has certainly made his contributions. And the body of work by Mr. Bentham is without equal. Hannah More is another for whom I hold a great respect. And there's also a young scholar I admire greatly, James Mill's son."

"Would that be John Stuart Mill?"

"You've read him?" Mrs. Phillips asked incredulously.

Harry chided himself for not quelling his usual authoritarian demeanor. He must remember to behave in a far humbler manner. He shrugged. "'Twas a name that popped into my head. I must assure you, Mrs. Phillips, I truly need your guidance."

She silently watched the passing carriages. "Poor Mr. Mill, the younger, was recently imprisoned when all he was doing was trying to help the less fortunate."

"Pray, what was he doing?" Harry asked, concern in his voice.

"He was instructing the ignorant masses on

methods of birth control," Louisa answered matter of factly.

Edward coughed. "Daresay it's a lovely day for a ride in the park."

Ellie, turning scarlet now, avoided eye contact with her companions. "Yes, it is," she said in a thin voice. "I do so thank you for showing me around London. I am enjoying it excessively."

As Edward and Miss Sinclair talked of pleasantries, Harry was determined to convince Mrs. Phillips of his sincerity in learning about the liberal thinkers.

"You must direct me to the younger Mill's writings. Your recommendation is a hearty endorsement, to be sure."

A flickering smile played at her lips. "When we return to Wycliff House, I will make my library available to you."

He studied her profile again, unable to imagine her as the wife of the unscrupulous Godwin Phillips. "Tell me, Mrs. Phillips, did the late Mr. Phillips share your enthusiasm for the liberal thinkers?"

Her face went cold. "While he did not share my beliefs, he allowed me to purchase whatever books I desired. When he was alive, I kept them in my chambers. Now, they are in the library."

He decided to probe further. "Did you have your Tuesday meetings when Mr. Phillips was alive?"

She shook her head, and he detected malice in her expression. "No. I went to many meetings, but in deference to my husband's opinions, I did not bring the bluestockings into his home. Or to what I thought was his home."

"Am I correct in thinking your husband would

not have approved?"

She swallowed. "You are correct."

He sensed she no longer wanted to speak of her husband when she said, "I do believe you should start by reading Mr. Bentham."

Harry's carriage pulled up in front of Wycliff House. It was still impossible to look upon his former home without being swept up in powerful emotions. As badly as he wanted to regain the townhouse, he knew that possessing it would not bring back the happy times and familial intimacy associated with it -- nor would it ever be the same without his mother.

God, but he needed to see it, to reclaim it. He would spare nothing to gain possession of it.

While Ellie and Edward took a stroll through the square's park, Mrs. Phillips took Harry to her library and stripped it of volumes that would enlighten the uninformed aristocrat.

* * *

Two days later, Louisa sympathetically watched a dejected man walk away into the crush at Lord Seymour's ball. She had been there but half an hour and had already turned down half a dozen men who had begged her to stand up with them. Surely young Mr. Dithers would be the last to approach her. She fixed her gaze on Lord Wycliff, who stood at her left, and found him appraising her with an undeniable look of heated desire. It was the same look that had been on his face when he called for her and she had come down the stairs wearing her new lavender gown. At the memory, color crept up her cheeks, and she broke eye contact.

Perhaps the new dress had not been such a good idea, after all. Though she had made it

herself, it had taken a rather dear length to
fashion it. She could ill afford to part with the
money that went to the linen drapers. At least not
until she knew how much was left in Godwin's
estate.

The time had come to put her half-hearted
mourning behind her. When she had stood in
front of her looking glass before Lord Wycliff
called tonight, she was almost embarrassed at
how the soft silk hugged the curve of her breasts
and swept across her other curves in a most
revealing way. Even though her neckline was not
nearly as low as most other women here tonight,
she could not deny that the gown was
provocative.

Which wasn't at all what she had intended. All
she had wanted was to appear pretty enough to
draw Lord Seymour's attention. He was a most
powerful man, and she desired nothing more than
to channel his power toward her pet projects of
reform.

She had to admit Lord Wycliff was becoming
sensitive to her views, despite that he was a
noble. She detected no embarrassment in his
manner tonight when he informed his friends of
her radical ideals. In fact, he even spoke of her
projects to those men. "Mrs. Phillips opposes the
idea of allowing only freeholders to vote," he
would say. Or, "Mrs. Phillips promulgates
compulsory education," he would tell another. To
another, he said, "I say, Mrs. Phillips's
suggestions for a hierarchy of criminal offenses --
for the purposes of incarceration -- have much
merit."

To which she replied, "Though I should love to
take credit for such brilliant ideas, Jeremy

Bentham is the genius who devised the scheme."

Harry addressed his companions: "Consider, if you will, a man stealing a leg of mutton to feed his hungry family, getting caught, and hanged. How can so petty a crime merit the same punishment given a cold-blooded murderer?"

Louisa beamed as she watched Lord Wycliff's friends' faces brighten with enlightenment.

After seeing him every day this week, she was beginning to realize not all nobles were committed to the status quo that was so advantageous to wealthy landowners like themselves. Lord Wycliff's progressive ideas had blossomed like spring flowers under her tutelage these past several days. She was not only learning that all nobles were not opposed to change, but also that not all men were totally selfish. If Lord Wycliff would sit in Parliament next session and endorse the idea of extending the franchise, he would gain Louisa's undying admiration.

Even though he would be shooting himself in the foot.

"Lord Seymour has left the receiving line," Lord Wycliff said. Though it was difficult to be heard over the sounds of laughter and conversation as well as the strains of the orchestra, he leaned closer to her and whispered, "Come, let us speak to our host. Lord Seymour has rather a penchant for pretty young things. You are quite the loveliest woman here."

"Pray, my lord, do you see me as young?"

"You *are* young. I must be ten years older than you."

"How old are you, if I might ask?"

"Three and thirty."

The beastly man was right. She was gravely

disappointed to learn Lord Seymour could possibly prey on young women. Men! Worthless the whole lot of them.

Of course, Lord Wycliff *had* said she was the loveliest woman here. Her heart went to fluttering – despite that she had never before wanted to be the object of men's desires.

And she hated herself for such shallowness.

When his hand rested at her back as he led her to Lord Seymour, she experienced an odd feeling of pride. She had been acutely aware that her escort was the recipient of seductive gazes and gushing flirtations from half the women present.

Their host was a distinguished looking man in his fifties. Though slight of build, his voice was commanding, as was his presence. He had obviously grown a swooping mustache as a younger man to add maturity to his slim person. Now it was his trademark, making him easily identifiable in political cartoons.

Louisa detected a glint in his green eyes when she approached with Lord Wycliff.

"I see, Wycliff, you have brought your charming companion." Lord Seymour turned his gaze to Louisa. "Mrs. Phillips, is it not?"

"It is," Louisa answered timidly. She knew she would have to gain firmer control of her voice if she hoped to merit this notable Whig's favor.

"Mrs. Phillips desires to speak with you on matters of reform," Harry said.

Seymour's brows elevated. "I am always happy to discuss reform, my dear Mrs. Phillips."

She moved closer to the notable Whig and favored him with what she hoped was her best smile just as the orchestra quit playing the set. The relative silence that ensued greatly pleased her. Now Lord Seymour could hear her much better. "I particularly desire to impart to you the importance of extending the franchise."

"What? No plea to regulate child labor? Or to reform the penal system?"

Now her convictions overtook any timidness. She was on firm ground expressing her beliefs. "While I am seriously troubled over the exploitation of children and the unfairness of our penal system, I believe the most serious problems will be solved if the vote does not rest with a privileged few to the exclusion of those most affected by our country's laws. If votes could be cast by those whose loved ones are transported for the most minor infractions, we could be assured the severe penalties of today's laws would be lessened."

"Well spoken, my dear," Seymour said, his eyes twinkling. "You must be influenced by Philip Lewis, a man I greatly admire."

An intoxicating feeling of pride bubbled within Louisa, and she had to fight the desire to shout *I am Philip Lewis!* Instead, she bowed humbly and said, "I, too, admire him." She fairly gagged on the necessity of calling her alter ego *him.*

Just then Lord Seymour's excited niece came scurrying up to her uncle and placed a possessive hand on his forearm. "Uncle! *He* is here. Won't you come meet him?"

Lord Seymour excused himself and left in a flurry on his niece's dainty heels.

After he had gone, Louisa turned to Lord Wycliff. "I am most grateful for the opportunity you afforded me of speaking with Lord Seymour, my lord."

He looked down upon her from his

considerable height. There was a distinctly admiring look on his face when he spoke to her. "Then I beg you to repay me by waltzing with me."

There it went again. That ridiculous fluttering in her chest as he took her hand within his strong grasp and led her to the dance floor. He had not even allowed her to protest. And when he actually took her in his arms, she feared she would swoon. Unaccountably, he had not seemed a real man until now. He was a nobleman. An inanimate object to be scorned.

But the man whose hands clasped hers so firmly was very real. And very appealing: tall and solid and ripe with masculinity. She blushed as she fleetingly thought of his sexual appetites. She supposed he was a most practiced lover. He had probably had his way with many women in this very room, judging from the jealous stares she now drew.

A pity there was no such thing as a trustworthy man.

* * *

Dancing with Mrs. Phillips filled Harry with an odd sense of pride. Though not dressed nearly so grandly as most of the woman here tonight, she still outshone the others with her simple beauty. Her crepe dress flowed softly from beneath her rounded bosom, clinging to her smooth curves. He found himself wondering what she would look like with her hair long and draping over her smooth bare shoulders.

Putting her beauty aside, he had to admire her. She had not wavered from her purpose in her brief meeting with Parliament's leading Whig. Her knowledge and vast capacity for compassion far exceeded that of all the other matrons here added together.

He looked down at the top of her fair head where candlelight cast a silvery glow over her smooth tresses. "Thank you," he murmured.

She looked up at him. It was difficult for him to get his thoughts straight while gazing into the porcelain perfection of her face. "For what?"

"For directing me. I spent all of last night with Mr. Bentham's writings." God, but he was an insincere lout!

"You found them enlightening?"

"Not only enlightening, but I've discovered that my whole life has been misdirected."

She smiled, and he thought perhaps her slender hand pressed his own a little more firmly.

* * *

Later that evening Louisa was overjoyed to find herself seated to the right of her host. Had Lord Wycliff interceded in her behalf? Or did Lord Seymour himself desire to further the acquaintance?

Throughout dinner Lord Seymour directed a great many comments toward her. "Mrs. Phillips is possessed of a deep concern for equality," he told the guests at the head of the table. "She has expounded with authority on empowering the citizenry with the franchise."

"I declare," Mrs. Aker-Jones said, glaring across the table at Louisa, "is the unfortunate woman mad? The ignorant masses would likely throw open all the prisons, and utter chaos would result."

"I am not an unfortunate woman, nor am I mad," Louisa retorted. "Though *you* must be possessed of inferior intellect if you imagine such a scenario."

"Well, I..."

"Please ladies," Lord Seymour interjected. "I had no idea my remarks would stir such controversy."

"I am used to being surrounded by controversy," Louisa said. "If I have offended you, Lord Seymour, I am deeply sorry, but I cannot help but speak my mind. As you know, I am most single minded in my pursuit of justice."

Lord Seymour placed his thin white hand over hers. "A noble pursuit, to be sure, but may I add that life is most unjust, my dear, a fact you will come to understand when you are my age."

As if she knew nothing of injustice! "I hope I shall never be so cynical that I do not desire to help those trodden-upon individuals who have no voice."

Lord Seymour surprised her by squeezing her hand.

"I hope so, too," he said.

* * *

Harry sat across from Mrs. Phillips at dinner. He was unable to remove his gaze from her and strained to hear her smooth voice, which was no easy task since Mrs. Aker-Jones seemed bent on engaging him in conversation and in telling him the merits of her daughter, whom he considered rather a beanstalk. As he observed Mrs. Phillips's confidence when speaking to the powerful lord about her causes, Harry unexpectedly swelled with pride.

He admired her more than he agreed with her.

Though she should have been like a fish out of water, surprisingly, she was not. She bespoke eloquence with her speech and with the elegance of her appearance. She was also the loveliest woman here.

One matter did concern Harry. Lord Seymour. Though the man held enormous respect in the House of Lords, his private dalliances with beautiful women was less than admirable. As Harry watched the man paw at Louisa, he vowed he would never allow Seymour to initiate the intimacy with Mrs. Phillips that the Whig so obviously desired.

Oddly, Harry felt unexpectedly protective toward her. Her bravura, he knew instinctively, only masked her innocence.

When he deposited her at Wycliff House a few hours later, she said, "Tomorrow, I shall direct you to the solicitor."

This was what he'd been wanting for. He should be elated.

Instead, he felt like a traitor.

$\mathcal{C}$hapter 4

"I declare, Louisa, you are looking ever so much prettier than when I arrived," Ellie said. "I suppose it's the wearing of color." The young woman's eyes rounded, and her flattened hand flew against her mouth. "Though really, Louisa, you should be wearing black. It's not at all proper not to mourn one's own husband. Even if you didn't love him. Think of propriety!"

How different she and Ellie were, Louisa thought. Despite Ellie's claims to emulate her sister's unorthodox beliefs, at heart, Ellie's tastes were catholic. Louisa wondered if her own tastes might have conformed to the norm if her life had been more normal.

Louisa hastily finished pinning up her hair. She was guilty of spending unaccustomed time on her toilet these past several days. For the first time in years she actually wanted to look pretty.

And for that she felt excessively guilty.

But she felt absolutely no guilt over not wearing mourning for the husband she had never been able to love. "To mourn someone I abhorred would be the embodiment of dishonesty, and you know I have no tolerance for liars."

"To be sure," Ellie said. "If you will not wear mourning, I am most happy you have cast aside your dislike of femininity, and I daresay Lord Wycliff approves, too. I believe the earl has romantic feelings for you."

Louisa had little patience with her sister's foolish romantic notions. The very idea of a nobleman having amorous feelings toward her was absurd. "I assure you Lord Wycliff tolerates me solely in order to improve his mind -- and to learn who owns his former house." She whirled away from the looking glass. "Even if he were in some way attracted to me -- which I assure you he is not -- a match between a nobleman and me is quite unacceptable to both of us."

Before leaving the room, Louisa took one last look at the glass, rather pleased at the way her saffron-colored dress hung. She thought it made her look somewhat taller -- which was a very good thing. Then she fastened on her gold earrings, angry at herself for this newfound desire to look pretty when a visit from his lordship was pending.

As they walked downstairs she continued to think of what Ellie had said. *I believe the earl has romantic feelings for you.* Louisa could not deny that Lord Wycliff had held her a little closer than necessary during the waltz at Lord Seymour's, and his lingering gaze that swept over her last night had made her feel completely undressed. His flirtatious ways had not stopped there. She thought of the way he held her hand a bit longer than necessary when handing her into his carriage, and the way he always sat next to her in the carriage, his powerful thigh brushing against hers ever so slightly.

Such behavior, no doubt, was exhibited by all noblemen, especially one who was as young and virile and available as Lord Wycliff. She was sure these men cared for nothing save their own gratification. Wastrels the whole lot of them!

Then she neared the bottom of the stairs to find him standing there. She had not even known he'd arrived, and here he stood, his boots planted sturdily on the marble floor as he gazed up at her, looking at her with a somber, unfathomable look. She did likewise, running her eyes from the dark hair he wore uncovered to his well-cut coat that hugged his broad shoulders and tapered down to his trim waist. She could understand how empty-headed women could be enamored of a man such as Lord Wycliff.

Thank goodness she was not an empty-headed female.

Once again, Lord Wycliff's warm brown eyes flickered along the length of her. She could not have felt more undressed had he removed her clothing. Had Godwin looked at her in such a way, she would have become nauseated and wished she had never been born. Lord Wycliff's longing gaze, on the other hand, brought a quiver to her insides and a not unpleasant stirring deep and low. She felt unaccountably feminine and, oddly, desirable and beautiful.

And infuriated with herself for feeling so.

She offered him her hand -- a gesture she would not have done two weeks earlier -- and gritted her teeth at her own ease in accepting him.

"Ah, Mrs. Phillips, how lovely you look today," he said pressing her hand to his lips. Then he hastily glanced at Ellie, who was a step behind her sister. To her, he merely nodded. "Good day, Miss Sinclair."

His youthful cousin, twirling his hat in his

hands, stepped forward and bowed to the two young women, his eyes solely on the younger sister. "Good morning, ladies."

As they all gathered in the foyer, Louisa turned to Ellie. "Do allow Mr. Coke to take you for a stroll about the square. I am sure you will find the information I have to impart to Lord Wycliff rather tedious."

Louisa noted the amusement twinkling in Mr. Coke's eyes before he donned his hat and offered Ellie his arm as the two strolled away.

Unaccustomed to being alone with Lord Wycliff, Louisa's heart fluttered as she turned to him. "Won't you follow me to the library?"

To her consternation, he took her arm, just as his cousin had done to her sister. Did Ellie feel as light and silly as she did right now? She had been so entrenched in her own world she had given nary a thought to Ellie and her relationship to the pleasant Mr. Coke. Now that she thought about it, she realized Ellie had recited any number of favorable comments about the young man. He *did* seem rather nice. And he acted with great propriety toward her sister. Still. . .Louisa had never known a man worthy of her trust.

She took a seat on the library's silken settee facing Lord Wycliff. For a moment she forgot his presence. She took note of her elegant surroundings and realized such grandiose furnishings meant nothing to her. She neither needed nor wanted such expensive finery. But she did need a roof over her head, though that roof would never be in Kerseymeade. She would beggar herself on the streets before she would ever step foot in her father's house again.

Her stomach twisted at the memory that even

though she had been a dutiful wife to Godwin, he had not had the goodness within him to provide for her future. She had received no money this quarter, and the solicitor she had asked to investigate the matter had not reported back to her.

The thought of being penniless as well as homeless sent a sinking feeling to her stomach.

"You were quite the loveliest woman at the ball last night, Mrs. Phillips," Lord Wycliff said.

"You know little of me, my lord, if you think such a comment a compliment. Were you to say Lord Seymour would speak to Parliament on behalf of my principles, that, sir, would turn my head."

A wry grin slid across his handsome face. "We shall continue to work to that end, ma'am."

"We?"

He nodded. "I confess you have made a convert of me. You and I shall foist ourselves into Society with the sole aim of *enlightening* the idle nobles."

She threw a dubious glance in his direction. Was he serious? Had she really converted him? Would he really gain for them admission to the *ton* in order to educate the lords on the need for reform? Somehow, she could not quite believe in Lord Wycliff's sincerity. Except for the first day they met, he had been nothing but sympathetic to her ideas, but for some unexplainable reason, she doubted his earnestness.

"Does that mean you will take your seat in Parliament, my lord?"

His answer was not as quick in coming as she would have liked.

"I shall. Once I have my personal affairs in order."

She stiffened. "And one of those personal affairs, of course, is reclaiming Wycliff House."

"Yes." He watched her somberly.

Her breast heaved. "Very well, my lord. I shall not only tell you the name of the solicitor, I shall allow you to take me there this morning." That would save the fare for the hackney, she thought with satisfaction. Two weeks previously she had sold her cattle and carriage and been forced to dismiss the groom when she'd learned there was no money.

She detected a flicker of satisfaction in Lord Wycliff's face as he stood.

Her eyes passed quickly from his muscled thighs to his flat stomach, then up to his strikingly wide shoulders, and she drew in her breath as she stood.

"Do we have the companionship of my cousin and your sister for our sojourn?" he asked.

She put hands to hips. "It is *not* a sojourn, my lord. Merely a business meeting. It so happens that I have business myself with the solicitor, business of a private nature."

"But you have not answered my question, Mrs. Phillips."

She gave him a puzzled stare. Why did the man rattle her so? Why did his presence have the ability to make her thinking not quite straight?

"Do you need the chaperonage of your sister?" he asked.

Did he think she as senseless as a schoolgirl? Or an easy conquest? She would show him, arrogant aristocrat that he was! "Of course I don't need a chaperon. I'm a woman who was married for eight years. As a woman of such vast experience I am not easily victimized by scheming men."

He gave out a laugh. "Pardon, but surely a woman with such vast experience does not attach that *scheming man* label to me."

"That, Lord Wycliff, remains to be seen." Then she swept from the room and called Williams to fetch her spencer.

"On the other hand, Lord Wycliff," she said to him as she waited for her butler to return, "I would rather not leave my maiden sister in the clutches of your worldly cousin." *Worldly cousin?* Such a dubious description of the thus-far-worthy Mr. Coke sounded false even to her own ears.

Lord Wycliff threw back his head and roared in laughter. "I assure you my cousin is a most honorable man."

Louisa swung around to face him, her blue eyes flashing. "Does not his father keep mistresses?"

Lord Wycliff's face went white and stern. "Did we not agree on our first meeting that each man is an individual and should be judged accordingly?"

Her face went red. She swallowed. "Of course, you are right. Mr. Coke deserves to be evaluated on his own merit. I apologize."

"I give you my word Edward is an honorable man."

As if *his* word meant anything, but she dare not question that now. She merely nodded, unable to meet his scathing gaze.

Since it was so fair a day and since Louisa knew Ellie and Mr. Coke would be bored beyond toleration at the solicitor's, Louisa suggested leaving the two young relatives behind.

"It is better that Miss Sinclair and my cousin

continue their enjoyment of the park outside," he agreed.

After giving the solicitor's direction to his driver, Lord Wycliff handed Louisa into his carriage, and to her surprise, took his regular seat beside her. They had never before been alone in the carriage. Ellie and Mr. Coke had always sat on one side, she and Lord Wycliff on the other. She knew she should scold Lord Wycliff and insist he sit across from her, but her voice failed her. To ask him to do so was to imply there was something improper in their sitting next to one another, and it would embarrass her exceedingly for him to think she could imply such things.

So during the ride to The City, she sat beside him, outwardly complacent while a great quivering rocked within her. It was some time before she trusted her voice not to tremble as she spoke. "Should you prefer to meet with the solicitor, Mr. Twining, in private?"

"I have nothing to hide from you, but Mr. Twining may. You see, if I don't get from him the information I seek, I plan to bribe the man."

Louisa knew she should act with outrage at his arrogant actions, but instead she felt mildly pleased that he was being truthful with her. Truth, she had found, was alien to most men. "Then by all means, see him alone," she said. "Will you mind waiting while I speak to him of my affairs -- which I heartily want to hide from you, my lord."

He grinned. A devastatingly handsome grin. The deuced man!

"Take as much time as you like."

The carriage turned to the right, and she leaned into him, their thighs as close as pages in a book. And once again that overwhelming deep-down stirring did havoc to her.

She avoided his gaze and hastily moved back.

A moment later they were at Mr. Twining's business establishment.

Lord Wycliff insisted she conduct her business first.

When Louisa entered Mr. Twining's interior office, the solicitor stood. He was the age of Godwin and had been Godwin's solicitor since long before she and Godwin were married. Like Godwin, he was fat, the buttons on his waistcoat straining across his round belly. She averted her gaze to his pleasant face, where his bushy gray sideburns drew her attention.

"I'm so sorry about Mr. Phillips," he began, his eyes sweeping over her pale – non-mourning – dress.

"As you observe," she said curtly, "I chose not to wear mourning. I am not here to discuss Godwin but to learn in what financial circumstances he has left me."

Without being told to do so, she sat down in front of the solicitor's desk in a broad chair with wooden arms.

A look of -- what? Mistrust? Disapproval? Or pity? -- flitted across his jowled face as he took a seat. He coughed, then rang for his clerk. When the young man entered his office, Mr. Twining instructed him to bring Mr. Godwin Phillips's papers.

A moment later these papers were in Mr. Twining's possession. He rifled through several pages, his eyes skipping over the print. He coughed again. It was not a cough of substance but one of hesitation.

"As I told you two weeks ago, Mrs. Phillips," he began, "your husband did not own the house in Grosvenor Square. He was actually more or less its caretaker for his benefactor."

"His benefactor?" she asked incredulously. Godwin had no close friends and, goodness knows, he wasn't likeable enough to have a benefactor. Then she remembered those nights when Godwin would tell her not to come down, that a very important personage would be paying him a clandestine visit. A Lord Something or Other he was. Not that Godwin had shared such information with her. But because of the secrecy, she had stolen through the dark hallways and tried to listen to the men talk. The only thing she heard was her husband referring to the man as *my lord.*

"Who is this man?" she asked.

"I am not at liberty to say."

Her hands fisted in her lap, her mouth went taut. "Then tell me what this man's relationship was to my husband."

"That I am not privy to."

She shrugged. "Did my husband provide another – smaller -- home for me?"

He sadly shook his head. "I'm afraid not, Mrs. Phillips."

"As his only beneficiary, I am entitled to my husband's estate."

"I do not deny that, Mrs. Phillips. It is just that there is little to his estate. When he moved to London permanently at the time of your marriage, he sold everything else he owned, and as you know, your late husband had rather expensive taste. His bills were enormous. Why his fees at Waiters alone--"

"I am not interested in Godwin's expensive lifestyle. I know the details only too well. What I require, Mr. Twining, is the exact figure of what is left from his extravagant spending. How much do I get?" *What a mercenary hussy Mr. Twining must think me.*

She leaned forward.

He cleared his throat. "As you know, none of the furnishings within the Grosvenor Square house will come to you." He rifled through papers, then coughed again. "I believe Mr. Phillips had a total of thirty-seven pounds in his bank at the time of his death. That will, of course, come to you."

She nodded, her anger swelling.

"Then, of course, all the jewelry and clothing he bestowed on you are yours to keep."

That much she had known. Not that Godwin had been all that generous to her. For the occasions they had gone to fetes and balls, he had lavished her with jewelry she found gaudy and wore only on those occasions when he insisted. These she still possessed, and they should fetch enough to purchase a cottage, but she certainly could not live the rest of her life on thirty-seven pounds! Surely there had to be more money. After all, Godwin had been a man of means.

"And as you know, Mr. Phillips settled your father with a very generous amount of money upon your marriage."

Her stomach turned over, and rage swept through her. "How much?" she demanded.

"One thousand pounds."

An exorbitant sum! She could have lived on such a sum for many years. She swallowed hard.

"I don't want to know of Godwin's expenses. I want to know what's left."

He coughed again. "Actually, that's all, Mrs. Phillips. The money in the bank and your personal possessions. Also, if you care to sell any of Mr. Phillip's personal possessions, such as snuff boxes or fobs or--"

"I get the idea, Mr. Twining." She stood up, regal and proud. "Tell me when I am to vacate my home."

"The house's owner has graciously said you can stay there until the end of next month.

As she mentally calculated that Godwin's possessions might fetch twenty or thirty pounds and that she had a little over a month to find a new home, she rose and bid the solicitor a curt good-day.

* * *

Harry did not like the worried look on Mrs. Phillips's face as she left the solicitor's office. He fought his unexpected urge to take her in his arms and smooth away her troubles. Even if she was a bloody bluestocking.

He stood and met her somber gaze with one of sympathy, then he squeezed her arm as he walked past her and entered Mr. Twining's office, shutting the door behind him.

The clerk had announced him as Lord Wycliff. Mr. Twining met the peer with a broad smile on his round face. "What can I do for you today, my lord?"

"I'll not beat around the bush, Twining. I want Wycliff House back, and I'm ready to negotiate with the proper owner."

The smile of Mr. Twining's face faded. "I will, of course, convey your wishes to the owner."

"And who would that be?" Harry asked.

Mr. Twining coughed. A more false cough Harry had never heard.

"I must exercise a solicitor-client privilege in not communicating that information to you, my lord."

"Come, Twining, every man has his price. What's yours? How much do I have to pay you to get the address of the owner of my former home?"

He withdrew a bag of gold coins and set it on the solicitor's desk.

Mr. Twining looked from the coins to Harry, his eyes glassy. Sweat beaded on his brow. Then he shook his head. "I'm an honorable man. I shall not disclose such privileged information."

Harry wasn't used to being turned down. Everyone had a price, but he knew this man would not bend. Not because he was honorable.

Because he was scared. The last time Harry had seen such fear on a man's face was when he'd been prepared to run a sword through the man.

$\mathcal{C}$hapter 5

The return journey to Grosvenor Square was solemn. Mrs. Phillips had obviously been as disappointed as he. Oddly, her sorrow disturbed Harry more than his own. Even if he never regained Wycliff House, his comfortable life would continue much the same. When Louisa Phillips left Wycliff House, a bleak future was all she could expect. Where would she live? What would she do for money?

For Harry knew the contemptible scoundrel who had been Louisa Phillips's husband had left her nothing. How could a man be so dishonorable?

Louisa's estrangement from her family, he had learned, was irrevocable. Her parent was as loathsome as her husband had been. How could they have played her so cruelly? What was a woman of gentle birth to do when thrust into London with neither money nor the protection of a husband? Other women in the same deplorable circumstance -- especially a woman as beautiful at the widow Phillips -- would seek to marry, but not Louisa Phillips. She was not like other women.

She hated men.

Harry spent the better part of the coach ride

trying to determine how he could help the unfortunate widow. The problem was that she was too bloody proud. She would never accept his charity. He must think of a way to help her anonymously.

He flicked a glance to her. And his heart could have bled for the somber desperation he saw on her troubled face. It was all he could do not to gather her into his arms and comfort her.

God, but he wanted to!

When he left her at the door to Wycliff House, he merely said, "We must think of some way to extricate you from this situation." His knuckle nudged under her chin as he lifted her face to meet his gaze. "Don't despair."

* * *

As foolish as it seemed, Lord Wycliff's words gave her hope. She felt less forlorn as she mounted the stairs to Godwin's chamber.

Though it was late afternoon, his bedchamber was as dark as a cave. Louisa shivered as she entered it. The cold was only partly responsible for her shivers. She told herself the room was cold because there had been no fires in the room since he'd died. A chill slid along her spine as she crossed the room and opened the heavy red draperies. She disliked this room ever so much. As she had disliked the man who had inhabited it.

Instead of experiencing exultation from her liberation, she cowered in fear, half expecting Godwin's corpulent presence to show itself.

She had never remembered the room smelling so foul. It was a stale odor that reminded her of death. He had died here.

Now that the room was flooded with daylight,

she could expunge Godwin from her memory. The eight years with him had been but a bad dream. She would never again have to lie beneath him. He was dead. And she was free.

She began to walk about his room, looking for things of value. There was his silver penknife. She took it up and placed it on the bed. Then she came across his ivory snuff box. It, too, went into the pile on the bed. She slid a gold band from her own finger and tossed it on the heap.

When she finished gathering everything of value she could find, she pulled the bell rope, and when Williams answered, she gave him her instructions. She first pointed to the meager pile on the bed. "I desire that you undertake a mission for me," she said.

"Anything you say, Mrs. Phillips."

"I wish for you to sell my husband's things I've collected on the bed."

He glanced at the bed.

"Also, I would like for you to take all of Mr. Phillips's clothing and leather goods to a second-hand clothier and obtain for them as much money as you can. It appears your former master has left this earth with no settlements for you or for me, Williams."

His lips folded. "A pity, ma'am. I'll do all I can to get a fair price for Mr. Phillips's goods. Ye can count on me."

She smiled. "Thank you, Williams."

* * *

The following morning, while Ellie was still asleep, Louisa left the house with Williams as her escort. They went to a jewelers on Conduit Street. A very reputable jeweler from whom Godwin had purchased many of her jewels.

Williams stayed outside as Louisa strolled confidently into the store and deposited a bag overflowing with jeweled necklaces and matching bracelets and earrings. She proceeded to dump the contents of the bag on the jeweler's counter.

The jewelers' eyes rounded.

"I wish to inquire as to the worth of my jewels," Louisa said confidently.

Without a reply, the jeweler popped a magnification device onto his left eye, then picked up the sapphire necklace. A moment later, he put it down. "I'm afraid, madam, that while these look quite lovely, they are comprised of very inferior stones. The sapphires I can give you no more than twenty pounds for."

She snatched them from him and began to put all the jewels back into the bag. "I shall go to another jeweler for another opinion," she said.

"I regret that they will give no more than I," he said. Now a shadow of some emotion -- was it sympathy? -- passed over his face. "Perhaps I could raise the amount to thirty pounds, Mrs. Phillips."

She froze. "How did you know my name?" She had never been there before.

"I remember your jewels, madam. And your husband." Another, less sympathetic, shadow crossed his face. "Your husband desired that I make a dazzling necklace from fake jewels. I refused. Then he asked that I make one of flawed jewels. He was adamant about wanting a necklace that gave the appearance of great wealth -- which he no doubt did not possess."

She softened toward the jeweler, who was old enough to be her father. He wasn't trying to cheat her, after all. She knew the man was telling the truth. He knew Godwin well. "Your assumption was correct, sir. I am learning that my husband's wealth was all a sham. Now that he is dead I find myself quite penniless."

He nodded sympathetically, putting the glass once again to his eye and examining the remainder of the jewels. When he finished, he removed the glass and looked at her with sadness in his eyes. "I will give you one-hundred pounds for all of them. I assure you no one else will do better. I know this because I am willing to give you exactly what they cost your late husband."

She knew he was being more than generous. "I accept your offer."

* * *

Later that afternoon, as Louisa sat sewing in the upstairs study, Williams entered the chamber. Assured that he and Louisa were alone, he gave her a fistful of coins. "This is all I could get for the master's things," he told her as he counted out a little less than seventy-two pounds.

She took the money and put it into her sewing bag. "I'm very grateful to you, Williams."

"It's grateful to you I am, Mrs. Phillips, for not puttin' me out on the street."

She smiled at him, hoping she could continue to put a roof over his head. If only she could find a nice little cottage that didn't cost so very much. Then perhaps she wouldn't have to dismiss Cook and Williams. Like her, they had nowhere to go.

After he left the room, Louisa put away her sewing and took up her pen. She had best concentrate on her writing. Every shilling counted, and it looked as if she was going to have to earn her keep -- and Ellie's and Cook's and Williams' -- through her writing.

But no sooner had she dipped her quill than Ellie moved into the room with a length of sarcenet. "I do believe I'll begin a new dress. Mr. Coke is sure to think I possess but two dresses."

Louisa looked up at her lovely sister. "And what Mr. Coke thinks matters to you?"

Ellie giggled. "Despite that he's a man, and you hate men, Mr. Coke is all that is amiable. Can you not agree?" She fixed her sister with a smile.

"I know nothing bad about him," Louisa said, "though I must say I don't think of him as *a man.* He seems rather boyish to me."

"He's *four and twenty.*" Ellie said this as if she were saying he was a hundred.

My own age, Louisa thought, realizing that she was not so very old after all. Actually, she would not be that age until her next birthday.

Compared to his elder cousin, Edward Coke seemed neither manly nor mature. Thinking of Lord Wycliff, she imagined she heard his voice. A moment later, Williams confirmed that he and his cousin were downstairs.

Ellie's hand flew to her hair. "I cannot go downstairs until I make myself more presentable."

Louisa smiled as she rose and spoke to her sister. "I'll tell them you will be down in five minutes."

"Five minutes! That's not nearly enough time," Ellie protested.

Louisa attempted to sound firm. "That will be enough time, my pet." Then she strolled from the room and told herself that if that wretched Lord Wycliff were standing at the bottom of the stairs gazing admirably up at her again, she would completely ignore him. *I will not let the man's attention rattle me.*

Fortunately, he was in the morning room, not at the bottom of the stairs. Unfortunately, he stood when she entered the room, and as always his eyes lingered admiringly over her from the top of her head to the tip of her satin shoes.

She tried to ignore him. This she did by addressing his cousin first. "Mr. Coke, how good it is to see you and your cousin." An almost imperceptive nod was directed at Lord Wycliff.

Not to be ignored, Lord Wycliff stepped forward, swept into a bow, then took Louisa's hand and pressed his lips to it. For a bit longer than necessary.

Curse him! She chose to address Mr. Coke again. "My sister will be down in a moment."

"Capital!" he said. "'Tis a lovely day. I thought to persuade her to do me the honor of accompanying me on another walk in the square."

"Which is an excellent plan," Lord Wycliff added, looking at Louisa, "for I have business of a very personal nature to discuss with you, Mrs. Phillips."

Good lord! He's looking at me again with those dangerously dark eyes. The way he said 'personal' brought color to her cheeks. Now she was acting more the schoolgirl than Ellie.

Soon Ellie was in the room, and then she wasn't. And no one was there except for Lord Wycliff and his wretched eyes. Louisa got up and walked to the window and watched her sister, who was dressed in light blue, as Ellie put their key into the lock on the gate to the park in the center of Grosvenor Square.

Louisa turned back and faced Lord Wycliff. "What is it you wish to discuss with me, my lord?"

"First," he said, "I wish to discuss the most

brilliant piece of writing -- of philosophy -- I've ever read."

"Pray, of what author do you speak?" she asked as she moved toward him, her brows lifted.

"Jeremy Bentham. I've just read his Classification of Offenses. You had told me about it, but this was the first time I had actually read it."

Now her eyes alighted as she went to sit on the settee. "He presents it all so logically and with such ease, one is instantly baffled as to why no one ever proposed so simple a solution to imprisonment before." Lord Wycliff suddenly saw the light.

He smiled as he came to sit on the settee across from her. "My feelings exactly. Classifications have been commonplace since the days of Plato's dialogues. That it has taken us hundreds of years to apply classification to punishable acts is incomprehensible."

"I agree completely!" she shrieked. "It should have been as obvious to us as the noses on our faces."

"If Mr. Bentham never wrote another word, his Classification of Offenses would have been enough to secure his position as one of the world's greatest thinkers."

Louisa beamed at Lord Wycliff. "I am so very happy you understand."

"And I am so thankful to you."

She faced him, her brow hitching. Had he not said he wished to speak to her of something *personal*? "You said *first* you wished to discuss Mr. Bentham. Pray, what else did you wish to discuss?"

"My lack of success with your solicitor

yesterday."

She sank back into the settee. "Then you were unable to coerce him into giving you the information you desired?"

"The man was impervious to my money."

"How novel, my lord."

"Come and sit beside me, Mrs. Phillips. I dislike shouting across the room."

For reasons she would never understand, she obeyed the arrogant man and sat on the settee next to him. "I am here, my lord. Are you happy?"

His eyes looked black today. And they sparkled with mirth. "My, but you are a saucy vixen."

"Do I take that for a compliment?"

He could not seem to repress his smile. He settled back and pinned her with a knowing stare. "How much did the late Mr. Phillips's things fetch?"

A flash of anger swept over her face, and she stiffened. "How do you know so much about my affairs?"

"Because I need all the leverage I can get."

"And your vast amounts of money cannot buy that?"

"I don't know. I'm prepared to settle a handsome sum on you for the information I failed to obtain from Mr. Twining."

"The identity of my husband's *benefactor*?"

He nodded, a morose expression on his handsome face.

"That I cannot give you. I honestly do not know the man's identity."

* * *

He gave her a long look. Gone was her flippancy. And her anger. She was telling the truth.

His face was grim, his voice low when he spoke. "You really don't know, do you?"

She shook her head.

"Did your husband never discuss the man?" God but he hated to call the despicable man her husband.

"Only to tell me to stay abovestairs when a lone man came two or three times a year. A man -- I think he's a lord -- who my husband addressed with great reverence -- and great secrecy."

That would fit, Harry thought. "Did you ever get a glimpse of the man?"

"Actually I did, once, from a very great distance."

Before she could say more, Ellie and Mr. Coke burst into the room. "You will never believe it!" Ellie squealed. "Even though the sun is shining, it has begun to rain!"

Ellie and Edward were not so wet that they could not sit down and join in the conversation, which soon turned to Jeremy Bentham's impending visit for a speaking engagement in London.

"I cannot believe that I will actually get to hear the great man in the flesh," Ellie exclaimed.

Edward cast a bemused glance at his cousin while Harry made every effort to show the proper respect toward the ladies' pontificating idol. That deuced Edward had better not betray him. It was imperative that the widow believe he enthusiastically shared her political views.

"When will we have the pleasure to hear Mr. Bentham's address?" Harry asked.

"He comes next week."

Hopefully he would be spared the boredom of hearing Bentham. Hopefully, by next week he would have the information he sought.

Chapter 6

Louisa was grateful for the opportunity to stay home this evening. She really must put pen to paper to turn out another essay. In the past her essays were the result of strong feelings she wanted to express about the rights of man -- and of women. Now, though, she sought to write merely for the money. She felt guilty writing for the wrong reasons, writing solely for the money.

She had been sitting here for the past hour trying to decide upon a topic. With no vituperative feelings begging to come forward, her pen was stilled. She could write about the franchise, but she had already done that. Child labor, prison reform, and birth control were subjects that also had been addressed by her.

She looked up at her sister, who sat across from her sewing on her new dress. Ellie's face lifted, and she caught Louisa's stare, taking it as permission to speak. "Are your writing one of your famous essays, Mr. Lewis?" A cocky expression lighted her youthful face, and she giggled.

Louisa sighed. "If only my muse would return." She put down her pen. "What are you sewing?"

Ellie's voice became animated. "A promenade dress for one of my wonderful walks with Mr. Coke."

"Whatever do the two of you find to talk about during these walks?"

A far-away look in her eyes, a satisfied countenance on her face, Ellie answered. "Mr. Coke and I have a great deal in common. First of all, he is as enamored of his cousin as I am of my elder sister. Then there is the fact that we were both tutored at home. We are both country bred. And he is just so very amusing.

"There is more to him than that," Ellie went on. "He allows me to expound endlessly on the merits of Mr. Bentham and on the wisdom imparted in Mr. Lewis's essays, and I believe I'm converting him to our way of thinking -- which is rather a coup, given that he hails from a noble family."

"You must not be impressed by the circumstances of his birth. Remember that his class has done nothing to earn respect."

"He tells me Lord Wycliff built his fortune by his own cunning after his father squandered away their lands and possessions. Do you not find that commendable?"

"I would find it far more commendable were Lord Wycliff to give his fortune to the poor," Louisa said.

"As much as I want to agree with you, I find that notion most unrealistic."

Louisa sighed. "You are, of course, right. I suppose the most I can hope for is that Lord Wycliff and others like him use their influence in Parliament to enact laws beneficial to the less fortunate."

Ellie's gaze flitted to the pen and paper before her sister. "You cannot believe how difficult it is for me to withhold your authorship from Mr. Coke. I am so very proud of you, and so close to him that it is quite an accomplishment for me not to confide in him."

Louisa's face clouded. "I beg that you never even consider revealing my identity to the gentleman – or to anyone. It's imperative that no one ever suspect I am a female – I mean, that Mr. Lewis is a female. If his gender were to become known, my work would never again have the opportunity to be widely distributed."

"Don't fear, Louisa. I shall never reveal that you are Philip Lewis."

"Labor unification!" Louisa shrieked, picking up her pen and beginning to write furiously.

* * *

Edward looked at the dog-eared volume reposing in his cousin's lap across the carriage from him. The sunlight reflected off the worn gilt on the edge of the pages. "Surely you're not going to tell Mrs. Phillips you read the book last night when you spent the whole of the evening at your club and didn't make it home until daylight!"

A sly smile slid across Harry's tanned face. "I thumbed through it enough to expound to her on its merits."

"You can't believe that ridiculous poppycock in those foolish treatises."

"Oh course not, my good man, but if I hope to accomplish my goals, I must have the widow on my side, and the best way to gain her trust is to feign appreciation for her bloody do-gooding reforms."

"But you even indicated to Lord Seymour that you sympathized with the reformers."

"I did no such thing," Harry protested. "I merely introduced him to a beautiful young woman, who then expounded on her beliefs as I stood silently beside her." The thought of how lovely Mrs. Phillips had been the night of Lord Seymour's ball left Harry weak inside and anxious to see her today. The woman was indeed a feast for the eyes. For the remainder of the carriage ride to his former home he reflected pleasurably on her silky skin and golden hair and the perfect oval of her incredible face.

And he grew impatient to see her.

* * *

The foursome seemed to have fallen into a pattern. Mr. Coke and Ellie would walk in the park that centered Grosvenor Square while Louisa and Lord Wycliff discussed the latest reading she had given him. As they had done on the previous day, Harry and Louisa sat next to each other on a settee in the library.

Despite her distrust of peers, Louisa had bestowed her favor on Lord Wycliff, whose earnestness impressed her. He had even told her he would take his seat in Parliament. This was obviously her most important conquest to date, and she owed it to him to help him regain his property so that he could fulfill his duties.

"When we were interrupted yesterday," he said, "you were saying that you once saw the man you believe was your husband's benefactor."

She settled back on the settee, crossing her legs at the ankles. "Yes, I thought about it a great deal last night, and I've decided the mysterious man must be Godwin's benefactor, though the Lord only knows why a man like Godwin would merit a benefactor."

"I have some idea," he said bitterly.

She gave him a probing look, then continued. "I only caught a glimpse of him once, and Godwin would have. . ." she hesitated a moment. "He would have been extremely angry with me had he known I peeked from over the upstairs balustrade to see the man."

Harry's eyes flashed. "What did the benefactor look like?"

"He was quite old. Older even than Godwin. And he had silver hair. He was tall, yet stooped, and I think he must have been handsome as a younger man."

"Could you identify him if you saw him again?" Lord Wycliff asked.

She thought for a moment. "I believe I could."

"Tell me," he said, "how long had your husband's valet been with him?"

"I don't really know. For many years. He was here when I came."

"Where is he now?"

"He's here. He's training to be my butler, but I don't know how long I'll be able to afford to keep him."

From nowhere Lord Wycliff's large hand curled around her forearm. "That husband of yours left you nothing?" Lord Wycliff asked, his voice tender and concerned.

She gave a bitter laugh. "Nothing."

"Death was too good for him."

She agreed, but would not admit it aloud.

He removed his hand. "Do you suppose his valet would know the identity of the benefactor?"

"I can ask."

His voice softened again. "I appreciate all you've done for me, especially since trusting a peer was repugnant to you but a few weeks ago."

She tossed back her head and laughed. "Oh, it's still repugnant, but in your case, I am learning to trust you. You've made an impressive effort to amend your ways." She got to her feet. "I'll go talk to Williams now."

* * *

He watched as she walked from the room, her back straight and her step light. She was a joy to watch.

While he waited for her to return, Harry cursed his own deceit. He had done many things that made him ashamed, but this deception stung deeper and with more regret.

She was such a passionate little thing, bursting with ideas and schemes to aid the masses. She had enough on her plate without having to worry about surviving with no money. *Damn Godwin Phillips.* Harry did not know if he hated the man more for treating his lovely wife so shabbily or for yanking her from the schoolroom and veritably purchasing her. His hand fisted, and he shocked himself by uttering a curse.

He got up and walked to the window and watched Ellie Sinclair and Edward walk about the small park. Edward seemed genuinely fond of the girl. God knows, she was pretty enough. She was a more youthful version of her sister. But she seemed so much younger and, frankly, stupid. He could not imagine Louisa Phillips ever having been so silly and carefree.

Then, with a thud in the vicinity of his heart, he realized Louisa Phillips had long been a married woman by the time she was Ellie's age. And he once again cursed Godwin Phillips.

He turned from the window, deliberately kicking his boot against the patterned carpet as he did so. The least Harry could do for the poor widow was to see her settled in a little home.

Perhaps that would assuage his conscience.

Damn, she trusts me, he thought with shame.

When she returned to the room, he read disappointment on her face. "Any luck?"

She shook her head, then returned to the settee. "Like me, he knew of the man's importance to Godwin, but Godwin was careful to shield the man's identity. Williams does know where the man came from, though."

A smile on his face, Harry sat down. "And, pray, where might that be?" He was getting close.

"Somewhere in Cornwall. And I was right about him being a lord. Williams confirmed it. Apparently the man was somewhat of a recluse."

Harry's mind spun. He tried to remember a lord from Cornwall, but the only one he knew -- Lord Robartes -- was an honorable man who took his seat in the House of Lords and was far from being a recluse. There must be any number of lords residing in Cornwall. The problem was to find one. The right one.

Say!" Harry said. "Have you a *Debrett's*?"

She got up and went straight to the book. "How clever of you!" She began to thumb through its pages. "Though I daresay it will take hours to go through all these names and titles and determine which of them live in Cornwall."

He took the tome from her. "We'll need paper and pen."

"Of course. We shall have to draw up a list." She went to the desk drawer and removed several sheets of velum and set them on top the desk. Then she pushed a second armchair up to the desk. "Come to the desk, Lord Wycliff. We can both sit here."

"Shall you record the names?" he asked. "I

daresay no one, not even me, can read my handwriting.

She nodded.

He sat beside her and placed the opened book on the desk. "You're right. This will take a great deal of time."

She sat and watched as he silently scanned page after page.

"Is Tyndrum in Cornwall?" he asked.

"No. It's in Scotland. Cornwall and Scotland retain many Celtic names." She moved to get up. "What's needed is a map. I'll make a list of the towns and villages of Cornwall. Will that be helpful?"

"It will, indeed."

She fetched the map and spread it over the top of the desk, then took pen and paper and began to list the names of Cornish towns. "I shall attempt to put them in alphabetical order," she said. "Bodmin. Boscastle. Cambourne. . . "

Her list was drawn up in less than ten minutes. And still he had not found a single peer who lived in any of the cities. She scooted her chair closer to him and began to peruse the information within the book. "Why do you not take the even numbered pages, and I'll take the odd?"

Without removing his gaze from the page, he nodded and moved the open book closer to her.

They read for another half hour until they found a peer who hailed from Cornwall. "Lord Arundel!" Harry exclaimed.

Louisa took her pen and wrote down his name and seat.

Then they commenced reading again.

By the time they had finished, they had

discovered there were six lords residing in Cornwall.

Next, Harry took the map and studied it to determine where each of the lords lived.

"Why do you need the map now?" she asked.

"Because we'll just have to go find the mysterious benefactor."

"We?"

"Yesterday," he said, "I told you I would help you financially if you could help me to regain this house. I am now ready to make a specific proposal to you, madam."

She cocked a thin brow.

"I am prepared to bestow on you a small home and an annual pension for as long as I live. I want you to travel to Cornwall with me and help me find the benefactor."

"But I can't possibly do that," she protested.

"You are afraid of the impropriety of traveling with a man?"

"Of course not," she countered. "But there's Ellie to think of, and. . ." She withdrew her gaze from him and stared into her lap. "Could we bring Ellie?"

"I see no reason why we couldn't."

"When would you want to go?" she asked.

"As soon as you can pack."

"But Jeremy Bentham's visit is but days away."

"Is that more important than a lifetime free of financial woes?"

She hesitated.

"Do you plan to take care of your sister indefinitely, or does she return to your father's home?"

"She will never return there," Louisa snapped, anger in her voice.

Why did she feel so strongly about keeping her sister with her? "Then, may I suggest you think of your sister's welfare. You certainly would not be able to make a home for her if you had no funds."

God but he could barely make eye contact with her. Her eyes were so soulful. There was another emotion in the depths of those incredible eyes. Was it controlled anger? Why would she be angry with him? He was merely trying to help her.

She lifted her chin defiantly.

He got to his feet. "Think on it tonight. I'll be here with my travelling coach in the morning."

Minutes later Ellie came flying through the door. She had gone out without her bonnet, and her face was flushed from the sun. "Mr. Coke has agreed to come see Mr. Bentham speak! Is that not wonderful news?"

Louisa looked at Ellie sympathetically. How could she keep her poor sister away from Jeremy Bentham's talk? He was growing old, and this might be Ellie's only chance to ever see the great man.

That night sleep eluded Louisa. She wanted the things Lord Wycliff offered, but could she really trust him? It was not, either, right to force Ellie on a trip that would not only take more than a week but would also prevent her from seeing Jeremy Bentham.

She thought about leaving Ellie behind and going to Cornwall alone with Lord Wycliff, but she did not think being alone with the man for days on end would be a good thing, especially since he had a most unsettling effect on her. Not to mention that he was a man, and they were not trustworthy.

It was almost dawn when she made her

decision.

$\mathscr{C}$hapter 7

By the time a bright sun streamed through her chamber window, Louisa was completely dressed in a traveling costume and sat at her desk writing a note to Ellie.

> *My Pet,*
> *I am sorry to say I've been called out of town to attend to affairs dealing with Godwin's estate. I doubt if I'll be back in time to see Mr. Bentham deliver his speech. Mr. Coke will do me the goodness of escorting you to see Mr. Bentham, and you must have Cook accompany you as chaperon. It wouldn't do to tarnish your reputation. Mr. Coke, especially, would not care for that at all. All my love.*
> *Louisa*

She dried the quill, then wrapped it in a piece of old cloth and placed it in her portmanteau with the rest of her things. Perhaps she could finish her essay on labor unification during the journey that lay ahead.

She heard the wheels of a coach rattle on the street below, and she lifted the bulky bag and carried it downstairs.

Once she edged open the front door, Lord

Wycliff bounded up the two steps and relieved her of the bag. She noted that he too was dressed for traveling. No silken finery today, nor his ever-present black. Today he wore fawn colored pantaloons with boots and a greatcoat.

He gave her bag to the coachman, who placed it on top the carriage before he opened the door for Louisa and his master.

"Before we leave London," Louisa said, "I beg that you impart to Mr. Coke the necessity of him escorting my sister to see Mr. Bentham."

"I have already done so."

Her brows winged together. "How did you know I didn't wish to bring her with me?"

"Because I knew you couldn't deprive her of the pleasure of seeing Mr. Bentham."

She shot him an angry glance then lifted the curtain to peer from the glass. Louisa didn't at all like the look of the skies. Clouds were gathering, and rain seemed imminent. Which would considerably slow their progress. It was cool, too. Much colder than it had been in weeks.

Lord Wycliff handed her into the coach, and she was pleased that he had provided a rug for her.

When he started to sit beside her, she protested. "I think not, my lord. There are just the two of us. We can each have our own seat for the journey."

"Ah," he said, sitting opposite of her, "unlike me, you are thinking quite clearly this morning. I fear I am a creature of habit."

"I trust you were up late last night reading one of the books I provided for you," she said mischievously.

His black eyes sparkled. "To be sure." Then he

cocked his hat and slid down in his seat, giving
every appearance of a man taking a nap.

She knew so very little about him. Had he
really been up late reading her book, or had he
spent the night gaming and womanizing as other
men of his class did? From their rides at Hyde
Park and from the ball at Lord Seymour's, it was
clear that Lord Wycliff was well known in the *ton*,
especially among the women. Their unabashed
flirting with him had given Louisa a peculiar
surge of pleasure that was not unconnected to
possessiveness.

Despite that she was tired this morning, she
continued to peer from the window. It had now
begun to rain. The streets quickly filled with mud
and water and noxious odors. She could not say
that she would regret leaving behind this city with
its sooty skies and stinking air and pitiable
creatures at every turn.

She looked away from the sight of a small boy
who could not have been more than five years old
but was alone on the pavement, wearing shoes
several sizes too large for his tiny feet. The poor
lad didn't even have a coat to shield him from the
day's cold.

She gathered the rug about her and grew
morose. Her thoughts, like the skies, turned
melancholy. She knew she must direct her
energies even more potently toward helping
children like the lad she had just seen.

Perhaps she did need to continue living in
London. Once he got the information he desired,
would Lord Wycliff continue taking her to events
where she could meet men of power? Would he be
true to his word and take his seat in Parliament
in order to promulgate the beliefs she had

imparted to him? Or was his interest feigned in order to gain what he wanted?

Again, Louisa realized she knew very little about the man who reposed across from her, his long muscular legs taking up a great deal of the inside of the carriage. She stared at his solid thighs and realized they were nearly as big around as her waist.

She took note of the quality of his well tailored pantaloons and the workmanship of his boots. They were obviously very expensive but not showy like something Godwin would have worn. The difference between Lord Wycliff's class and Godwin's aspirations to emulate it was as distinct as night from day.

However, that was not to say she liked the peer. His worth had yet to be proven. Her approval would continue to be withheld from him. After all, he was a man, and God knows none of them were trustworthy.

By the time Lord Wycliff's coachman had paid at the last London tollgate, the rain was falling onto the carriage roof likes buckets being emptied. She felt terribly sorry for the poor coachman, for in addition to the pounding rain, it had become bitterly cold.

And through it all, Lord Wycliff slept.

Louisa was discovering the rug, thick and tightly woven wool though it was, offered little protection against the chill that seeped to her very bones. *How could Lord Wycliff sleep through such discomfort?* Then she remembered her elder brother, who had an unfortunate drinking problem. Frederick, after a night of overindulging, was oblivious to everything. She remembered the time Ellie had poured icy water on him in a vain effort to awaken him for Sunday services. He had merely turned over and continued snoring.

Could Lord Wycliff be sleeping one off? With such thoughts ringing in her brain and her arms tucked under the heavy rug, she finally did as Lord Wycliff. She drifted off to sleep.

*   *   *

When Harry awoke, Louisa was asleep. He was unable to remove his gaze from her. He had seen many beautiful women asleep beside him, but none compared to Louisa Phillips. There was an innocence about her, not just because she was fair and petite and young looking, but also because of the naiveté of her hopes for reform and because of her true compassion.

Which made him even more ashamed of his deception. She was only now beginning to trust a man, and he was about to turn around and blow up the little ground he had gained for his gender.

Though Louisa Phillips professed to eschew the strictures of society, Harry was determined not to blacken her reputation.

He turned his attention to the matter of securing a room at an inn. Since the rain had seriously impeded their progress, they would probably be forced to spend several nights in posting inns. How were they to do that while sparing her reputation?

An idea came to him, but he knew the widow would not like it.

He apprised her of it when she awoke. He had watched her awaken, gathering the rug tightly about her as she pulled herself to a sitting position. When she looked across at him, she blushed. Did the prospect of a man watching her sleep cause her embarrassment?

"Rather cold, is it not?" he said casually.

"Would that we had a hot brick," she lamented. "But I should not be so selfish when the poor coachman has none of the luxuries we enjoy."

"Do you always direct your thoughts to the plight of others who are less fortunate than you?"

She gave him a most straightforward stare. "Someone must, my lord."

"And you prefer that someone be a person in a position to do something to evoke change?"

"Of course. That's what I've worked toward for a very long time."

"And I shall be your instrument."

She nodded. He liked the way her blue eyes danced like those of a child impatient to open a present.

"Are you not exceedingly cold without a rug, my lord?"

His pulse quickened as he thought of sitting next to her, sharing her rug. "It is rather unpleasant."

"Then you thought to share the rug with me?"

A coy smile slanted across his face. "I did."

He enjoyed watching the guilt wash over her.

"Very well," she said with reluctance. "You may move to this side, but I will not have any part of you touching me. Is that clear?"

"Like a bell, madam," he said as he stood to a stooped position and moved to her seat.

"I believe we need to discuss the matter of rooms at the inn," he said. "I know you don't care a fig about the opinion of the *ton*, but you need to realize that in order to work with them you have to earn their respect."

"What does that have to do with rooms at the inn?"

"Were it to be discovered that we traveled together, I fear your good name would be ruined."

She gazed at him through narrowed eyes. "What, then, do you propose, my lord?"

"That we use other names. Registering as, say, a Mr. and Mrs. Smith would neither attract attention nor draw scrutiny. On the other hand, were we to secure separate rooms under other names, any intercourse between us would be sure to draw censure."

Her eyes rounded. "You're proposing that we sleep together?" There was disbelief and irritation in her voice.

"I promise not to touch."

"And I'm supposed to trust you?" she questioned. "My dear Lord Wycliff, you are a man, and I've yet to find one worthy of trust."

"I don't know what else I can say or do to warrant your acceptance."

"The matter is out of your hands."

He leaned back into the window, allowing cold air to rush beneath the rug in the gap between them.

She haughtily pulled the rug away from him and hugged it to herself.

* * *

Night came early. Just before five in the afternoon, the coach pulled into an inn yard in Reading. It had taken them all day to travel forty miles. Despite that the rain was still coming down in sheets, Louisa would be happy to stretch her legs.

And to get away from Lord Wycliff. The audacity! He really expected that she would allow him to sleep in her room! The man was completely insufferable.

He held an umbrella over her as they ran to the inn.

Once inside, he bespoke a private parlor "for my wife and me."

Louisa was about to protest when she felt very strong hands squeeze at her arm. Then, she realized a scene would attract a great deal of attention. She would merely shake it off for now, then later insist the obstinate man obtain separate sleeping rooms. Right now all she could think of was her desire to plop down in front of a bright fire and drink a cup of warm milk.

Since they were the only occupants of the private parlor, she and Lord Wycliff were at liberty to take a seat immediately in front of the hearth. Soon the chill in her bones faded, and she felt her cheeks growing hot. She also felt Lord Wycliff's eyes on her and finally looked up to meet his gaze.

"Really, Mrs. Phillips," he said, "you mustn't worry about your virtue. I assure you the last thing I want is to share a bed with a man-hating reformer."

Even though the last thing she wanted was to share a bed with a man, she was oddly piqued by his remark. "Then how would you suggest we share a room without sharing a bed?"

"How do you know I couldn't lie with you without wanting to make love to you?" he asked.

She hoped he would mistake her blush for flush from the fire. "I know that you're a man, and all men want the same thing."

"I assure you, Mrs. Phillips, the thing you allude to I can have whenever I want. It has not been so long since I was with a woman that I would lower either my preferences or my expectations."

Now she was really mad. *Lower his expectations indeed*! She took a long drink from her mug of milk and avoided eye contact with the conceited, arrogant, obnoxious peer of the realm.

Before long the innkeeper's wife brought each of them a plate of mutton and hot bread with freshly churned butter.

Lord Wycliff cut, but did not eat, his mutton. "I see I have offended you," he said. "I thought you would be pleased that I do not find you desirable."

She lifted her chin haughtily. "I am."

"Then we can sleep together?"

She bit into a thick slice of crusty bread and slowly chewed it before answering. "I can scream quite loudly, you know."

He smiled before biting down on a forkful of meat.

Chapter 8

Butterflies danced in Louisa's stomach as she and Lord Wycliff mounted the steep, ill-lit stairs to the bedchamber they would share.

He inserted the key into the iron lock and eased open the door. A candle already burned beside the bed, and a fire blazed. The room's wooden ceiling was low, which together with the warmth, gave the room a comforting feel.

She stepped into the room, a chill inching down her back despite the room's warmth. Her portmanteau had been placed beside the bed.

Lord Wycliff stood in the doorway. "I go to the tavern now. I have the key and will let myself in later." His voice dropped to a husky whisper when he added, "I daresay you'll be asleep when I return."

Louisa looked at him with surprise, but he was already turning away to descend the stairs. She crossed the room and locked the door, then began to remove her wrinkled traveling clothes. First the pelisse, then the gown. And still she wasn't really cold. She decided the innkeepers must keep a fire burning even when there were no guests. She would have to ask Lord Wycliff to give the innkeepers an extra sum in appreciation of the accommodations. Lord Wycliff could obviously afford such a trivial expense. After all, he was going to settle her for life, merely for accompanying him on this journey.

Her chest suddenly tightened. What if he was not a man of his word? Did he truly plan to recompense her so well for a few days of her time? As she had so thoroughly been reminding herself all day, she knew not what manner of man he was. In spite of the many hours they had spent together over the last few weeks, he had revealed nothing of himself.

She stopped midway through donning her woolen night shift and wondered what she really knew of him. That he possessed a great deal of money was a certainty. His cousin boasted of Lord Wycliff's ability to build a sizeable fortune after being left virtually penniless by his squandering father. Louisa also knew without doubt that the lord who was to share her room was fiercely devoted to his mother. An admirable trait in a man, she thought.

But what else did she really know of him? She recounted their many visits together and realized she knew only the little he had allowed her observe, and little of it was personal. She had no idea even of how he had amassed his fortune. Nor did she know if he had ever been close to matrimony. She wrung her hands, learning just now as she was about to share her bed with him that the handsome nobleman was a virtual stranger.

She donned her night rail, slid beneath the warm blankets and blew out the candle. Weary from the day's travel, she went to sleep almost immediately, careful to take less than half of the bed.

* * *

Lying beneath the warm covers some hours later and listening to the rhythmic breathing of the feminine creature beside him, Harry could barely hold back the desire to laugh. The silly woman had actually believed him when he told her he had no desire for her. With every rise and fall of her breasts, he wanted her. His desire for her was more keen than even the desire to command his first ship. Or the desire to reclaim Wycliff House. Or to regain his mother's portrait.

Yet he had instinctively known Louisa Phillips was not a woman to be taken lightly. She would certainly not give herself to a man who did not plan to make her the center of his life, and Harry knew the complex reformer was not the woman for him. Why, she didn't even like men!

He gave himself to trying to unravel the puzzle that was Louisa Phillips. Why did she hate men with such vehemence? The source, of course, pointed to the vile man who had been her husband. What manner of man would leave a young thing like that without provisions for a roof over her head?

From something she had begun to say before amending her words, Harry felt certain that Godwin Phillips had raised his hand to his young bride. Harry could barely hold back his curse. If Godwin Phillips were still alive, Harry would take pleasure in beating him until his ugly face looked like a can of maggots.

As he lay beside her, Harry vowed he would see that Louisa Phillips was comfortable for the rest of her life. Whether she aided him in his quest or not.

* * *

The following morning they ate a hearty breakfast before renewing their journey. He had awakened before she did, slipped on his pantaloons -- for he had slept only in his silken shirt -- and gone downstairs without disturbing her.

That she had survived the night with her virtue intact undoubtedly loosened her tongue this morning when she met him in the parlor for breakfast. Gone were the scowls of the night before.

Through his restraint, he had earned her approval.

"I believe the innkeeper keeps fires blazing in the rooms so they are warm when guests arrive," Louisa told him between spoonfuls of porridge. "You must be generous to the man, my lord."

An amused grin lighted his tanned face. "As you wish, madam."

"From the indentation on the bed I surmise that you slept in our room," she said, "but I declare I never knew when you came."

He watched as her cheeks grew rosy. He had learned to detect her propensity to blush when things embarrassed her. "Have I earned your trust, madam?"

She shyly nodded. "I daresay it's because I hold no appeal to you."

He would play along with the charade. "Please don't think you're not attractive, ma'am. I vow that any number of men would find you desirable."

Her scowl returned. "Then you lied when you said I was the prettiest woman at Lord Seymour's?"

He fairly spit out his tea. "Not at all, madam.

You were the prettiest woman there. It is just that I like women who are a bit more. . ."

"Free with their favors?"

"I confess to having a certain amount of experience with women of that description."

"Women like Lady Davenwood?"

How in the deuce did she know of his affair with Fanny? "A gentleman does not discuss such matters, Mrs. Phillips."

That blush of hers returned.

"I do find your liberal opinions at odds with your own lifestyle," he said.

"How so?" she asked.

"Do you not espouse the principals of free love?"

"I do," she said. "Marriage as we know it is nothing but a sham."

He raised a brow. "I'm afraid I don't follow you."

"Surely you know how freely ladies of the *ton* share their beds with men who are not their husbands."

She really does know about Fanny. He nodded sheepishly.

"Which appears to be perfectly all right because they are married women. Then there is the fact that few women are truly given the opportunity to choose their own husbands. Circumstances of birth determine who marries whom. You must admit a man of your birth would never marry a flower woman at Covent Garden."

"Nor would a lovely young woman from Kerseymeade choose to marry an aging card shark."

Her eyes rounded. She was silent for a moment, then her voice dropped, and she spoke without hesitation. "My father sold me for a thousand pounds. My significant abhorrence to the match was irrelevant."

He felt the pain in her words and reached across the sturdy wooden table to take her hand. "So that's why you hate men," he whispered. "They've done nothing but hurt you. Not only your husband, but also your father."

She withdrew her hand and stiffened. "You're selfish creatures, the lot of you."

"I can see why you think that," he said solemnly, his voice low. Now he knew why she would never return home, why she wanted to get Ellie away from their father. Harry finished the last of his tea, then put on his coat and helped her into hers. "Let us hope the weather is better today."

It was still raining as they walked around puddles in the inn yard, and his coach pulled in front of another in order to save them a few steps of walking. Harry handed her into the conveyance, then took his seat across from her and watched with amusement as she tucked herself beneath the heavy rug.

He wasn't cold yet. He was still warm from the parlor -- and from the intimacy of their conversation. It was as if a barrier between them had been removed.

She looked out the window. "I believe the clouds are breaking up," she said cheerfully.

With a lump in his throat, he watched her. There was such a child-like quality about her, despite the tough facade she had erected. In the weeks he had known her, her demeanor had softened considerably. She dressed far less somberly, and acted far more femininely. If only he had more time to spend with the lovely lady.

He almost regretted that he would no longer see her once he located Godwin Phillips's benefactor, but since Harry had no intentions of becoming a member of the House of Lords, nor of embracing Mrs. Phillips's liberal politics, he knew he would have to steer clear of her once he regained Wycliff House.

Why should he wish to extend the franchise and allow his cottagers to usurp his rights, rights that had been enjoyed by the Earls of Wycliff for the past two hundred years? The notion was utterly ridiculous. He would be sorry to disappoint her, but his money should salve her anger and bruised pride.

"It's a pity man's future is determined by his birth," she said. "Take John Coachman. It's his lot in life to brave the elements, the cold chilling his bones and the wind cutting through him, while it is your lot to sit inside the coach, warm and dry."

"Would it please you if I sent him to join you and I take his seat on the box?" Harry asked, mirth in his voice.

"That is not my point at all," she protested. "It is a sad fact of life that while some children are coddled with nurses and tutors and protected within their nurseries, others are left orphans to beg strangers on the street for their next meal."

"I regret that I am unable to feed and clothe all the orphans of the world, Mrs. Phillips. My pockets are only so deep."

She heaved a sigh. "That is not the point, either. Don't you see it is the right of every child to be able to play and learn, not to work to earn his keep? It is the responsibility of thinking people like you and me to equalize people."

"And by that, we would all benefit."

She tossed aside her rug. He loved it when those pale eyes of hers flashed. "Yes!" she said. "A well fed and well educated citizenry would automatically reduce crime and could even reduce diseases which I am convinced are spread by sheer ignorance."

"I had no idea your education extended to the field of medicine, Mrs. Phillips."

She glared at him. "You're making fun of me."

"Not at all," he protested. "I find you exceedingly intelligent, and I have great respect for your intellect."

Growing cold, she took up her rug again. "What of your intellect, my lord? It seems to me you have carefully concealed your own ideas from me."

He felt pangs of guilt. "I admit I have spent much of my adult life amassing a fortune, giving little thought to the wisdom of the great thinkers of today. I am now trying to fill that void -- with your help." He sounded convincing, even to himself.

She met his gaze with a frank stare. "Tell me, Lord Wycliff, how did you make your fortune?"

Additional pangs of guilt vibrated through him. "I was in the shipping business."

She nodded. "Were I to go into the shipping business, could I make vast sums of money?"

"You're a woman."

"Exactly. Doors are closed in women's faces."

"The next thing I know, you'll be demanding the franchise for women, too."

"And why not? We comprise half the population."

"I don't deny that we need women, but their principal purpose in life is to bear children."

Her face looked wounded. "Are you saying that since I have borne no children, I have no worth?"

"Damn it, woman, that's not what I meant!" Despite himself, he tried to imagine her with a child. He did not at all like to think of her bearing Godwin Phillips's child. Not to say that she wouldn't have been a fine mother. And wife, too, had she been given the chance to marry a man who owned her heart. She might not realize it herself, but with her capacity for compassion she could have been a great wife and mother. *Had her circumstances of birth been more fortunate*. Had she not been born to the abominable father who could sell his spawn for mere money. The muscles in Harry's face tightened. How he hated the man for what he had done to his own daughter.

Harry's thoughts flitted to his own father. As angry as Harry was with him, he knew his father always loved him and his mother above worldly possessions. A pity his father's weakness had led to Harry's mother's death. Harry remembered how broken his mother had been when she lost first her home, then her husband.

Louisa's declaration that the clouds were breaking proved correct. When it was time to partake of a nuncheon, the skies had cleared, and they were able to depart the carriage and stretch their legs. Then Harry spread a blanket on the damp grass beside the road, and the three of them sat down to eat the generous repast packed by the innkeepers' wife.

Chapter 9

The grass was wet, but their blanket seemed to absorb most of the moisture. After they ate, the coachman went to tend the horses and Lord Wycliff leaned back, his weight on his elbows, his long legs stretched out beyond the length of the blanket as he gazed up into the now-blue sky. It was warm enough now that he'd removed his greatcoat, and Louisa -- with Lord Wycliff's assistance -- had taken off her black cloak.

She tried to avert her gaze from Lord Wycliff's limbs. They reminded her of one of those statues of ancient Greeks she had viewed in the British Museum. Like them, he was all firm planes and smoothly rounded muscles that must be as hard as the marble from which the Grecian men were carved. Her eyes traveled from his muddy boots, past his thighs and settled just above his waist, where there was not an ounce of fat on his well constructed bones.

She was once again reminded of her first impression of him when she had thought him too manly to be clothed in the finery worn by fops of the *ton*. Not that he sported the frivolous frills worn by dandies, either. She could see him sparring with the likes of Jackson or keeping his balance at the helm of ship, his sword drawn in defense of his schooner.

"What keeps you so pensive?" he asked, making no effort to sit up.

She watched him intently. The endless fields of wheat behind him framed his head like a golden halo in a Renaissance painting.

A week ago she would have lashed out in anger at his presumptuousness in asking her so personal a question. But this was now, and their close proximity had slowly been weathering away the armor they both had worn for a considerable period of time.

"I was wondering why you hate your father."

He sat up and drilled her with his dark eyes. "How do you know I hated my father? I never told you."

"You didn't have to say the words. Do you take me for such a fool that I would not notice that you adored your mother, yet said nothing about your father?"

He relaxed, taking a sip of the wine that had been in their basket. "You know that my father lost everything."

"I know he lost Wycliff House to Godwin at cards one night at Waiters."

He looked as if a brace of candles had been lit within his gaze. "How could a man who had nothing to leave his wife amass a fortune great enough to play for stakes that would include one of London's finest townhouses?"

Now the brightness of her eyes matched his. "The benefactor!" she said. Godwin had certainly never been able to hold onto money. Not with his obsession for gaming. And for lavish living.

"That has to be it," he said.

They both stayed silent a moment, lost in their

own thoughts. Finally, she spoke. "Do you suppose the benefactor chose his prey?"

He slapped at his knee. "You are positively brilliant!"

"You are just learning that, my lord?" She laughed.

"That you are considerably smarter than other women of my acquaintance I learned the day I met you."

The corners of her mouth lifted into a smile. "Lucky for me and my need for a good night's sleep that you are not enamored of intelligent women."

A mischievous glint flashed in his eyes. "Indeed."

Somehow, his answer seemed to lack sincerity.

He began to gather up the leavings of their luncheon, and she stood and stretched, lifting her arms straight toward the heavens. The stiffness in her back from hours of riding in the coach had lessened considerably, but she knew it would return once they resumed the journey.

To her surprise, he came to her and gently covered her shoulders with her cloak. Unexpected warmth surged through her.

* * *

That night he repeated his practice of leaving her to dress for bed while he went to the tavern. Only this night she was awake when he came to bed.

Lying there in the dark, she pretended to be asleep as he stood before the window and removed his pants. Her heart accelerated when she beheld him, his wondrous body bathed in moonlight. Then he tossed aside his jacket. She could no more remove her eyes from the glorious sight than she could cease to draw breath.

Had Godwin looked like that, she might not have found his presence in her bed so repugnant. She wondered what it would be like to lie beneath a man like Lord Wycliff. She watched as he moved toward the bed, lithe and powerful and dark like a panther, and she wondered how many women he had been with.

He climbed beneath the covers, careful not to touch her. After the brief whiff of cold air from lifting the covers, she felt his heat.

She lay there for a very long time, her back to him. She waited to hear his breathing change as a man's does when he drops into slumber, but she heard no such change.

Was he, too, wondering what it would be like to take her into his arms?

It was a very long time before she finally heard the pattern of his breathing change. He had finally gone to sleep.

Only then did she do likewise.

* * *

The following day, Harry consulted the map.

"How long before we reach Cornwall?" she asked.

He flicked a glance toward her. "We shall sleep in Cornwall tomorrow night."

"Do we go to the northern coast first?"

He smiled. "I see *you* know how to read a map." His glance darted back to the map. "We should make it to the River Tamar tomorrow evening -- if the weather holds out."

"Then Lord Arundel is our first prospect?"

He gazed at her with amusement in his eyes. "You are also in possession of a good memory."

She held herself proudly. "I believe I can even

predict the route you wish to take, my lord."

"Indeed?"

She nodded. "Tintagel first, then south to Bodmin, and from Bodmin to Polperro on the south coast. From Polperro, we'll continue west along the south coast to Penryn. From Penryn we'll head directly north again to Curthbert. And Falwell -- being nearly at Land's End -- and shot her a devilish glance. "I see your map skills -- and your logic -- are excellent. He frowned. A pity she was a do-gooder. He rather enjoyed having for a companion a woman of superior intellect.

The weather continued unimpeded, and they slept at an inn in Minehead that night. Harry was disappointed that Minehead was some miles short of Devon. He had assured her they'd be sleeping in Cornwall the following night.

Then she grew dejected. "I daresay I never realized when we embarked on this trip that it would be four days before we even reached Cornish soil. Which means it will probably be two weeks before we return to London. I deplore leaving poor Ellie for so long."

"She'll scarcely miss you, she'll be so elated over the Bentham chap."

Louisa continued to frown.

"What do you know of Tintagel?" he asked.

"There's a shell of a castle there where it's said King Arthur ruled."

"Perhaps our Lord Arundel is a descendent of King Arthur."

"If one were to believe in Camelot," she said solemnly.

Harry gave her a solemn look. A pity she could never believe in Camelot or in happily-ever-afters.

The following day, as the afternoon sun shone

its brightest, Louisa was looking out the window of the coach and seemed almost startled by his voice. "I think it's time for me to send the coachman to the next inn while you and I begin to explore the coastline on foot."

Since the weather had turned fair, they made excellent progress and were now travelling along the first part of the Cornish coast.

"An excellent plan," she agreed. "Glad I will be to stretch my legs."

Harry and Louisa disembarked, with the coachman given instructions to bespeak rooms for them at the inn in Boscastle. "Aye, Mr. Smith," the coachman said, winking with great emphasis. "Take good care of the Missus."

"Get on with you!" Harry ordered, a chuckle in his deep voice.

Louisa wrapped her dainty hand around his proffered arm as they began to walk along the single cobbled street of this village that was not to be found on their map. "I trust you are looking for our lordly friend," Harry said facetiously.

"To be sure, my lord."

In mere moments, the village lay behind them, and they followed the mists that would surely lead them to the sea.

Their instincts were correct. After traversing a craggy land, they heard the roaring of distant waves and tasted the salty air that seemed to cling to them like wool to sheep. Soon, they began to walk along the coastal path where they could see the dark seawater ringed by white far below. "I'm assuming Lord Arundel is a man of wealth, and it's my bet that he lives near the coast," Harry said.

Now that no one watching them, Louisa

released her hand from Harry's arm and skipped ahead of him, stopping to pick a crocus blooming in the midst of rocky crags.

Had he been a painter, Harry would have painted her stooping to smell the flower that grew wild on the gray cliffs. With the wind catching her pale hair, Louisa Phillips was undoubtedly the loveliest creature he had ever beheld. Almost as refreshing as the complete lack of artifice in her beauty was her total lack of conceit. Did she have no idea how beautiful she was?

His eyes narrowed from the sun, Harry stood watching her as if he were as rooted to the land as the nearby elm. She looked up at him then, puzzlement on her face. "Are you unwell, my lord?"

He stepped forward. "I have never been better. It is a fine day, is it not?"

She stood up. "Wonderful, I should say. I've never been to Cornwall before. Have you?"

She looked like an inquisitive child. "No I haven't, and I quite agree with you. There's a loneliness about the land, but also a peace."

Waiting for him to come even with her, she watched him, a puzzled look on her face. "That's a most poetic thing for you to say, my lord. I had no idea you were so sensitive."

"Please," he urged, "do not imbue me with qualities I do not possess."

She took his arm again though he had not offered it. He was glad she did.

"There's absolutely nothing to be ashamed of in having the ability to express one's feelings. Lord Byron did so, and to my knowledge, he never lacked for suitors."

Harry laughed. "Then perhaps I shall become a

poet."

"Come, my lord, I hardly think you have to begin writing poetry to woe women."

"But according to you, all my suitors are women of easy virtue. Where's the fun of the conquest?"

She removed her hand from his arm. Though she continued to walk beside him, he detected a stiffness in her manner. Was she angry at his remark? Did she take it personally? Surely his restraint last night as he lay beside her throbbing with need assured her of the honor of his intentions. He had best change the subject before he angered her further by confessing his desire for her.

"Tell me, Mrs. Phillips, where is it you wish to make your next home?"

His comment relaxed her. "I had thought to buy a little cottage in a rural village, but as we left London yesterday I realized I am needed there."

"Needed?"

"I must see the poverty first hand if I am to do something to relieve it."

"And you think you can singlehandedly change it?"

"I am not naive, my lord. But with your help in Parliament, we can move forward."

God, but he felt as slimy as Godwin Phillips right now. Like all the other men in her life, he was using her.

She stooped to pick more wild crocus, then she leaned over the precipice of the cliff to tug at a huge flower that bloomed there. When she pulled the flower, the dirt around it came away, and the ground beneath her crumbled.

Harry watched in horror as she plunged over

the cliff.

$\mathcal{C}$hapter 10

Harry's heart nearly stopped beating. In one blindingly quick second Louisa bent at the precipice, the wind blowing her flaxen locks, a flower clutched in her hand. The next second she was gone, a whirl of tumbling skirts, then nothing.

He raced to the cliff's edge, not really wanting to look down, but knowing that he must. He was prepared to see no sign of the lovely Louisa who had surely been swallowed by the raging sea a hundred feet below.

At first he didn't see her. Then the distant echo of her wails reached his ears among the sounds of the roaring seas and the ever-present winds of Cornwall.

And he saw her hand on a ledge not ten feet below. It was grasping the edge with a life-saving grip that could not possibly last much longer. Though he could not see the rest of her, he knew her body dangled beneath the ledge, the clutch of her slim hand the only bridge between life and death.

He had no time to think, only to react. He threw off his coat to allow himself greater flexibility, then squatted at land's edge, lowering first one leg, then the other downward. He had known he could not jump to the ledge below. Not because it was a distance of ten feet, but because the impact of his considerable bulk could disturb her tenuous grip.

As fast as he could, he shimmied down the rugged face of the cliff, oblivious to the scraping of its jagged surface removing the flesh from his arms. His only thought was of getting to Louisa before she fell to her death.

With relief, his boots hit solid ground, and he quickly turned to see where Louisa was. He lunged toward the ledge's edge and dove to grab her wrist with a lock as permanent as a welded chain.

From his vantage point he looked down at her and was rewarded with a view of her smiling face looking up at him, hope shining in her eyes.

From then on, the rest was easy, and his erratic breathing returned to normal. In a moment he had pulled her up, and she sat beside him on the ledge, which was no larger than his carriage.

She looked up at him with eyes full of gratitude. Then she saw his bloody arms and gasped. "You've hurt yourself!"

He looked down at the maze of bloody scrapes on his arms. "I assure you, I feel nothing -- save relief that you're alive."

To his surprise, she reached up and lovingly stroked his face. No words of gratitude could have spoken as eloquently or been as appreciated.

"Thank you," she said softly, then looked away.

"What's wrong?" he asked, touching his knuckle to her chin and turning her face toward him.

"I've just realized how much I wanted to live,"

she said, laughing bitterly.

A fierce wave of emotions washed over him. He wanted nothing so much as to take her in his arms, but his restraint won out in the end. After the damned Godwin Phillips, she would likely have an aversion to physical contact with men. What she needed now were kindly delivered words of assurance of her worth. "My dear Mrs. Phillips, think of how much work you have yet to do on behalf of mankind, of how many people you can help."

She merely looked at him with a dazed expression.

Then, he thought of one last advantage to her living. "What would happen to Ellie if something happened to you?"

A slow smile spread over her smudged face. "I do have a lot to live for, do I not?"

He reached to wipe the dirt from her forehead. "Indeed you do."

She surveyed their little plot of firm ground. "May I ask how we are to get off this spot, my lord?"

He chuckled though he felt far removed from levity. "A good question, Mrs. Phillips." With no rope and no one to help them from above, going upward was completely out. Then he gazed at the shoreline below. Going down would mean certain death. "It is hoped my coachman will come looking for us if we do not return at dark."

"But it's far too dangerous to ride a horse so near the cliffs at dark," she said.

He frowned. "You do have a point there."

"What are we to do?"

"I shall have to think on it," he said, his voice upbeat, a smile on his face.

The wind grew stronger now, whipping her hair away from Louisa's head in horizontal sheets. It was wretchedly unpleasant here with no coat. And damned if his arms hadn't begun to hurt like the dickens. Of course, he would never tell her. As he sat there on the cold limestone, he thought and thought. There had to be a way to get them off the deuced ledge. It was a certainty no one would ever find them here. Their slip of rock was, after all, not visible to anyone traveling the high road.

He got up and carefully inched his way to the edge. A series of ledges climbed up the cliff. He believed he could leap from one to another. It was no different than jumping from deck to deck, his sword at the ready. He had done it any number of times. Of course, Mrs. Phillips could not be expected to follow him.

He looked up at her. "Do you remember those steps we saw a couple of miles back?"

"The ones that led to the sea?"

"The very ones," he said. "I believe I'll scurry down those rocks." He pointed to his left. "And when I reach the beach, I'll walk back to the steps and come back to fetch you in no time."

"You'll be killed," she protested.

"Nonsense. I'm said to be rather acrobatic."

"Dying here of the elements and of hunger would be preferable to watching you plunge to your death."

"I am flattered, madam." He rose. "Nevertheless, I believe I shall begin our rescue."

With those words, he squatted at the precipice, and in but a second had disappeared from her sight.

* * *

Along with his presence, her breath seemed to have vanished. She tried to scream, but no sound came forth. With her pulse fluttering madly, she scraped up the courage to move to the precipice and watch Lord Wycliff as he bravely jumped from one ledge to another. He was like a hero from one the novels she had read when she was young. Before she married Godwin and lost all dreams of love and happy endings.

Finally, she could no longer see him clearly. All she saw was the white of his shirt. Then he did reach the beach. And she could breathe again.

The fear that had gripped her for the past hour vanished like her perception of the cold. She knew she would be rescued. And all because a noble man had risked his very life to save her. She forgot that the wind pierced her. She forgot that she had, literally, come within an inch of life. All she thought of was the warmth that spread through her.

Because of him.

She could not have said how long she sat there on the scant ledge waiting for Lord Wycliff to rescue her. All she knew was that the sun was low in the sky when she heard the crunch of rocks above her and looked up to see him smiling down at her.

"Did you find help?" she yelled up at him.

"We don't need help," he shouted, taking his greatcoat and tying its sleeve to the sleeve of his jacket, careful to use the trusty sailor knots. Then he laid on his belly to where his arms hung over the cliff's edge, the coats dangling down to just above Louisa's fair head.

She had almost fallen when she stood up. Her knee must have been injured in the fall. She could only barely put weight on it. She reached and tentatively took hold of the sleeve that hung nearest to her. Surprised that it held her weight, she held tightly as she began to rise. She looked up into Lord Wycliff's face, strained as he hoisted her to the top of the upper ledge.

As she reached his hands, he firmly grabbed her wrists and lifted her to where she was even with him. The man possessed incredible strength.

"Be careful," he cautioned as he backed up, causing her upper arms to be bruised on the jagged rocks.

Then they were on firm ground, three feet from the precipice.

"Promise me you won't pick any more flowers," he said with levity as he pulled her up to stand next to him.

When he saw that she was unable to put weight on her knee, a look of worry flashed across his face. "You're hurt."

She looked up at him and nodded solemnly.

"Bloody hell!" he said, giving her a mock scowl. "Now I've got to carry you four miles to Boscastle."

"I most certainly can limp."

"The hell if you will!" He picked her up.

"Put me down at once!" she commanded. "I can wait here until your man comes back for me."

He looked up at the darkening skies and at the setting sun in the west. "I'll not allow my carriage or my horses here at night."

Her lower lip stuck out. "If you don't put me down right now, I'll never speak to you again, Lord Wycliff!"

"A severe punishment, indeed."

"You, my lord, are making fun of me." Her

stiffened arms remained at her sides.

"You wrong me, Mrs. Phillips."

She burst out laughing then, and hooked her arms about his neck. "Really, my lord, you have certainly been through enough today without having to carry me for four miles."

"You weigh no more than a sack of grain, and I assure you I have carried many of those in my day."

It seemed quite odd that a peer of the realm had actually toted sacks of grain. But, then, Harold Blassingame, the Earl of Wycliff was not just any peer. She was beginning to feel a great deal of remorse for all the wicked things she had said about him and about the worthlessness of his lot.

He had been right the day they met to ask her not to judge him as she judged others who were born to a title. "My lord?"

"Yes?" he answered in a much winded voice.

"Perhaps we should stop to rest for a spell."

He obliged her, spreading out his coat for them to sit upon.

She waited for him to catch his breath. "My lord?"

He looked at her with eyes full of warmth. "Yes?"

"I am very sorry for the wicked things I have said about you and your class."

"Then I am sorry for the wicked things I said about bluestocking ladies -- in the past."

They both laughed.

"Perhaps we could begin again," she proposed. "Maybe we could be, simply---"

"Harry and Louisa?"

She smiled. "I'd like that."

He took an apple from the pocket of his coat and offered her a bite. "Hungry?"

She took a bite. "There's another thing I need to tell you, my--"

"Harry," he said firmly.

"Harry," she said, smiling. "It's. . .it's that you have made me realize that not all men are selfish, horrible creatures like my father and husband." How many men could have spent three nights in the bed of a woman possessed of some beauty and not have tried to take their own pleasure with her? And how many men would have risked their lives to save a highly opinionated bluestocking who purported to hate men?

His voice was soft when he spoke. "I sincerely hope I can continue to earn your trust, Mrs.--"

"Louisa," she urged.

"Louisa."

Brown eyes locked with blue.

"Nothing you could have said," he continued, "could have meant more to me. I wager you say the same thing to all men who rescue you."

They both laughed. She was grateful that an easy camaraderie had developed between them. Then she saw that his arms were still bleeding.

He followed the path of her gaze.

"Are you in pain?" she asked, compassion in her voice.

"Probably not nearly as much as you -- from your knee."

"But I don't have to carry another person."

He got to his feet, and she thought he looked like a dark god. She forced herself to look away.

He lifted her, and without thinking, she wrapped her arms around his neck, which was still warm from the waning sun.

As they trod over the moorland, she rested her face against his chest and could never remember feeling such contentment in her entire life. It brought to mind the reassurance she had felt as a small child when her mother, rest her soul, had read her nursery rhymes and Bible stories in her soft, loving voice as Louisa lay tucked beneath her blankets.

She could hear the steady beat of Harry's heart and his labored breath, and she was intensely sorry she was such a burden. In so many ways.

She vowed to do everything in her power to aid him in his quest to regain Wycliff House.

She was almost sorry when they reached the inn in Boscastle, for he would have to put her down. She fleetingly wondered if she would ever again feel such warmth in her life.

She rather doubted it.

Chapter 11

As they sat across from one another over dinner at the tidy little inn, the fire to Harry's back, Louisa thought she had never before felt so comfortable with another person. That was not to say she and Ellie did not enjoy an easy camaraderie, but with Harry she not only felt completely warm inside, she seemed to glow on the outside. Something about being with him set her to sparkling like sun glancing off a bed of crystal. She found herself hoping it would be many days before they found their mysterious lord.

For she knew that when his quest was over, she would return to her dreary life of meetings with those man-hating bluestockings who had been her only social life. Now, companionship with such women held little allure.

She supposed they had filled a deep and retching need in her at the time. Now, though, she felt another need, though she could no more put a name to it than she could understand it. All that she knew for sure about it was that it had something to do with Harry.

Calling him Harry seemed quite natural now, though she found it hard to countenance, as would others who might hear her address him in such a manner. So sitting there in the private parlor of the Cock and Stock, she came to the decision that she would never address him so familiarly in front of others. It would be like her mother's miniature portrait, something she could pull out and take comfort in when she was alone.

"This is the most I have seen you eat on the journey," he commented, his eyes not removed from her clean plate.

"Then the four-mile walk must have tired me, I dare say." There was levity in her voice and an amused glint in her eyes.

He cocked his brow. "A pity it was so exhausting for you. I found it rather invigorating."

She laughed then moved forward ever so slightly and with a feather-like touch ran gentle fingers across his bandaged arms. "I cannot tell you how deeply I am indebted to you."

* * *

Her gentle touch was much like that which she had used when she had tended to his wounds upon their arrival at the inn. Instead of allowing him to look at her knee, she permitted him to carry her up the wooden stairs to the room his coachman had secured for them. And there on the high feather bed they had sat facing each other. He had followed her instructions to remove his shirt so she could minister to his wounds. He wasn't sure, but he thought her breath swooped as his shirt fell to the counterpane.

She had been quick to gain control of herself as she deftly cleaned and bandaged his mangled arm.

A pity he had not recovered as quickly as she had. His close proximity to her and the feel of her soft breast brushing against him as she bent over his arm affected him emotionally as well as physically.

Once she finished bandaging his arm, she bent over and lightly kissed his arm, then looked up at him, a flush creeping up her face. He could tell she was embarrassed and wished he could put her at ease.

"I'm. . ." she stammered. "I didn't think of what I was doing," she explained. "I used to kiss Ellie's wounds after I bandaged them when she was little."

He set his hand on her frail shoulder. "You've nothing to apologize for. My mother did the same to me when I was small, and to this day I believe it aids in the recovery."

When his remarks did not seem to put her at ease, he ruffled her hair and laughed. "Rather amusing that you think of me as a child."

"Oh, no!" she protested, looking up at him. "There's nothing at all childish about you. In fact, I believe you must be the bravest man I have ever known."

He made light of her compliment, changing the subject. "I believe we should ask for another bottle of wine."

"Pray, Harry, it's already made me lightheaded."

He became pensive. "I like it when you call me Harry."

"I confess, it seems most inappropriate."

"But there are those who find John Stuart Mill's actions inappropriate, though you and I know his vision is correct."

"You speak of his efforts on behalf of birth control?"

He nodded.

"You had not told me before that you approved of the younger Mr. Mill's efforts."

"You never asked me before," he said.

He could almost see the years of woe peel from her like layers off an onion as her voice became animated, her face lively. "Tell me, how do you feel about slavery in the colonies?" she asked.

"Until I met you, I confess I had never given it a thought." He caught the serving maid's attention and told her they needed another bottle of wine.

"And now?" she asked.

"Now I have decided it is not a good thing."

"Why?" she challenged.

Darn the chit! What was he supposed to say now? He'd never given thought before to African men. Then he remembered Thomas Paine's *Rights of Man*. He had not read the blasted thing, but the title gave him a clue as to its contents. "Regardless of the color of the skin, a man is a man, and as such should have the right to be his own master and to be treated with dignity." He was completely surprised at his own eloquence. Perhaps he would have made a good show in Parliament.

"Oh, Harry," she beamed. "I cannot wait until we have your voice in the House of Lords."

He experienced a wretched feeling in the pit of his stomach. He had so carefully earned the girl's trust, and now as he held it as securely as a vault, he was about to trample it. Which just confirmed his own low opinion of himself. A pity he was not the man he pretended to be. That man could have been quite noble. Not conniving like Harold Blassingame, the Seventh Earl of Wycliff. Former pirate of the high seas. Murdering and stealing his way to an extremely comfortable station in life.

The return of the serving lady saved him from having to make a response.

"Tell me, if you will," he said to the serving woman. "Is there a Lord. . .What was that man's name, my dear?" he asked Louisa.

Playing along with him, Louisa said, "Goodness me, I cannot at all remember it."

Harry pretended to act drunk. "Can't remember the chap's name. What is the name of the local lord in these parts?"

"We have no local lord, sir," the woman said. "The closest one's Lord Harley over in Binghampton some forty miles from here."

"Is that in Cornwall?" Harry asked.

"Oh, no, sir. It's in Devon."

He watched somberly as the woman poured two more glasses of claret, wishing for the first time in a long while that he could drink himself into oblivion.

* * *

Edward Coke sat next to Miss Sinclair in his curricle as he made his way back to her house after Jeremy Bentham's first talk of the series. It had been difficult, indeed, not to burst out laughing at the most peculiar assortment of individuals he had ever seen in his four-and-twenty years. Reminded him of the first day he had stepped foot at Uncle Robert's former townhouse and faced Mrs. Phillips's room full of man-hating bluestockings. For today he had seen many of those same faces. At least he believed he had seen many of the same women. Though if push came to shove, he would have to say he hadn't actually looked -- really looked -- at any of their ugly mugs, either that first day or today.

Then, too, today there were any number of gaunt men that he'd wager a quid were Methodists. Not a Weston coat in the whole lot of them. In fact, they dressed so somberly they could have been at a wake.

Though none of these peculiar things had Miss Ellie Sinclair seemed to notice. He slid a glance at her rather taking little face. Unfortunately, the chit was still ecstatic over the peculiar little man they had heard speak this afternoon. She kept telling him how enlightening was Mr. Bentham, how brilliant was Mr. Bentham, how this had been the happiest day of her life.

For the life of him, he could not understand the attraction in Mr. Jeremy Bentham. The man's cravat was a disgrace, and he'd wager a quarterly the Bentham fellow had never run to foxes in his life. Probably didn't even know how to fence.

Nevertheless, Edward continued to feign enchantment over the weasel for the girl's sake. He had grown rather fond of her. Not just because she was the prettiest thing he'd seen in a very long time, but there was about her a certain innocence he found delightful.

And, besides, Harry had said he was to look out for Miss Sinclair during her sister's absence, and he had always done whatever his elder cousin asked.

However, looking out after her was far easier said than actually done. He supposed it was because she was country bred, but the girl was possessed of a ridiculous notion that all men had designs on her virtue. He'd like to ring the neck of the governess -- Miss Grimm was it not? -- who filled the poor girl's head with such nonsense.

He'd had the devil of a time getting Miss

Sinclair to consent to allow him to escort her to the series of lectures. He glanced behind to assure himself the Phillips's cook was riding in Harry's gig, keeping a sharp eye on his actions with Miss Sinclair. Did the fat old hog also think he had designs on Miss Sinclair's virtue?

He inwardly sighed over the realization that he had to endure three more of these horridly dull talks. The things a man does for the lovely lady.

* * *

The longer Harry sat in the fire-lit room looking at Louisa, the room's only other occupant, the more persistently he wanted her. That, he told himself, would never do. He had finally earned her trust, and he was not about to destroy it.

He looked down at the bandages on his arms. Which reminded him of the feel of carrying her over the moors. His arms had grown tired, and his breath seemed to come only at great difficulty, but he would do it all over again without a moment's hesitation.

Though Louisa had little fat, there was about her tiny body a real softness, a frailness, too, that evoked every protective instinct he had ever possessed, instincts he'd not even known he possessed. Yet they were instincts he enjoyed awakening.

He would always cherish the memory of holding her against him, of her arms secure about his neck, her sweet face resting against his chest as they made their way across the moors to the Cock and Stock Inn.

The more he looked at her face bathed in the glow of the candle, its light flickering in her hair, the more he remembered the heavenly feel of her in his arms, and the more he realized how difficult it would be to sleep with her tonight.

He took another swig of the wine. "I shall carry you upstairs now." He moved to her and gently lifted her into his arms and carried her to their chamber. "I go to the tavern now," he said simply.

Her eyes seemed melancholy when she nodded.

As Louisa dressed for bed, she heard rain beginning to pelt the window of their tiny room. By the time she had put on her woolen gown and slipped beneath the bed's chilly sheets, a full-fledged storm whistled and roared outside the inn. Then thunder boomed and lightning blazed across the night sky, and she pulled their blankets tightly around her.

Her thoughts drifted back to the day's events. She was sorry she had yet to aid Harry in his search because she wanted to repay him for all he'd done for her. Otherwise, she looked back over the day with no regrets.

She regretted that the trip must come to an end. She had never enjoyed anything so much. She remembered the fear that had robbed her breath when she had watched Harry descend the cliffside, fearing he would fall to his death any minute.

Looking back on it, her heart unaccountably swelled with pride over his actions. He had not only earned her trust today, he had earned her deep and abiding admiration.

Then she thought of the utter contentment of being swept up into his strong arms and of being held against his solid chest. Had anything ever felt so good in her life?

Despite the whooshing winds outside and the hard rain coming down on the roof over her head, she smiled.

Soon Harry would be lying beside her.

She went to sleep with the candle burning beside the bed, a smile playing at her lips.

That is how Harry found her an hour later. He was grateful she was asleep. Had she so much as said a single word to him, he would have been powerless to prevent himself from scooping her into his arms and destroying the progress he had made.

He stood for a moment looking down at her. *The wine.* She must have drunk nearly a bottle. No doubt it had made her very sleepy.

Which was a good thing.

$\mathcal{C}$hapter 12

Fully dressed, Harry stood before their bed the following morning, offering Louisa a cup of hot tea.

She opened first one eye, then the other.

"Good morning, my dear," he said.

She rubbed her eyes. "I'm not your dear."

"I expect you have the headache from the wine you drank last night." He handed her a glass. "Here, I've made you an elixir that has served me well when I've . . .shall we say, overimbibed?"

She shot him an angry look, pulled herself up to a sitting position, and took the proffered drink.

"How's the head?" he asked.

"Quite as awful as you think it is." She drank from the glass, then made a face of disgust. "That odious concoction had better work."

"You have my word on it that it does." He continued to watch her, thankful her woolen night shift climbed up to her throat.

She swung her leg over the side of the bed, and to his surprise she began to lift the wool to reveal her knee -- with not a shred of modesty on her part.

Then he saw that her knee was bruised and swollen, and he moved to her, kneeling at her feet. He gently moved her calf down, then back up. "I don't believe it's broken," he said. "Since you did not scream with pain at movement, I'm guessing it only hurts when you put weight on it."

She nodded solemnly.

"Stay off it for a couple of days, and I believe it will mend," he said.

She frowned, then reached for the cup of tea he he'd brought and took a sip. "The chamber's far colder now than it was last night."

He got up and walked to the hearth where he picked up a poker and stirred. "The fire's died, and I asked that the maid not disturb you to lay a new one."

She nodded appreciatively. "Also, I believe it's turned colder outside."

"To be sure," he said, his back still to her. "I just came from the stables, and I can attest to that."

A moment later he sat in a wooden chair facing her and watched silently as she drank her tea.

She set down her cup and gave him a quizzing look. "Why is it you know so much of wounds and of other things a gentleman of substance is not supposed to know? What is it you did those twelve years? How did you really make your fortune?"

Good God, did she know? Why would she be thinking on it if she had not already guessed? A concerned look sweeping across his face, Harry went to her, dropping to one knee at her bedside. "If I tell you the truth I will lose any respect I have worked hard to earn from you."

Her indigo eyes looked into his as if she could see through to the soul he had long ago lost. "You were a pirate, weren't you?"

He closed his eyes and muttered an oath, then

got up and walked to the hearth. He bent low and attempted to stir the embers once again.

"I see I've hit upon the truth," she said somberly.

He merely nodded, then moved to the door. "I'll go down and order your breakfast."

* * *

Because of the injury to Louisa's knee and the wetness of the weather, walking was out of the question. Harry carried her to his coach. The rain which had continued throughout the night had left the roads soggy.

The farther south they went, the cooler the temperature became. It was as if the heavy white mist followed them inland. Louisa lifted the curtain and pressed her face into the foggy glass. Progress was slow the first hour of their journey southward as the coach rattled sluggishly along the hilly terrain. Once the hills were behind them, the somber landscape leveled out, and the carriage picked up speed.

In the midst of the barren land that now surrounded them, Louisa beheld a most peculiar natural phenomenon. At least, she assumed the towering, cylinder-like rocks were natural. Though, for all the world, they rather resembled giant candles jutting up from the soggy earth.

"Pray, Harry, what are those things?"

He scooted across the seat opposite and inched his face closer to hers. "I've never seen them before, but I believe they're tors."

Her brows drew together. "Tors? Like tornadoes?"

He sat upright and shrugged. "Don't know where the word came from."

She continued peering from the window. "I

suppose these vast stretches of wasteland where no trees are growing must be the moors."

"The Bodmin Moor," he said.

She let the curtain drop, and she straightened up, her spine touching the back of the seat. "A light mist is beginning to fall. I do feel so sorry for the coachman."

"I assure you, your worries for him are greater than his own. He's well used to physical discomfort."

She frowned. "What is the name of Lord Blamey's abode in Bodmin?"

Harry answered without consulting his notes. "St. Alban's Abbey."

They rode along in Harry's coach, and for mile after mile through the Bodmin Moor, villages were scarce. Harry peered through the foggy window for any sign of habitation.

Though it was early afternoon still, a charcoal blanket covered the skies, and the wind whistled alongside their vehicle. Harry knew Louisa must be cold and tired, but not once had she asked that they stop nor had she complained of hunger.

The second time he had to brave the weather and help the coachman dislodge a wheel from the muddy mire, Harry knew further progress would be impossible until the rain that had begun an hour ago let up -- most likely not until tomorrow.

He grew impatient to learn the identity of the mysterious lord who had orchestrated his father's downfall. More than anything, he wondered why someone would hate his father with such vengeance. Except for his squandering of the family fortune, his father had been an amiable, well-liked man.

Could his father's political views have made

such an enemy? Harry thought back but could remember nothing that his father could have done that would have warranted such punishment. Perhaps the elder Lord Wycliff had angered a foreign power through his fierce patriotism to England during its war with France. He remembered the sacrifices his father had made in order to purchase weapons for soldiers in the Peninsula in 1808. He had not only bought the munitions with his own money, but he had spent considerable time searching for qualified men to take the supplies from Portsmouth into Portugal -- all using his own funds.

But if his father had angered a foreign power, why would Godwin Phillips's mysterious benefactor be a *lord from Cornwall?* Perhaps Louisa had been wrong.

He watched Louisa as she rubbed the fog from the inside of the coach window. They had barely spoken all day. He knew she would never be able to condone the manner in which he had amassed his fortune.

The woman was far too fine to be sitting with the likes of him.

While one side of him was sorry that his silence had confirmed the truth, and in so doing had lost Louisa's respect he'd only just won, the other side of him was somewhat glad that he'd told her the truth. For some inexplicable reason, what they had gone through the day before brought them as close together as two people could be. She had even let him probe on her leg without a blush hiking up her smooth cheeks.

He decided to cut through the barrier that had once again been erected between them. "Are you sure the benefactor was addressed as a lord?

Could he have been a count or a marquis or one
of those titles the bloody French like to use?"

She shook her head. "Oh, no, I'm certain. And
that's what Williams said, too."

Harry frowned. So much for that theory. At
least she had spoken to him. He dwelled for a
moment on the melodious, childlike quality of her
smooth voice. Was there nothing about her he did
not find admirable?

Oh, yes, he told himself. She was a bloody do-
gooder.

If the woman would not hold a civil
conversation with him, perhaps she would at
least discuss her bloody causes. Anything would
be preferable to sitting across from her do-
gooding self scorning him with every turn of the
wheels.

"Tell me," he began, "What are your feelings
about penal reform?" He crossed his arms across
his chest and settled back to smugly watch her
leap to life.

"If I were a violent person -- which I'm not," she
said, throwing him a haughty glance, "I would be
violently opposed to the practice of depriving
persons of their lives for minor infractions like
stealing a day's food to feed one's family. I think,
perhaps, the death penalty should be reserved for
only the most heinous crimes."

He sat straighter and uncrossed his arms.
"Like murder."

Her eyes flashed with satisfaction. "Yes. And I
am completely against transportation, too."

Her opinions exactly reflected those imparted
in the essays he had read by Philip Lewis. As he
said the name in his mind, something sparked.
Philip Lewis. Louisa Phillips. Quicker than the

flash of lightning, he knew they were one and the same.

He knew Louisa's secrets as well as she knew his. The knowledge afforded him great satisfaction. He slid into the corner of the coach, a cocky arch to his brow and a mischievous smile playing at his lips as he watched her.

A puzzled look flashed across her face. "Whatever do you find so amusing, my lord?"

"Yesterday I was Harry."

"That was before I knew that you were a thief."

"I admit I stole. I stole from ships owned by men who had profited by my father's loss."

Her lower lip worked into a pout. "It was still stealing."

"I do not deny it." He watched her sulk for a moment before renewing his banter. "Have you never done anything for which you have been ashamed?"

She thought for a long moment. "I have certainly many regrets over how my life has been lived, but I have none over actions which I controlled."

"Have you ever lied, Louisa?"

"Mrs. Phillips."

"I'm not going to call you by the despicable man's name, Louisa. Answer me, have you ever lied?"

She refused to answer.

"Perhaps it was not a lie but an omission," he said. "Something like purporting to be a man. Say a man like Philip Lewis."

She went rigid. Her lips parted, and her eyes grew round. "How did you know?" she asked.

He got up and moved to her side of the coach and drew his face close to hers. "I know you as well as you know me, Louisa. You guessed correctly about my secret as I guessed about yours."

"Will you tell?" Her voice was thin and frightened.

He stayed there in the darkened coach nose to nose with the most beautiful woman he had ever known. He peered into the depths of her frightened eyes and spoke gently, like a whisper of the night. "I will never hurt you, Louisa."

Then the coach came to a stop.

"What the deuce is going on?" Harry demanded, scooting to the door and opening it.

There the coachman stood, his oilskin dripping, his hat nearly covering his bearded face while all the while rain beat down on him and thunder spiked the air like the clashing of cymbals. "There's no inn in this village, my lord."

"Mr. Smith," Harry mumbled, wiping the water from his face.

"I'm sorry, Mr. Smith."

Harry uttered another oath. "Well, man, go to the tavern and make inquiries. I will pay handsomely for a room for my bride and myself for the night."

The coachman nodded, his sweeping hat scattering water, and he walked off toward the town.

Harry, by now completely wet, slammed the coach door and took his usual seat across from Louisa. It had grown so dark, he could barely see her.

"Will we go on to the next town if we don't find a room here?" she asked.

"My good woman, you know little of traveling country roads if you think these passable, and you know little of a man of wealth if you don't realize there is little that cannot be bought, given that one has enough money."

She straightened her shoulders and shot him a defiant look. "I mustn't forget that your plundering has made you a most wealthy man, my lord."

"Louisa," he said, his voice soft and pleading.

They sat in silence until the inside of the coach became completely dark. The only sound was the dripping of rain on the roof and the scattered boom of thunder in the far-off skies. It grew colder, too. He was bloody miserable in these wet clothes.

A half an hour passed before John Coachman returned, hopped up on the box and drove them to a farm house a mile from the village.

Harry did not wait for the coachman to open the door. He was bloody tired of being cooped in the blasted coach and bloody tired of Louisa's refusal to speak to him.

He was not so angry, though, that he did not hold open the carriage door for her and give her his hand as she climbed down. Then he remembered her knee. Uttering yet another curse, he scooped her up and stormed up to the house, ignoring Louisa's protests.

As they drew near the house, his voice lowered. "Remember, my dear Louisa, these kind persons who have opened their home to us believe us to be on our honeymoon. Act the loving wife."

If she glared at him, he couldn't see it as he swept through the opening door, putting Louisa down and charmingly greeting the farmer's matronly wife. "Harold Smith, ma'am, and my bride, Louisa." Removing his hat, he said, "I do thank you for providing us shelter."

The woman extended her hand. "I'm Millie Winston." She turned to Louisa. "Are you unwell, my dear?"

Louisa shook her head. "I've just injured my leg is all."

"You'll want to get dry, I'm sure," the woman said. "Then you'll be hungry. I wasn't expecting anyone, so our fare is quite simple, but there's plenty. Now, let me show you to what used to be our daughters' room -- before they got married and moved to homes of their own."

They followed her up a simple wooden staircase.

"Our girl Meg married the blacksmith over in Penwick. She's increasing now with her fifth babe. I'll be going to her soon."

"How many children and grandchildren have you?" Louisa inquired.

"Three daughters, and our son helps with the farm. He and his wife live just next door. Altogether, Mr. Winston and I have sixteen grandchildren."

"You've been blessed, indeed," Louisa said.

Harry fleetingly wondered if Louisa regretted that she had borne no children. Though he did not like to think of her bearing the seed of Godwin Phillips.

Their hostess walked across the room and, using her own candle, lighted a tallow beside the room's only bed. "It's not been dusted nor cleaned in here in a good while, but the bedclothes are clean though most likely damp."

Louisa began to unbutton her pelisse. "I'll come down and help you with dinner, Mrs. Winston, while my husband changes into dry clothes,"

Louisa said, as Harry helped her out of her pelisse and hung it on a peg on the wall.

My husband. The words had tumbled naturally from her lips. Harry liked the way they sounded.

"I can't allow that," Mrs. Winston protested. "Not on your sore leg."

"She's right, my dear," Harry said. "You need to stay off that leg."

My dear? Why did the endearment not offend her?

Chapter 13

As soon as Harry closed the door to their chamber, Louisa spun around to face him, anger flashing in her eyes. "Have you no shame? Telling that nice couple we're on our honeymoon?"

He shrugged from his wet coat and hung it on a hook a foot from her pelisse. "You know little of human nature if you do not realize the Winstons are delighted to be of assistance to us. I fear their glee would vanish if they were to be apprised of the truth."

"I suppose you're right," she agreed, hands on her hips as she watched him standing there facing her, a look of sheer devilment in his black eyes. "But how am I to get into dry clothing with you standing there gawking at me?"

"I shall turn around and gaze at the wall until you notify me you are dressed."

"Very well," she snapped, "turn around." She watched as he presented his back to her. Why did the man have to have such broad shoulders? His size intimidated her. Looking at him, she backed away but was still not able to undress, even though she trusted him. Though the man had his faults, she had to admit forcing himself on a woman was not one of them.

She slowly unbuttoned her dress.

"If you need assistance, I shall be happy to oblige," he said mischievously.

"Just keep looking at the wall." She took a dry worsted dress from her portmanteau, then began to slip out of her wet travelling dress, clutching its skirt over the personal parts of her anatomy. Throwing one last look at him to assure herself he was not watching her, she quickly stepped into the dry dress and buttoned it.

"I am dressed now," she informed him. "I shall sit on the bed and turn my back so that you may don dry clothing."

"You can look if you like," he said teasingly.

"I don't."

Once they both were dry, Harry moved over to the bed and picked up Louisa. "I'll carry you downstairs. Taking stairs is the worst thing you can do for a bad knee."

She could not argue his point. Her knee was already throbbing from the weight she put on it while dressing. Though she allowed him to lift her, she vowed she would not put her arm around him. Which really was awkward, keeping her arms pressed against her sides.

When they got downstairs they found the Winston's linen-covered table set in Sunday finest and spread with an array of steaming bowls.

Louisa fleetingly thought of the warmth and privacy of the dining parlors she and Harry were used to and vaguely missed them.

But as soon as they sat at the kindly couple's table, her misgivings vanished. This little farmhouse possessed more warmth and feeling of love than any impersonal inn could possibly offer.

Mrs. Winston could not have been more hospitable, and her quiet husband, dressed in

Sunday wear that had become faded and shiny at points of use, was amiable.

"They're on their honeymoon, Jonah," Mrs. Winston informed her husband. Then, turning her attention to the presumed newlyweds, asked, "When did you get married?"

Louisa looked at Harry to answer.

He put down his fork, looked up at the farmer's wife with a smiling countenance, and said, "We married at my wife's home in Trent on Saturday and are now journeying to Penzance, where we shall make our home together."

"You are from Penzance?" Mr. Winston asked in a surprised fashion. Had Harry's lack of a local accent raised warning flags?

Harry nodded as he buttered his roll.

"However did a man who lives in Penzance meet a bride who lived so far away?" Mrs. Winston asked.

There was not even a second's hesitation on Harry's part. "My wife was introduced to me by my cousin, who also lives in Trent."

The man was a natural-born liar! My wife this, my wife that. Lying appeared to come quite naturally to him. Like stealing.

"Millie and I've known each other all our lives," Mr. Winston said. "Known since I was twelve I was gonna marry her."

Louisa smiled at this. "Was there never anyone else?"

Mr. Winston looked at Louisa as if she'd blasphemed the Lord he so obviously honored. "There weren't no one else to shower my affections on, lest you count Rosemary Penthorn, who weren't all right in the head, if you know what I mean."

All except Mrs. Winston laughed at this. The round, white-headed woman put her hands to her hips in protest. "I'll have you know, Jonah, I had my pick from four different lads, and you're the one I wanted to spend the rest of my life with."

At this, Mr. Winston lowered his head to his bowl of soup and began to slurp.

Louisa and Harry exchanged amused glances.

When Mr. Winston finished with his soup, he turned to Harry. "A little old aren't you to be marrying for the first time?"

"What makes you think it's the first time?" Harry asked.

Louisa felt her stomach drop.

"It's not?" Mr. Winston queried.

"Yes, it actually is the first," Harry said with a chuckle. "It took me three and thirty years to find my sweet Louisa. I'd given up hope of ever finding one such as her."

Oh, please. Lord Wycliff had certainly missed his calling on the stage. A pity he did not make his fortune there. Then, thinking of the manner in which he *had* regained his fortune, she grew angry once again, and turned her complete attention to her sturgeon.

"What do you do in Penzance, Mr. Smith?" Mrs. Winston asked Harry.

Louisa was astounded over the huge amount of food Harry had consumed as she watched him cut his fish and answer his hostess.

"I'm in imports and exports."

At least that was somewhat true.

"You have a boat?" Mr. Winston asked before shoveling peas into his mouth.

"Let's put it this way," Harry said. "My bank and I have a boat."

Hogwash.

When they were finished with their meal, Louisa insisted that she and *her husband* be allowed to clean up. "Please, Mrs. Winston, we have been sitting in a carriage all day and are longing to stand for a while. You and your husband go rest by the fire. You both have put in a hard day's work."

The old woman shuffled off, mumbling protests under her breath.

Once alone in the kitchen, Louisa lashed into him in a sing-song voice of mockery. "My wife and I this, my wife and I that. My bank and I. . .Honestly, my lord, you are a scheming, lying, cheating, good-for-nothing peer of the realm if ever there was one." For good measure, she added, "I do declare!"

His mouth twisted into a wry smile. "Don't forget to add thief."

She huffed. "If it weren't for the bandages on your arm I would hit you."

"But if you did, I wouldn't be able to help you with the dishes."

"As if you know your way around the kitchen." She issued a harrumph.

"Do you?" he asked.

"Of course." She took Mrs. Winston's apron and tied it about her slim waist. "The real question is if you know *your* way around a kitchen."

His face fell. "To be truthful, no."

"You wouldn't know the truth if it bit you on the nose."

"A very poor analogy, Louisa." He picked up a roughly hewn stool and placed it before the sink. "I order you to sit down."

She shot him an angry glance, sat on the proffered stool and began to run a wet cloth over a plate several times. "I told you not to call me Louisa."

"And I refused." He took a dry cloth and began to dry the plate Louisa had washed.

They worked side by side for some time, lost in their own thoughts, no conversation uniting them.

When they were more than half way through, he spoke. "It's clear that you detest your father, but what of your mother?"

She continued washing. "I loved her very much, but she died giving birth to Ellie."

"So you were almost like a mother to Ellie."

She nodded solemnly. "I suppose so."

"Did your father never remarry?"

"No, which seemed peculiar, given his delight in ordering others to do his bidding."

"But he was so selfish a man, he probably didn't want to feign affection for another that he did not feel."

She stopped washing and looked at him. "I believe you're right. He never needed anyone but himself. The only person he cared a fig for." Then she took up her cleaning again.

"Louisa?"

"Yes," she answered, averting her gaze from him.

"Is there nothing I can do to regain the affection I felt from you yesterday?"

She thought for a moment. "You could show your remorse by giving your money to the poor."

"You know I can't do that," he said somberly.

She turned to him, hardness in her steely eyes.

"It was never about the money," he said softly.

"Always it was about family. My family. Not only
the ancient title and the wealth that had once
gone with it, though those things were important
to me.

"It was pride in my family name I wanted to
recapture. I want to rebuild what my father had
torn down." He dropped the cloth to the counter.
"More than anything on earth I have wanted to
rekindle the feeling of love I had known so
thoroughly as a child. I wanted to reestablish
that. I want my old home back. I want a woman
whom I can love as my father loved my mother. I
want a son who will proudly carry the title of Earl
of Wycliff and grandsons and great-grandsons."
He turned back toward her. "Are you
understanding any of this?"

She swallowed. "I think so," she said, her voice
wispy.

He felt a closeness to her he had never felt with
anyone else. Why else would he have revealed so
much about himself and become so vulnerable?

When the kitchen was spotless, Louisa and
Harry said good-night to their host and hostess.

"Mrs. Winston," Louisa asked, "How did you
know we were newlyweds?"

"My dear, I knew by the way Mr. Smith looked
at you. It was the same as Jonah Junior looked at
his bride the day of their wedding."

Louisa's cheeks grew hot. She left the parlor to
climb the stairs to their room, grabbing onto the
banister to carry her weight from her bad knee.
Harry followed, picked her up and began to march
up the stairs while holding her to him. How did he
expect her to dress for bed with him in the room?
A pity there was no tavern for him to go to
tonight.

The taper Mrs. Winston lit still burned on the bedside table. The room was cold. Terribly so. Since there was no hearth in this room, Mrs. Winston had brought extra blankets.

Now Louisa knew why. "Turn around and close your eyes," she ordered.

For extra preservation of her privacy, she too turned around, her back to him as she quickly undressed and hurried into her woolen night gown.

Then she sat on the bed. "You may turn around and remove your shirt. I need to redress the bandages on your arms."

"Would you like me to come stand in front of the candle as I remove my shirt?" he asked teasingly.

She bent down to pick up her shoe and throw it at him. "You odious man!"

The flying shoe just missed one of his bandaged arms. She was all contrite when she said, "Oh, Harry, I'm so sorry. Did I hurt your arm?"

He stood beside her and slowly began to unbutton his shirt, not removing his eyes from her.

Embarrassed, she turned away until he had removed his shirt and came to sit on the bed next to her. "You called me Harry again," he said gently.

She was in no mood to be seduced by a thieving pirate. "Let me see your arms," she said harshly.

She proceeded to remove the bloodied bandages from his arm, gasping as she did so. "I am afraid infection may have set in," she solemnly announced.

He picked up the candle and held it to his arm. The gashes were still oozing, and his entire arm had begun to swell.

"No wonder the blasted thing's bothered me so much today."

Her voice was soft when she spoke. "You never said anything."

"We weren't speaking. Remember?"

She looked contrite. "I don't know what we can do for it. What have you learned about such treatment in your vast experience?"

"To bloody well hope it gets better. I'd rather not lose my arm."

She gasped. "Oh, that's terrible, and it's all my fault." She removed clean linen from her portmanteau with shaking hands.

"I'm sure it will be all right," he soothed.

She ignored him as she gently cleaned the wound and began to wrap it in a fresh bandage. Then she leaned across him and began to minister to his other arm "This arm isn't nearly as bad as the other."

"I'm not such a bloody idiot that I don't already know that."

"Don't be so cross," she scolded. Then she was sorry she had snapped at him when he was obviously in a lot of pain. "I'm sorry if I'm hurting you, Harry. Would you like for me to go downstairs and see if Mr. Winston has some whiskey for you to take to dull your pain?"

"I don't need it," he said. "I've been through worse."

She saw by the scar low in his belly that he spoke the truth.

"Besides," he snapped, "you can't go down those stairs on your knee."

She stopped what she was doing, met his devilish eyes and began to giggle. "If we aren't a pair for sore eyes!"

He began to chuckle, his voice low and hardy.

When they stopped, she gave him a solemn look. "I shall put you in a sling in the morning. Perhaps that will help your bad arm."

"Perhaps it will."

She put the rest of the clean bandage back in her bag. "I suppose we had best blow out the light and go to sleep."

"I suppose we had."

She blew out the candle and scooted under the covers, shivering with cold.

Harry had walked around to the other side of the bed. She heard him removing his pantaloons and was terribly thankful he could not see the blush creep into her cheeks once again.

Chapter 14

As he had done the day before, Harry awakened Louisa with a cup of hot tea. "Sit up, sleepy head."

She sat up and stretched and gratefully picked up the warm cup and drank. "I declare, I have never been so cold in my entire life."

Harry nodded. The blasted cold had awakened him several times during the night -- which was no wonder since Louisa had pulled the blankets from him and wrapped herself in them. All of this, of course, occurred while she slept. Being a gentleman, he could hardly remove the blankets from her. So he had gotten up and fully dressed, and anxiously waited for the first light of dawn so he could go downstairs and stand before a fire.

He watched with satisfaction now as Louisa curled her hands about the warmth of the cup.

"Let me have a look at your knee," he said when she finished.

She obliged him by swinging both legs over the side of the bed and lifting the hem of her woolen gown until both her knees were revealed.

Her lack of womanly modesty surprised him. This was, after all, the same woman who grew crimson at the mention of bosom. He dropped to one knee and visually examined her swelling first.

Then he flexed her leg, first down then up. "You've made great improvement in one day," he told her. "The swelling's half what it was yesterday."

"Does that mean you'll allow me to walk downstairs by myself?"

"It does not," he said. "The worst thing you could possibly do is to negotiate stairs." He reached to pull her gown back down, surprised at what an intimate gesture it seemed. "I shall carry you."

He got to his feet and announced, "I will tell Mrs. Winston you're ready for breakfast."

"Not until you put that arm in a sling, Harry Blassingame, Lord Wycliff."

He rolled his eyes. "You remembered your threat."

"I did indeed." She began to rummage through her valise until she found a length of linen which she fashioned into a sling. He obliged her by allowing her to tie it around his neck before he left their chamber.

A moment later he rejoined her, lifted her into his arms, and proceeded to walk down the stairs before placing her in a dining room chair.

The cheerful Mrs. Winston, wearing a white apron and carrying a tray of scones, entered the dining room and proudly laid the table with food. "I hope your room wasn't too cold last night," she said.

"The quantity of blankets compensated for the room's chill," Louisa said.

Harry coughed.

Louisa picked at her food, and after a few moments turned to Harry. "I've been wondering about something."

"Yes?"

"Where does your coachman sleep and eat while all of our physical needs are being met?"

Harry finished slathering the clotted cream on his scone. "Last night he slept in the barn where there were horses and cattle and a wide assortment of blankets to keep him warm -- which is what he's used to in London. As far as his meals are concerned, he ate in Mrs. Winston's kitchen not half an hour ago."

"What about when we stay at an inn?" she queried.

"I pay for his night's lodgings, same as ours," he said with mock outrage. "Surely you don't expect that I would not make arrangements for his accommodations."

There was indignation in her voice when she answered. "Of course I didn't think you would forget the man."

She took a bite of her scone. "I cannot help but to wonder how the truly unfortunate survive in the cold when they have no roof over their heads."

He lowered his lashes as well as his voice when he replied. "I believe your fears are well founded, madam. Many of them, unfortunately, succumb to the elements."

She pushed away her plate. "I cannot eat when I think of all the suffering that goes on in the world."

Mrs. Winston scurried back to the table with another pot of tea.

"I assure you, my love," he said, "your eating or your not eating will not change the spots on a leopard."

"The Missus isn't eating?" Mrs. Winston asked with disappointment.

"Yes I am, Mrs. Winston," Louisa said.

"Everything's delicious."

The matron went back to the kitchen, a satisfied smile on her kindly face.

"My love, indeed," Louisa mocked. "Must you lay it on so thick? I declare, Lord Wycliff, you have missed your calling on the London stage."

"Mustn't disappoint the old girl. After all, Mrs. Winston is convinced that I look at you like a lovesick schoolboy."

"I daresay the woman's vision has gone completely."

He laughed to cover his embarrassment. For Mrs. Winston's observations had not been far from the mark. The longer he was with Louisa, the fonder he became of her. Except for her ridiculous reforming notions, she was everything he'd ever wanted in his countess. She was not only beautiful and intelligent and compassionate, she also had the ability to understand the complex emotions that made him the man he was today. She knew him nearly as well as he knew himself.

A pity she detested the man he was.

"If the bedchamber was as cold as it was," he said to change the subject, "one hates to imagine how cold the coach will be today."

She affected a mock shudder. "It will be easier to bear if we think of poor John Coachman."

Did she always have to think of others? The woman could grow quite tedious.

He assisted the coachman in loading their bags onto the coach, gratefully accepted the basket of food Mrs. Winston gave him for their noon meal, paid her handsomely for sharing her hospitality, and they were once again on their way.

They had to drive through miles and miles of

dreary moorland in order to get to the next village. Harry's predictions about the cold in the carriage had, unfortunately, been right on the mark. Though it was not raining, the temperature was below freezing, and the wind howled a lonely wail outside their carriage. Harry was miserable as he watched Louisa wrapped completely in the rug.

Finally she took pity on him. "I suppose if I can share a bed with you, my lord, we can use this rug together." She made an opening for him, and he quickly and gratefully crossed the coach and sat next to her under the rug. As he had been careful to do every night as he lay beside her torturing presence, he made sure he did not touch her.

He was sorry she had reverted to calling him *my lord* again. The intimacy of calling one another by their Christian names had been a balm to his loneliness of the last decade.

"You know, you took all the covers last night," he said as if he were commenting on the weather.

She gave him an incredulous stare. "I did not! I would surely know it if I had."

"I beg to differ, madam."

"If that is the case, I heartily apologize, my lord. May I hope that you took them back?"

"That would hardly have been gallant."

"Do you mean to tell me that you spent the whole of the night in that freezing room with no blankets covering you?"

"I do."

"Oh, my poor Harr---" She stopped herself, that blush creeping up her face. "I am terribly sorry, my lord."

He had heard enough. A woman who hated him would hardly refer to him as *my poor Harry*.

So she doesn't completely hate me, he thought with satisfaction.

* * *

The terrain between the Winston's farm house and the town of Bodmin was much the same. Barren moorland. It was past noon when they reached Bodmin. Louisa would not have been surprised had she turned completely blue from the cold -- which made her think of the coatless lad she had seen as the left London. Had the poor boy gotten a coat by now? She rather doubted it.

At the local tavern, Louisa fairly leaped at the prospect of warming herself in front of the fire while Harry made inquiries about the lord of these parts. Not only did she crave a hot drink, but she also had a mighty wish to stretch her legs.

Harry desired whiskey to make him warm, while Louisa ordered a glass of warm milk. When the serving woman returned with their drinks, Louisa could barely keep a straight face when Harry, using his most cultured voice, asked, "I say, a chap from my club in London said if ever I was in Bodmin I was to look him up. A Lord Blamey at St. Alban's Abbey. Would you know his direction?"

The serving woman put down the glasses and pointed west. "It's about five miles from town on the Hopping Road."

Harry gave the woman a shilling.

"Oh, thank you ever so much, sir," she said, dropping the coin into her ample bosom before going back to the public rooms.

"We dare not hope Lord Blamey would be coming to town on so cold a day, do we?" Louisa asked hopefully.

Harry shook his head. "No, I think not." Then

he took a long drink of whiskey. "I'll be back in a few moments."

His few moments turned into twenty. Louisa had long been finished with her milk and grown impatient when he finally returned.

"I bought a saddle," he boasted upon entering the private parlor.

"That is supposed to make me happy?"

His face fell. "Actually, quite the opposite, I'm afraid." He sat next to her, not across from her as he had done earlier. "I hate terribly to ask it of you," he began, "but since you're the only one who can identify our mysterious lord, you will have to go to his house."

"That much I had already surmised," she said.

"Alone," he added.

She nodded.

"On horseback," he added.

Visions of treading alone through snow came to Louisa, and she did not at all like it.

"We can hardly drive up in a coach and four without attracting undue attention," Harry explained. "So I propose to take you to the hedge nearest to Lord Blamey's house, then saddle one of the horses for you to ride to the front door. Perhaps you won't get so terribly cold since it is just a short ride."

"Why can you not go, my lord?"

He looked contrite. "I honestly wish I could, but I fear that since he's a peer he could quite likely recognize me, which would, of course, spoil our plan."

She nodded. "Yes, I suppose you do know quite a few men of nobility, despite your years away."

He looked offended. "I see that you don't believe me, but I assure you I do know a number of people. I happen to belong to London's most prestigious club. And I've been at Almack's any number of times."

Though she had never been there, she knew Almack's was where all the young maidens searched for respectable husbands. The thought of Harry looking among them for a prospective bride, quite oddly, disturbed her.

Though she wanted to protest having to go to St. Alban's Abbey by herself, she realized Harry was right in not allowing the lord to see -- and possibly recognize -- him. "Very well," she agreed weakly. "But how on earth shall I explain my presence there alone -- and on so wicked a day?"

Harry ran a finger across his lips. "Good point. We shall think on it all the way to St. Alban's Abbey."

She scowled at him as they left the tavern.

During the next forty minutes they suggested one scenario after another but found objections to all. She couldn't be asking for a job. She couldn't profess a prior acquaintance. She couldn't be a friend of his wife/child/brother/sister since she had no idea if he had a wife/child/brother/sister.

Finally they decided to forget about saddling a horse. They would drive up to St. Alban's Abbey in Lord Wycliff's impressive carriage, and Louisa would put her own plan into action.

* * *

The carriage securely in front of St. Alban's Abbey, Louisa bundled herself up into her cloak and muff and scurried up the front path, aware that her knee had greatly improved. The abbey was of an age to have survived the Dissolution. Barely. The east and west wing were in ruins. Only the central area, which must have formerly been a chapel, was in good repair -- though modestly small. For a peer.

Louisa strolled to the timbered door and knocked. A butler answered. *Drat.* She was hoping for the master himself. "Is your master within?" she asked.

The butler ran a most disapproving eye over her. "Who should I tell him is calling?"

"Miss . . .Miss Augusta Marks. I desire to speak with him on a personal matter."

The balding man raised a bushy eyebrow, turned on his heel, and left her standing in the doorway.

Louisa had no doubt the butler found her a fancy piece. After all, what decent woman would show up like this on a man's doorstep?

As she waited, she grew nervous.

Finally the butler returned, asked her to come in, and showed her to the morning room.

$\mathscr{C}$hapter 15

The longer Lord Blamey kept her waiting, the more nervous Louisa became. She rehearsed what she was going to say over and over, wishing she possessed Harry's gift for ad libbing.

All the while she waited, she forced herself to remember the one time she had seen the lord from Cornwall. That night she had brushed out her hair, gone to bed, and snuffed the candle. Then, with no light to guide her, Louisa had crept from her room and eased her way down the dark hallway, careful to walk as quietly as she could.

She waited for a long while until Godwin himself opened the front door, which only happened when his mysterious visitor came. Then Louisa crept forward to where the light from below reached the landing where she stood, and she stopped and stood at the end of the wall to which the banister was attached. Like a turtle poking its head from the cover of its shell, she moved around the corner and glanced below.

The two men had walked toward the library, the lord nearly a head taller than Godwin, who was no more than five-feet, seven inches. She had been struck by the other man's almost regal posture and the excellent cut of his clothing. There was something distinguished looking about his appearance. She was not surprised that Godwin had addressed him as *my lord*.

She snapped out of her reverie when the door opened, and she turned to see a man who was far younger than Godwin's benefactor.

Lord Blamey was much the same age as Harry. He sported a thick head of auburn hair and a thick waist he attempted to disguise beneath a striped waistcoat.

His brow elevated, his hand still on the handle of the door he had not shut, Lord Blamey closed the door and walked forward. "I am Lord Blamey," he declared as she stood up to face him.

"Forgive me for interrupting you, my lord," she said nervously. "I fear you will think me rather silly when you find out why I am here."

Lord Blamey gave her another quizzing look, but apparently satisfied from her voice that she was a lady of Quality, asked her to sit down.

Though she sat, he continued to stand as she began her story.

"I've been journeying from London in my traveling coach with only my dog, Cuddles, for company." She gave a little laugh. "As you can imagine, one must stop every so often so the little fellow can. . ."

"Yes, I understand," he said with a chuckle.

"The naughty fellow ran off into the woods not far from here. My coachman and I have looked everywhere but have been unable to find the little pooch. You can imagine how distraught I am."

"Yes, quite, but I assure you I have seen no sign of your dog."

"Allow me to describe him to you," she continued. "He is small." She lowered her hand to less than a foot off the carpeted floor. "He is ginger colored and answers to the name of Cuddles." She fluttered her lashes. "I would be ever so grateful if you and your servants would treat him kindly if you see him." She stood up, "And please send word to the tavern in Bodmin."

Then she peered at him and came to a sudden stop. "Your butler referred to you as Lord Blamey. I'm thinking I may have once met your predecessor in London. A tall, distinguished looking man?" She was prepared to further describe him, but that wasn't necessary.

Lord Blamey chuckled. "That is not my father. I'm afraid I am the image of my late father."

She dropped into a curtsy and walked to the door of the morning room. Just beyond the door stood a well dressed lady -- obviously Lady Blamey -- whose eyes raked over Louisa as if she were a lady of the night.

* * *

Once back in the carriage, Louisa patted the seat next to her for Harry to share, covered them with the rug, then burst out laughing.

After she told him her tale, he broke out laughing too. "I can see the poor bloke running about the park shouting, "Here, Cuddles," Harry said between laughs.

She tried to get serious. "I'm truly sorry, my lord, that we have not found your man."

He stopped laughing. "Are you sorry only because you are hungry to gain my money?"

"That's an unkind thing to say. I truly want you to regain your family's possessions."

"So I can give them to the poor?" he asked.

"No," she said with a pout. "So that you can speak on behalf of the poor in Parliament."

She made him feel bloody wretched. He *had*

told her he would take his seat in Parliament once he settled his affairs. It was just another of his blasted lies that the naive Louisa Phillips had seemed to believe. Which made him feel quite low. But then, he was a rather low person.

"How's the bad arm today?" she asked with concern.

"Somewhat bad, I would say."

Her face turned solemn. "When I said my prayers last night, I asked the Lord to spare your arm."

Bloody hell! Like a bloody Methodist or a Quaker, she was praying for him. Not bloody likely he had any points left with his Creator. Not after all he had done. Nevertheless, he was touched over her concern.

"I thought intellectuals were not believers."

"Then I must be a very poor intellectual, indeed," Louisa said quietly. "You will find I'm not nearly as pious as Hannah More has become."

"Which, I would think, is a good thing."

She laughed at this. "It would not surprise me that you, though you're not an intellectual, have little faith in an almighty power."

He felt uncomfortable. "You already know more about me than I ever wanted a woman to know."

A satisfied smile turned up the corners of her lips. "Then we are in the same boat, my lord, for you know far more about me than I would like for any man to know."

Now he smiled.

"Which brings up the matter of my alter ego. . .You have admitted you read -- and admired -- Mr. Philip Lewis when you thought he was a man. I expect now your opinion will change completely."

He thought for a moment, remembering the

essays he'd read in the *Edinburgh Review*. "Actually, I think not. Sound opinions that are fully supported with examples and logic are most difficult to refute."

"I am glad to learn that, my lord."

"Stop addressing me as *my lord*, Louisa.

"I will think on it," she said.

Lopping from side to side by the fierce winds, the carriage churned forward toward the south coast. The barren land gave way to more interesting -- though still sparsely inhabited -- terrain. The closer they came to the coast, the more the landscape became dotted with cottages and people and plump trees. The more, too, the sun shone, and warmth replaced the cold.

Harry pulled out the basket Mrs. Winston had packed for them. He gave Louisa a hard-cooked egg and a thick slice of bread that had been baked that morning. There was good country cheese and a large apple for each of them.

They ate their fill, then followed it with a jug of water fresh from the Winston's well.

Harry sincerely hoped Louisa did not notice how difficult it was for him to move his arm. The last thing he needed was a bloody bluestocking pitying him.

He could tell the swelling was becoming worse in his left arm, while the right one was far better today. At least, since he was right handed, he was glad that if he had to lose an arm, it be the left.

Such reasoning did little to cheer him. If he lost his left arm, he doubted he would be effective at sword fighting. And it would be quite difficult to hold the reins and whip the horse all at the same time. Then there was the matter of placing his arms around a desirable woman. He glanced at

Louisa, who was becoming more desirable with each passing day. Excruciatingly so at night when he would lay beside her, tortured with longing to take her in his arms and make her forget that a ruffian like Godwin Phillips had ever made love to her.

The thought of her making love to Godwin Phillips stung painfully.

He slid a glance in her direction. Her head had dropped, and her lashes swept low. A full stomach and the lulling movement of the carriage must be working together to make her sleep.

And he was the freezing one who'd gone without sleep the night before!

If only he could sleep. That would give him some relief from the blasted pain in his arm.

As wide awake as if he'd drunk a pot of strong tea, Harry watched as the coach rolled into Polperro, a quaint fishing village. The coachman went into the local inn to procure their rooms. Harry's eyelids began to grow heavy.

* * *

After the second of Jeremy Bentham's speeches, Edward was seeing Miss Sinclair home when she startled him by asking him if he carried a weapon.

"I have no need, ma'am. We are in Mayfair."

"Is that supposed to assure me that there are no cutthroats in Mayfair?"

He thought for a moment. "You will be quite safe here, Miss Sinclair."

"I don't feel quite safe. Just this morning I read in the *Gazette* that a woman's throat was slashed in Whitechapel."

He laughed. "If I were to go to Whitechapel -- which I'm not likely to do -- I *would* carry a weapon. The borough is notorious for crimes of every sort. I hear there are prostitutes on every corner, selling themselves for a penny."

Miss Sinclair's mouth opened to a perfect oval, and crimson crept into her cheeks.

"I beg your pardon, I should not have spoken so in front of a lady."

As they drew near Grosvenor Square, he glanced at her and spoke again, "I thought perhaps tonight you would do me the goodness to accompany me to Vauxhall Gardens. With your. . .er, cook to chaperon, of course." Demmed if he'd ever heard of young lady being chaperoned by her blasted cook! Edward would be only too happy to have his cousin return. It was most embarrassing traveling about London – and to a neighborhood he would not normally visit – with Harry's gig rattling behind him with the plump cook, who must be sixty years old, demmed near spilling out of the seat. Most embarrassing indeed.

The young lady's face turned white, and she grew stiff as a poker. "Miss Grimm said Vauxhall was no place for gently bred ladies."

He turned the corner that would take them to Grosvenor Square. "I take that for an insult, Miss Sinclair. Was just there last month with my sisters, and if they ain't well bred, I'll eat your bonnet."

"I mean no offense, sir. I am only repeating what was told to me by Miss Grimm, whom, as I have told you, had been with Sir Sedgeley's daughters the year before she came to me." Miss Sinclair said that as if he was supposed to know who the demmed Sir Sedgeley was.

If ever he met Miss Grimm, Edward would take great pleasure in throttling her.

When he pulled up in front of Harry's old house, Edward leaped from the vehicle and assisted Miss Sinclair in alighting from it.

Though he was not nearly so tall as his cousin, Edward towered over Ellie Sinclair. The top of her head barely reached the center of his chest. She looked up at him, her blue eyes smiling, and he was deuced glad he had spent the afternoon with her. Her blush had completely disappeared, leaving her skin the color of fresh snow. She was dainty and fair and had such a helpless quality about her that he would have been here with her even if Harry had not instructed him to do so.

"I cannot tell you how grateful I am that you have taken me to see Mr. Bentham. I don't know what I would have done if it weren't for you," she said.

He inclined his head. "It was my pleasure."

"Wasn't Mr. Bentham enlightening?"

He hadn't understood a word the man said. *Bloody intellectual.* "Oh, most enlightening."

"Poor Louisa, I know she must be sorry, indeed, to miss Mr. Bentham."

"Quite unfortunate," he agreed as the chubby cook swept past them.

* * *

Louisa woke from her nap when the carriage stopped. She was disoriented at first. She had been dreaming that she was in a warm bed at home in Kerseymeade, her mother bending over her lovingly.

When she awoke she realized she was in Lord Wycliff's coach. Then she realized Lord Wycliff's head was in her lap. Which seemed terribly out of character for him. She peered down at him. He seemed to be sleeping like the dead.

Unconscious of her own movement, Louisa gently swept her hand across his brow.
He was burning with fever!

Chapter 16

Had Harry been cold instead of hot, she would
have taken him for dead. For his body, blazing
with heat, had gone completely limp. She looked
down into his face. Rivulets of perspiration
streaked it. Her breath grew short and she
seemed paralyzed with fear. *His arm! The infection
had spread to the rest of his body. He was going to
die!*

She couldn't have said for how long she sat
there in a frightened stupor. *No, God!* she kept
saying until she finally realized her utter
helplessness was doing him no good. Running her
hand across his forehead once again, she called
his name.

He did not respond.

She raised her voice and called him again.
"Harry! Harry! Wake up!"

When he did not respond the second time, she
poked her head from the window and yelled to the
coachman. Not that he could restore Lord Wycliff
to good health. With her pulse racing, she sat
there waiting, stroking Harry's heated face.

Finally the coachman opened the carriage door.
His eyes darted first to his lifeless master, then
up into Louisa's frightened gaze.

"Lord Wycliff's terribly ill."

The coachman's dark eyes passed sympathetically over the lifeless form of his employer. Louisa realized the servant must have been as frightened as she.

"It's a good thing we've reached the inn." He flung the door open wider, then bent forward to help Harry out. But it was too much of a job for one man. Harry was too large.

"I'll help," Louisa said calmly, knowing that she must remain level headed for the sake of Lord Wycliff.

She extricated herself from him, and Harry's upper torso fell back into the soft leather seat, his legs sprawled in front of him. Then she stooped over him and wedged her left arm between his sides and his arm and heaved upward. She succeeded in bringing him to a sitting position while John gripped him from under his other arm. Together they hoisted Harry from the carriage, and with one of them on either side of him, walked toward the inn.

"My master's sick and has urgent need of a room," the coachman informed the innkeeper.

The swarthy innkeeper glanced behind them where the door was still open, affording a view of Harry's impressive carriage. "Come, put him in my room. There's a fire in there."

Located on the first floor, the innkeepers' room was far less tidy than Louisa supposed his guests' rooms were -- because of the personal items littering the room -- but the bed had been made, and at the hearth a fire blazed.

The innkeeper took over for Louisa and helped the coachman lift Harry onto the bed as soon as Louisa had pulled the covers back. Then he turned to her. "I'll send for the doctor."

Moving swiftly to Harry's side, she thanked him. She stood solemnly over Harry, wiping his brow. Though he was perspiring, he began to tremble as does one with chills. She pulled the blanket up to his chin and smoothed his brow once more.

John stood at the other side of the bed. "I don't understand it. He was right as rain this morning."

She looked up at him, her eyes hooded with shame. "It's all my fault. He took an injury rescuing me the day I fell, and I fear the infection in his arm has spread to his whole body." Her voice broke on the last few words.

John folded his mouth into a grim line. "I'll stay here with you, ma'am, in case the master needs anything."

She wished he weren't so nice to her. She deserved his wrath for her foolishness that had caused Harry to . . . she couldn't even think that her carelessness would lead to his death.

Yet as she stood there beside his bed, stroking his brow and trying to force water between his parched lips, she knew he was terribly sick. He had been one of the bravest, most vibrant men -- no, amend that to *the* bravest, most vibrant man she had ever known -- and because of her he was reduced to a shivering, helpless mass.

Impatient and frozen with fear, Louisa thought it was hours before the doctor arrived when in reality it had been less than one. The stooped old man wearing spectacles and sporting longish hair strode into the room, the innkeeper on his heels. "Well, what do we have here?" he asked.

Her words choked, Louisa said, "A very sick man."

"I don't understand it none," the coachman

added, "he was fit as a fiddle this morn."

The doctor gently pushed John aside. "Let me take a look."

Louisa stood at the other side of the bed. "You might wish to examine the wound on his left arm. I believe it has become infected."

"Let's get this shirt off," the doctor said, leaning down and beginning to unfasten the pearl buttons. He carefully lifted the shirt away from Harry's fevered body, then proceeded to unwrap the bandages on his arms. When he saw the yellow liquid oozing from Harry's left arm, he winced. "Nasty it is, I'll say. However did he come to bruise himself so badly?" He looked up at Louisa.

"He fell down a Cliffside."

"And lived?" the doctor joked. "Think I'll bathe the wound in a decoction of winter cresses and rebandage it. See if that will help stop the infection at the source." He turned now to John. "Fetch me a bowl of hot water, will you?"

By the time the doctor had removed his own coat and rolled up his sleeves, John was back.

Louisa stood helplessly watching the doctor clean Harry's wound.

When he finished he looked up at Louisa. "Now I'll bleed your husband."

Ignoring that he had addressed her as Harry's wife, Louisa stiffened and regained her sternest voice. "I will not allow you to bleed my husband."

"You don't want him to get well?" the doctor asked.

"Of course I do, but after reading the works of Dr. Heidbreder in Germany, I have decided that bleeding not only does no good, but it can also be harmful."

"Heidbreder, Schneidebreder. Never heard of the quack. I've been bleeding patients since I was a lad of twenty."

Anger flashed in her eyes. "And I'll wager you've lost many of those patients."

"I cannot keep to the earth what God desires in heaven," he defended.

Now she glared at the man. "I do not wish my husband to be in heaven, doctor." Her voice was harsh. She made eye contact with John. "Pay the doctor, John, for his services."

John removed a pouch from his pocket, and gave the doctor a half crown. He waited until the doctor had packed his bag, donned his coat, and left before he spoke to Louisa. "Are you sure the doctor should not bleed Lord Wycliff?"

Her face was grim when she answered. "I am sure." She fervently wished she were as convinced as she sounded.

For the next several hours, Harry went from hot to cold. She would hold and rub his hand and cover him snugly when he shook with chill, then she would take off his covers and wipe his heated flesh with cool water when he was hot. Hot to cold. Cold to hot. The hours dragged on. And Louisa's fear mounted.

Harry couldn't die! Although they had known each other less than a month, he was the only man -- the only person -- she had ever been truly close to. He understood her as she understood him. She knew his secret -- as he knew hers.

Louisa couldn't think about the immeasurable loss it would be to lose his voice in Parliament. That seemed as insignificant now as her foolish pride over the Philip Lewis' essays. All that mattered in her life right now was that Harry get well.

She tried to remember when she had ever been so frightened. She had been too young when her beloved mother died and too filled with scorn when the sixty-year-old gout-ridden Godwin had died. But were she to lose Harry. . .

She tried to tell herself that she would lose him anyway once he found Godwin's benefactor. But at least his vibrancy would not still. All that really mattered was that he live. She would always carry a place for Harry within her heart.

As midnight came, a parlor maid brought more wood for the fire, and Louisa told John to get some sleep. "I'll need you fresh in the morning to watch out for Lord Wycliff while I catch some sleep."

The tired old man nodded, then trudged off to his room.

Louisa took his warm hand within her own and sat down. She prayed some more until he began to flail about, tossing his soaking sheets from him. Then she stood up again and took the bowl of water in her hands and began to rub his burning flesh with her wet hands, oblivious to the fact her tears were dropping into the bowl.

As the hazy light of dawn began to squeeze into the room,

Louisa set down the bowl of water and stretched her arms high above her head. Her feet throbbed with pain, her back ached, and her wounded knee had begun to swell.

Then Harry opened his eyes, and Louisa thought she had never felt so wonderful.

"Harry?" she said softly, moving closer to his bed.

"Where in the bloody hell are we?" he groaned.

Giving no thought to what she was doing, she took his hand and squeezed it. "We are in an innkeeper's bedchamber in Polperro. You, my lord, have been very, very sick."

"Harry, not my lord," he corrected, a smile on his face as he squeezed her hand back.

"Yes, Harry, dearest," she said in a breaking voice, her eyes moist.

He smiled, turned over, and went back to sleep.

He was going to make it!

She climbed in the bed beside him and went fast to sleep.

In the days that followed, Harry showed a little more improvement each day. He grew stronger with each passing day, and the swelling on his arm -- like that of Louisa's knee -- diminished each day. His fever stopped on the third day, but his appetite had not returned, nor was he strong enough to get out of bed.

Louisa continued to sleep with him. After all, she had told everyone he was her husband.

As he regained his strength, he listened to John's tales of how he had been at death's door. During his recovery he gave a lot of thought to Louisa's slavish devotion toward getting him well. He pictured her standing over him, gently wiping him with cool water. And he kept remembering her words when he awoke. She had referred to him as *Harry dearest*. No accolade on earth could have been more welcome than those two words uttered by a sweet little blonde bending over him with worried eyes.

Despite her kindness to him in those days when he was recovering, he found himself growing short tempered with her and knew it was not because of anything she had done. It was his own self he hated. He wasn't worthy to touch the hem of her skirt, such an angel was she. He had no right to be the recipient of her kindness. He deserved to die.

Instead of keeping his feelings of self loathing within him, he took them out on her. He treated her with gruffness and displayed a consistent bad humor.

And at night when she would lay her weary body beside him on the big feather bed, he would shudder with his need to take her within his arms.

Then he would awaken the next morning and begin lashing out angrily at her. *The porridge was too cold. She'd awakened him up with her comings and goings to and from the kitchen. Why couldn't she let things bloody well alone? Was she obsessed with her ridiculous notions of ruling the world with her possessive ways?*

He winced and turned away to avoid seeing the pain in her face. Despite his own remorse, he knew his unconscious had its own way of keeping someone as pure as Louisa Phillips out of his sordid life.

* * *

One afternoon after Louisa was convinced Harry was on the mend, she left him in the coachman's care as she went to the church on the outskirts of Polperro.

She would be the only person at the church for it was a Tuesday. She opened the creaking timber door, entered the dark church, and strolled down the nave. She fell to her knees on the stone floors and gave thanks that Harry had survived.

A noise beyond the altar startled her. She

raised her lowered lids to see a young cleric – concern on his face – moving toward her. "Is there anything I can do to help you?" he asked in a gentle voice.

She shook her head. "I've never been better. I'm here to give thanks to the Almighty."

The young man smiled. "You're not from around here."

He had obviously determined a great deal from her voice. "I've come from London."

He nodded. "I'm the vicar here. Rouse is my name."

She stood up and curtsied. "I'm . . . " She started to say Mrs. Phillips. Then quickly said, "Mrs. Smith." Suddenly an idea occurred to her. "Does Lord Treleavens provide your living here in Polperro?"

His green eyes flashed with good humor. "He does. Do you know him?"

"No, but my husband may. Is he an older gentleman? Tall and lean?"

He chuckled. "Not at all. Trelly and I were at Oxford together. He's my age and rather portly, I'd say."

"Oh, dear. Perhaps it was his father my husband is thinking of. Was he tall and rather thin?"

"Actually, Trelly inherited at the age of twelve from his uncle. I never met the chap."

Then the uncle had to have been dead at least fifteen years, Louisa reasoned, for the vicar looked to be far closer to thirty than to twenty. Which meant neither the current Lord Treleavens nor his predecessor could have been Godwin's benefactor -- and the previous Lord Wycliff's menace.

"My husband will be so disappointed that Lord

Treleavens is not the man he had thought he might know."

"Did your husband attend Oxford?"

Louisa had no idea where Harry had gone to university. Then again, Harry would not want to be confronting anyone who might recognize him. "I'm afraid not. Mr. Smith went to Cambridge." She flashed the vicar a smile. "Thank you, Mr. Rouse, for your concern and for answering my questions." She curtsied and left.

* * *

Early the next week Harry was strong enough to travel. The weather had turned mild and sunny, and Louisa regained some of her feistiness.

In no uncertain terms she refused to let him sit on her side of the carriage. "To put it bluntly, my lord, I have no desire for you to touch me even in the most innocent way. If I had my choice, I would refuse to share a room with you at the inns, too, but I fear that might lead to the discovery of your true person, which would foil our plans."

Our plans. Despite everything, it came back to the simple fact that, like it or not, desire it or not, he and Louisa Phillips were as drawn together as those united by clergy. His heart's desire lay within the grasp of her small hands. And her heart's desire did not lie with him, he thought bitterly.

$\mathcal{C}$hapter 17

Leaving the Polperro innkeeper's chambers brought Louisa mixed emotions. On the one hand, she was sorry to leave the intimacy of the room where she had been for so many days with Harry, days of worry and of a closeness she doubted she would ever rekindle with another human being. On the other hand, she knew they needed to be getting along. She had never planned to leave Ellie for this long, and she was becoming worried over her sister.

Then, too, leaving Polperro might restore Harry to better humor. She tried to be patient when he was impatient with her. After all, a man like Harry was unused to being bedridden. No doubt, his pride was bruised over his infirmity.

Getting back on the road again was the best thing. They left the Polperro inn early in the morning, the *so'westerly* wind fighting against Harry's four matched grays. They drove along the coastal route, which was so vastly different from the desolate Bodmin Moors. Here there were spreading oaks and elms, and primroses bloomed everywhere, even though spring had not yet come.

It was warmer here in the South, too. Louisa flung off her rug an hour into the journey, and she eagerly viewed each village.

Underlying all her thoughts, though, was her worry over Ellie. When she had left London, she had felt certain she would return within a week. Now that week had stretched into almost three. They had covered half of Cornwall, but their search had thus far proved fruitless. She wished she could hop on a post chaise headed to London, but she had given Lord Wycliff her word she would help him identify Godwin's benefactor. And Louisa Sinclair Phillips had never gone back on her word.

Besides, were she to return to London without having proven successful, she would receive not a farthing from Lord Wycliff, and she and Ellie desperately needed the money.

Poor Ellie. Left alone in the metropolis that terrified her so with only the occasional companionship of the immature Edward Coke. The poor little pet must be quite miserable.

Louisa flicked a glance at Lord Wycliff, who sat across from her in the carriage. She was embarrassed to find that he was watching her. "In the next village," she said firmly, "I must post a letter to Ellie, and I beg that you will do likewise with Mr. Coke. Mr. Bentham has long ago finished delivering his talks, and I fear your cousin will have forgotten about my sister."

"That's hardly likely."

"Why do you say that?"

"Because my cousin is a gentleman and will feel obligated to offer your sister protection until we return. Besides, your sister is a lovely creature."

A sting of jealousy swept through Louisa. She did not at all like for Harry to find any other female attractive. Even if that female were her beloved sister. On further reflection, though, Louisa took his words for a compliment. After all, Ellie was but a younger, more petite version of herself."

"Could you please ask your cousin to take Ellie to the theatre or the opera? I believe she would find those most amusing." She smiled as she thought of Ellie's sweet countenance and innocence.

"Consider it done."

* * *

Being fully apprised of the nature of his cousin's business in Cornwall, Edward grew alarmed when the third week arrived and still he had heard no word from Harry. Had Harry located the mysterious lord and then been done in by him? Any manner of murderous scenarios flashed through Edward's brain, which was already given over to adventurous accounts of villainy and the triumphs of honorable heroes.

In the depths of his mental wanderings, Edward rather fancied himself a dashing hero. And now his opportunity had arrived. He would single handedly rescue his cousin from the grip of death – and the sword of a vile lord.

Though Harry had cautioned him not to impart to Miss Sinclair the particulars of his journey, Edward let the cat out of the bag one fine afternoon he was taking Miss Sinclair for a walk about the Grosvenor Square park, innocently telling her that he had grave fears for the safety of his cousin and her sister.

She turned her sweet face -- which he rather liked -- up to his. Most ladies of his acquaintance tended to be taller than him – such a pity that he could not have taken after Uncle Robert's side of the family and been tall like Harry.

He noticed that Ellie's eyes were wide with surprise.

"My sister is with Lord Wycliff? I do not believe you, sir. Louisa specifically told me she was seeing to matters of her late husband's estate, and Louisa would never lie to me."

He had gotten himself into rather a pickle. Harry expressly told him not to mention that Mrs. Phillips had gone away with him. Some ridiculous notion about not wanting to sully the widow's good name! As if a woman who delivered talks berating the state of matrimony and advocating free love had not already hopelessly tarnished her reputation. "See here," he said frantically, "you're not to know that your sister's gone to Cornwall."

"To Cornwall? Why Louisa doesn't know a soul there, and if you are trying to tell me my sister is having an affair with your cousin, I refuse to believe a word you say. She doesn't even like your cousin. He's an aristocrat!"

"I'm not saying that, either. Why must you keep trying to put the most ridiculous words into my mouth?"

She stomped her dainty heel. "I'm not trying to put words into your mouth. I'm merely trying to learn my sister's whereabouts. Has your wicked cousin abducted her with intentions of stealing her virtue?"

There she went again. Did she think every man in London went around stealing good women's virtue? Damn Harry for saddling him with a blasted chit who was still wet behind the ears. "My cousin need not steal any woman's virtue. He can have the most beautiful women in London merely for the asking."

"Are you saying my sister would willingly give your odious cousin her virtue? That my sister is nothing more than a harlot, sir?"

He rolled his eyes toward the heavens. "I'm saying no such thing, Miss Sinclair. I'm certain your sister's virtue is still intact. Bluestockings don't appeal to Harry."

She huffed.

He stopped and placed both of his hands on her shoulders. "Harry learned that the man who owns Wycliff House lives in Cornwall, and only your sister can identify him. Harry bribed her to go with him. That's all there is to it."

Ellie's mouth dropped open. "Louisa does not own Wycliff House?"

"I'm afraid not," he said gently, his hands still on her slim shoulders. "That brute of a husband of hers didn't leave her anything. That's how Harry got your sister to go with him. He promised her a house and a comfortable settlement for the rest of her life."

Ellie bit at her lip.

"But I'm afraid they've come to harm," Edward said. "The man they're searching for, whom I am told is rather unsavory, must have found out about them and decided to make sure they would no longer be a threat to him."

Ellie shrieked. "What can we do?"

"Not we, but I," he said forcefully. Puffing out his chest, he said, "I shall have to rescue them."

"But. . .you could be killed." She held both hands to her breasts.

"'Tis a chance I shall have to take." He turned away. "I had best have my man pack my things now."

She clung to his sleeve. "Take me with you!"

He stopped dead in his stride. "I can't do that."
"Why?"
"Because. . .it ain't proper."
"But my sister's with Lord Wycliff. If Louisa does something, that makes it right. My sister has an acute sense of right from wrong."
"Your sister has been a married woman. That makes her a great deal different than you."
"How so?"
"Because she's. . .you know."
"I don't."
"She's been with a man before."
"Of course she's been with a man. She's with another one as we speak."
"When I said *been with a man*, I meant, well, blast it, Miss Sinclair, your sister has lain with a man."
He watched with sympathy as the color crept up her cheeks. "Oh," she managed to squeak.
"So you see, you can't come with me."
"But you're a gentleman. I can trust you not to. . ."
Steal my virtue, he wanted to finish.
Instead, she said, "want to lie with me."
"Of course you can trust me not to try to do that. Nevertheless, I still can't take you."
"But you can't leave me alone here in London! I'm so terribly frightened."
He hated like the dickens to watch the pitiful little thing pleading in front of him like that, but the fact was he simply couldn't take her with him. It could be quite dangerous, not to mention the impropriety of it. "You'll have your Cook."
She stomped her slippers once again. "Oh, you odious man!" Then she ran off to Wycliff House, though, of course it wasn't called that any more.

Not since that contemptible Godwin Phillips had taken possession of it.

With an inexplicable feeling of lowness, Edward rode the phaeton back to the livery stable nearest his lodgings, and he instructed his man to pack some clothing. Then he realized a phaeton would mean poor travelling, indeed. But Harry had taken the coach, which would give excellent protection from the elements. Edward fleetingly thought of taking a post chaise, but that would hardly do. He had no idea where he was actually going.

An hour later, bag in hand, he returned to the stables to fetch his gig and rode off toward the west.

He was completely unaware that a young lady dressed as a tiger hitched herself behind his phaeton.

* * *

In the next village Harry and Louisa came to, they learned that a post chaise would stop for the mail the following morning. Harry scribbled out a message to his cousin, while Louisa, in the broad flourishes of her distinctive penmanship, scratched away a three-page letter to her sister.

"You don't need to write a bloody book," Harry quipped.

Louisa shot him an I'd-like-wring-your-aristocratic-neck look.

He franked the pair of letters, then they got back into the coach.

"I'm beginning to think I dreamed up our non-existent lord," Louisa told him, her voice – like herself – utterly tired.

"I have faith in you, Louisa."

It was the first civil comment he'd made to her

since he had regained his strength. In some small way, it helped to buoy her sagging spirits. She was as weary as she could ever remember being in her life. Her weariness coupled with Harry's brutish manner toward her had worn her down to the point she could collapse for a week.

His ill treatment bruised her, especially since the disturbing revelation that had come to her as she stood at Harry's bedside watching him weakly flail under the hallucinations of the high fever. And despite all the reasons why she should not, Louisa had come to realize that she did, indeed, love Harry Blassingame, the Lord of Wycliff. He was an arrogant aristocrat. He was far too handsome to ever settle with a single woman. He had been a lying, thieving pirate. To make matters even worse, he didn't even like her!

Nevertheless, she was in love with him.

And, God help her, she did not want to be.

* * *

When afternoon came, Harry suggested they walk along the cliffs now that her knee had fully mended. He sent the coach ahead to the next village.

"You know," Harry said solemnly to Louisa, "we will soon be reaching Penryn."

He did not need to say more. She knew what his thoughts were. That was the problem with Harry and her. They knew each other far too well, and he obviously did not like what he saw in her.

She felt an utter failure. She'd been unable to help Harry find the Cornwall lord, she'd axed any hopes of gaining that little house and a comfortable income, and she'd never have a champion in the House of Lords.

Worst of all, she would never know the love of

Harry Blassingame, Earl of Wycliff.

Had someone told her six weeks ago that she'd fall desperately in love, she would have committed them to Bedlam. She disliked all men as much as she disliked Godwin. Or so she thought.

But she had not reckoned on finding a man who read her thoughts, or on finding a man who would risk his own life to save hers, or of finding a man whose sensual presence invaded her very dreams.

She knew, too, he had a commanding enough presence and a keen enough mind to have been a force of great power in the House of Lords.

A pity the world would not know what a capable leader it had lost.

"I beg that you not pick any wild flowers today, my love."

My love? She looked at him with questioning eyes.

"Sorry. A habit picked up in front of innkeepers, I'm afraid."

If only he meant it. "I believe, my lord, I have learned *not* to pick crocus that grown wild at cliff's edge." She gave a little laugh and skipped ahead of him.

"What makes you so energetic today?" he asked.

"Three weeks of being cooped up either in a traveling coach or in an innkeeper's stuffy bed chamber."

He caught up with her and offered his arm, and she tucked hers into his.

"I apologize that I haven't told you before how grateful I am for your care while I was sick."

"'Twas nothing."

"Nothing indeed! You did not leave my side for

six days."

"Had it been me, you would have done the same."

He set his warm hand over hers. "I would, Louisa. It seems you know me far too well."

"As you know me."

"You're right, once again."

"I am most happy you realize that, my lord."

"Harry," he said in a throaty voice.

"Harry," she repeated, her voice soft as she squeezed his hand.

"I don't know if I'll ever become accustomed to night falling at four in the afternoon as it does here," he said. "It appears from my map that we'll barely reach Mevagissey by dark."

"Cheer up. We'll be in Penryn tomorrow -- and in time to make short work of finding Lord Kellow."

He frowned. "And I hazard a guess that my scheming Mrs. Phillips already has a plan in place for meeting the fellow."

Was she too scheming? Was that why he found her companionship so objectionable? Her lashes dropped. "I have no plan, my lord. Have you?"

He muttered an oath. "I will once I see the lay of the land."

They walked the last hour in relative silence, Louisa's only comfort her tenacious grip on Harry's proffered arm.

Chapter 18

A strange thing occurred at the inn in Mevagissey. Harry had instructed that two rooms be procured: one for him and one for his sister, Miss Smith. Louisa was fighting mad. First, she was deeply offended that Harry was so repulsed by her presence; then, she was furious that he'd traveled as husband and wife for the duration of their journey. Had he originally thought to seduce her?

She fumed. Was her rage only to mask her grievous hurt? Now that Harry had been in her company for three weeks, he had not only grown tired of her, he obviously had grown to abhor her. And she felt like crying.

The private parlor was already dark, though it was only half past the hour of four. Harry lit the candle for their table from the hearth and sat down across from her at a table near the fireplace.

She glared at him.

"Surely you're not still angry over the sleeping arrangements," he said, grinning. "Have you come to crave my body in your bed, madam?"

Her eyes narrowed. "The only thing I crave is your absence! I am excessively displeased that you did not think to travel as brother and sister three weeks ago. It's my belief you thought to seduce me." She glared at him. "I have lost all respect for you."

He shrugged, then picked up his bumper of ale.

His indifference stung. She sat up straighter and shot him a haughty glance, hoping she gave the appearance of being equally indifferent.

A timid serving woman brought their haddock and set it on the table without uttering a single comment. The two of them ate in silence. Toward the end of the meal, he said, "I beg that you play a hand of piquet with me after dinner. It's far too early for bed."

Still angry, Louisa stiffened. She had no desire to be accommodating to him. She forced a mock yawn. "I find traveling extremely tiring, my lord." She took her last bite of fish, then rose from the table. "I shall meet you back down here at dawn. We should be in Penryn by noon tomorrow." Then she turned on her heel and left.

* * *

Bloody hell! That woman and her haughty manner sorely tried his patience. 'Twas just as good that she did not wish to play cards with him. Every minute he spent with her was unmitigated torture. He had been unable to allow himself to spend another night in her bed. It had been all he could do not to force himself on her every night since he'd regained his strength.

Each time he gazed at her, he remembered how she had looked bent over his fevered body, worry etched on her beautiful face. He would remember her calling him *Harry Dearest*, and he physically hurt with need of her. Each night as he lay beside her, he thought of how desperately he longed to stroke her silken skin, to feel her breasts pressed against his chest, to touch his lips to hers . . . to bury himself within her.

'Twas just as well that he spend his evening in the tavern away from Louisa. He picked up his bumper and decided he just might drink himself into oblivion.

* * *

The following morning, they met silently in the parlor, and after coffee, toast, and ham, departed the fishing village of Mevagissey.

Louisa pushed back the curtains in the carriage to view the town's saffron cottages with their green porches. She watched a young boy carrying the slops to a common ditch and dumping them, and she viewed a girl fetching water and carrying it back to her family's granite cottage.

Soon, the village was behind them. The next signs of habitation were clayworks north of the coast. She had heard of the windowless huts where the claymen slept, but she had never before seen them. Now, she watched them with a fascination mingled with pity. How wretched it would be to be forced to sleep with a dozen others in a single room that had neither fresh air nor a window to allow a peek of the sun.

At least they had a place to sleep, she conceded. In London's East End, living conditions were much worse. Many did not have a bed on which to sleep; others paid a penny to hang up in a vertical position for a night.

She had many years of work ahead in order to improve such horrid living conditions.

They reached Penryn at noon, and they took a repast in the private parlor at Oddfellows Arms. They still did not speak to one another.

Louisa wanted to pump the serving woman for information about Lord Kellow, but she fought the urge to do so. It had occurred to her that Lord Wycliff might find her too domineering. A man preferred to be the dominant partner, the decision maker. She laughed a bitter laugh to herself. What did it matter if she were overbearing or meek? Harry already detested her, and nothing she could do now would ever change that.

Harry quenched Louisa's curiosity when he glanced up from his bumper of ale and caught the woman's attention. "Would you be able to give me the direction of Gulvall House?"

Lord Kellow's abode.

The fair young woman's eyes flashed with mirth. "I thought a fancy gent like ye might be acquainted with Lord Kellow -- especially seeings as how yer of the same age and all."

"I was trying to recall to my sister here," he said, glancing at Louisa, "how long it's been since his lordship inherited."

The young redhead raised her eyes toward the heavens. "A good question. Let's see . . . 'is firstborn is aboot ten, I'd say, and I know 'e 'adn't inherited when he wed the lovely lady from Lun'en 'cause everyone was a sayin' what a fine Lady Kellow she'd make one day. Sorry I'm no 'elp to ye."

"I'll just have to ask him when I see him. Where *is* Gulvall House?"

"Aboot three miles from town. Don't know me north from me south, but it's that away." She pointed north. "Take the road what runs along the heath. The road to Truro."

Harry gave the girl a shilling, and she curtsied her thanks.

Moments later, she returned with steaming food. After she left, Louisa asked, "Then you plan to confront Lord Kellow yourself?"

"I do."

She raised a brow. "But if the man is *of your age*, as the woman said, you run a risk that he will know you."

Harry thought on this for a moment. "It no longer matters if he knows me since it's not he -- but his father -- who is my sworn enemy. I care not if the son knows who I am. I have no ill feelings toward the offspring of my father's enemy. I only need to find out if his father was the Cornish lord."

"I hope the beast has died."

He stopped cutting his kidney. "You speak of the man responsible for my father's demise?"

She nodded.

"I'd rather he be alive. Only he can answer the questions I mean to ask."

Louisa shuddered and pushed away her uneaten food. "I think I should be the one to confront Lord Kellow."

Harry's eyes flashed defiantly. "You forget I have been out of the country for nearly a decade, and during that time the man who is now Lord Kellow has wed and started a family and is likely buried with duties of his Cornwall estate. It's not likely he's met me at my London club."

Harry twirled his glass in his hands and met her questioning gaze. "I believe it suits me that you become my wife once again."

"But it *doesn't* suit me," she snapped.

"I'm the one making the decisions. I'm the one holding the purse strings, Louisa."

She shot him an icy glance. "I'd best not defy

you, else you'll be sure to renege on the bargain."

"How low you must think me."

She shrugged. Let him think she was as indifferent as he.

He stood. "I wish to introduce you to Lord Kellow as my wife."

She rose and flashed him a defiant look that was completely at odds with her capitulation. "Whatever you wish, my lord."

* * *

During the carriage ride north of Penryn, Harry imparted his plan to Louisa. To her utter surprise, he procured a neat stack of cards that he'd had printed in London. Crisp black Roman letters identified him as Harold Smith, Esquire.

Since the weather had become quite mild, Louisa swept aside the velvet curtain and lowered the window. Sunshine and salty air filled the carriage. Louisa thought she could be quite happy in southern Cornwall -- if it weren't for the obtuseness of her traveling companion.

Some thirty minutes later, she was looking up at the aged gray stone of Lord Kellow's Gulvall House, which sprawled magnificently along the crest of a hill that was surrounded by verdant woods. A most advantageous situation, to be sure. The house had been accessed from a winding road that forced the coach to travel at a slow pace. It must have taken fifteen minutes to ride from its base to the modest portico of Gulvall House, where the carriage rolled to a stop.

Harry disembarked, then turned back and offered Louisa a hand. "Ready, Mrs. Smith?"

Despite her anger, being addressed as his wife filled her with a satisfying warmth, even though the title meant nothing. Especially to him. She placed her hand in his, climbed down and smoothed her skirts as she looked up at the aged, three-storey house.

Her hand on Harry's arm, she followed him to the front door, where he knocked.

The door was opened by a stiff-mannered man wearing worn and frayed gray livery and a powdered wig. He raised a brow at beholding the two of them.

Harry offered his card. "Please announce me – and my wife – to your master."

Eying the card but saying nothing, the servant closed the door upon them.

Louisa and Harry exchanged amused glances. "If the card had identified you as the Earl of Wycliff, I'd wager we would sitting in the morning room as I speak," she said.

He chuckled. "It's just as you're always saying, Mr. Lewis, people are unfairly judged by their rank, not on the basis of their individual accomplishment."

"Ssh," she said, lowering her voice to a whisper. "Someone might hear you address me like that."

"I'm not so foolish as to address you as your alter ego in public."

Before she could reply, the door swung open, and the servant begged them to follow him to the morning room. The room's green coloring seemed to make the chamber an extension of the verdant outdoors surrounding Gulvall. Her eyes sweeping across the richly decorated chamber, Louisa lowered herself onto a green silk brocade settee that faced the door. She cringed when Harry sat beside her.

The servant departed, closing the door behind

him. A moment later, a fair young man who was tall and lean strolled into the chamber. *Oh, dear,* Louisa thought, *he's built exactly like our lord from Cornwall.*

Harry stood and faced the man. "Lord Kellow?"

The young man, a quizzing look on his face, nodded.

Harry bowed. "Forgive me for coming unannounced, but your London solicitor would not forward my inquiries to you – and since my wife and I are travelling to Penzance for our wedding trip, I thought we'd swing down to Penryn and see you in person."

"My good man," said Lord Kellow, who stood almost nose to nose with Harry. "I do not have a solicitor in London. Perhaps you're thinking of the gentleman who handles my wife's father's estate?"

"Your wife's father was a peer?" Harry asked.

Lord Kellow shook his head. "Dear me, no. His name was Mr. Montague of Russell Square. Do you know him?"

"No."

"He's dead now." Lord Kellow glanced at Louisa and the settee where she sat, then his gaze flicked back to Harry. "Please sit down, Mr. Smith."

The host took a seat in a Tudor chair near the settee. "Now what is it you wished to see me about?"

Harry's dark eyes met the peer's. "About the Grosvenor Square townhouse."

The man's brows folded together. "What Grosvenor Square townhouse?"

"The one your father purchased."

"You cannot be serious, my good man! My father detested London, and I assure you he never purchased property there. In fact, my father could never have afforded to purchase property in the capital."

"Perhaps I'm mistaken," Harry said.

"Actually," Lord Kellow added, "I'm far more affluent than ever my father was – thanks to the present Lady Kellow's father's hefty purse."

"Does the present Lady Kellow not enjoy returning to London?" Louisa asked. As soon as she spoke, Louisa realized she was once again trying to take charge. No wonder Harry detested her and her authoritarian ways.

With smiling eyes, Lord Kellow met Louisa's gaze and shook his head. "She's quite as bad as my father was in her quickness to criticize London. After our first year in Penryn, she said she never wished to return to the Capital and its filthy black skies. And I must say, the asthma complaints that plagued her in London have completely disappeared since our marriage."

Harry grinned, nodding, then slid a glance at Louisa. "Come, love," he said as he stood and offered her his hand. "I'm afraid we've troubled Lord Kellow for nothing."

"No trouble at all," the man said as he stood up.

"Nevertheless," Harry said, "I must apologize for having mistaken you for another peer."

Kellow came closer. "Perhaps I can help?"

"I'm trying to purchase the Grosvenor townhouse," Harry said, "but I've been unable to contact its owner. I was told the owner was a peer from Cornwall. I had the odd notion that was you."

Kellow shook his head. "Dare say it's Arundell. His is the wealthiest family in Cornwall."

Louisa shook her head. "We started with him,

but he was not the man we were seeking."

Kellow lifted a brow. "I suppose it could be Tremaine. Nobody knows much about him. Reclusive and all that, but I've heard he's wealthier than anyone will ever know."

Tremaine. The next to last lord on the list, the last geographically. A peer whose seat was in Falwell, near Land's End. "What does he look like?" Louisa asked.

Lord Kellow shook his head. "Actually, I've never met him. As I said, he's rather reclusive."

"What age would he be?" Harry asked.

"I expect he's near my own father's age. Were he alive, my padre would be four and seventy."

Harry glanced at Louisa. She nodded. That would be the right age. He took Louisa's hand and moved toward Lord Kellow. "We're exceedingly sorry to have troubled you," Harry said.

"No problem whatsoever," Kellow mumbled. His brows lowered as if he were deep in concentration.

As Harry and Louisa left the spacious morning room and headed down the broad stone hallway to the front door, Lord Kellow followed them.

Even when they left the house and walked up to the carriage, he followed. They turned back to say goodbye to him, and he slapped at his head, a broad grin on his face.

"By Jove! Knew you looked familiar to me," Lord Kellow said to Harry. Then his eyes narrowed. "Though the name Smith doesn't match up. Why, Lord Wycliff, did you wish to deceive me?"

Chapter 19

Harry stiffened.

Kellow smiled and walked toward them. "Perhaps you would remember me as Tom St. John – my name before I ascended."

Harry's jaw dropped. "By Jove! At Eton, you gave no sign you would ever grow so tall."

A grin flashed across Kellow's face. "My mother claims I didn't begin to grow until I married!"

Since he had been no closer to Kellow – or Sinjun, as he was then called – at Eton than he was now, Harry did not feel he owed the fellow an explanation. "A pity your growth came so late. You'd have been a much more formidable opponent in sport."

"I doubt I could ever have bested you."

"I daresay your recollection of my abilities has dimmed with the years."

Kellow tossed a glance at Louisa. "Pray, is this really your wife?"

As much as he disliked lying to the fellow, Harry refused to allow Kellow to think ill of Louisa. "Of course!" he said with mock outrage, moving closer to Louisa and closing his arm around her. "We have our reasons for secrecy. Another time, perhaps, I shall be at liberty to discuss them with you."

"As you wish, Wycliff."

Harry turned his back on the man and helped Louisa into the carriage.

As the carriage pushed away, Louisa asked, "Were you not utterly dumbstruck when Lord Kellow recognized you?"

"Thunderstruck is more like it."

"I take it you two were not close at Eton?"

"Not particularly. Poor fellow was one of the last chaps picked for the matches."

"I daresay you were the one doing the picking."

Harry shrugged.

"Had you no desire to impart the truth to Lord Kellow?"

He leveled his gaze across the carriage at her. "None whatsoever. I'm not an idiot."

"I do abhor lying."

"As much as you abhor the idea of being my wife?"

She continued gazing at her gloved hands, then slowly lifted her lashes and glared at him. "Being your *pretend* wife."

He shrugged. "Pray, which is most odious to you? Lying or being my *pretend* wife?"

"I'm surprised you credit me with an intolerance toward fabrication, given my *nom de plume.*"

"Yes, you do live a lie. Somewhat."

She thrust hands to hips. "I can honestly say my pen name is the only time in my entire life I have lied, and my reasons for doing so more than justified my dishonesty. My work would never have found an audience had it been known the author was a female, and it was very important to me that my writings be published. I believe what I have to say promotes the common good."

"Utilitarianism. And you're justified in thinking so."

His compliment silenced her.

He stretched out his long legs and watched her beneath hooded brows. Undoubtedly aware of his scrutiny, she refused to glance in his direction. Instead, she lifted the curtain and peered at the verdant countryside.

"When will we reach Truro?" she asked a little while later.

"What makes you so sure I'm not going to skip Truro and go directly to the reclusive Tremaine?"

She spun toward him, her brows lifted. "You're not?"

He chuckled. "It's a possibility. What think you of it?"

Her lovely lips puckered in thought for a moment. "If I'm picturing the map correctly – and I am possessed of picture-perfect memory – going to Cuthbert instead of to Lord Tremaine's Falwell would actually take us back father to the east. And if Curthbert's Lord Walke is not our man – and I must confess it *does* seem more likely Lord Tremaine is our man – then we would have diverted from our path for naught. I say we should forget Cuthbert and head toward Land's End." She paused a moment, then meekly added, "If my opinion is being solicited."

He threw his head back and laughed hardily. "Your opinion is, indeed, being solicited." He tapped his signal to the coachman, then after the coachman stopped, Harry directed him to head toward Land's End.

"Aye, my lord, but I shall have to consult me map."

"As I would expect you to do," Harry said. John

was a good man. He not only knew his horses, but was also skillful at directions. Harry had the greatest confidence in his abilities.

While they sat there inside the unmoving carriage, Louisa gazed out the open window. Finally she looked back at him. "Pray, why did you think it necessary for me to play the part of your wife at Gulvall?"

"Because I knew Kellow was a fellow of my own age, and I realized there was a possibility he would recognize me."

She looked quizzingly at him. "And?"

"And I thought I would be less recognizable if I appeared to be a happily married man." He cleared his throat. "It seems I have a reputation as a . . . well, as a bit of a rake."

"And having a wife would erase your wicked past?"

"Having a wife as lovely as you could," he said throatily. *What the deuce was he doing?* He hadn't meant to give himself away. Wasn't he supposed to be convincing Louisa she was completely unattractive to him?

A deep flush crept up her cheeks.

He had to redirect the conversation. "Using your picture-perfect memory, I beg that you tell me what the next town we come to will be."

"I only memorized the routes we *had planned* to take. Since we're altering our direction, I cannot tell you. I did not memorize the name of every village in the Duchy of Cornwall."

He had gone and aggravated her again. Where Louisa was concerned, he could not seem to do anything right.

Fortunately, she softened. "Actually, as the crow flies, it's almost directly a straight line west to Falwell, but, of course, the roads never seem to go in a straight line."

"No, they don't," he said grimly. Surely the reclusive Tremaine had to be the fiend who had caused his father's ruin. Yet, a nagging doubt persisted. Everywhere they had gone, they had met with failure. All of this time spent could be for naught. No, he amended, a surge of an unfamiliar emotion washing over him. Not for naught. He could never regret one single, precious moment he had spent with Louisa. Even when he had lain in his fevered stupor, he counted himself fortunate for the pleasure of gazing up into his angel's face.

He gritted his teeth and forced himself to look away from her. *Bloody hell!* She was far too good for him. He wasn't fit to be sitting in the carriage with her. He moved to the opposite window from where Louisa watched.

At noon, they reached Marazion, where they stood gazing out to the medieval structure rising from St. Michael's Mount before changing horses and taking a quick repast. Harry smiled to himself when Louisa insisted on purchasing a comfit from the establishment next to the inn. She wished to give it to the coachman, and she refused to allow Harry to pay for it. No doubt, she pitied John Coachman because of his misfortune of being born to the working class.

Once they were on the road again and he was just about to close his eyes for a nap, Louisa startled him. "Why didn't we ask Lord Kellow about Lord Walke?"

A good question. Had they erred in deciding to dismiss Curthbert without making any inquiries about its Lord Walke? Since they had already eliminated four of the possible six lords, what would it have hurt them to try to find out everything they could about Lord Walke and his Padflow Priory? Harry bolted up and muttered an oath.

"I'm sorry," she said. "I had no right to be so negative. It's not as if we can't go right to Cuthbert if Lord Tremaine is not our man. Actually, it won't be a minute out of our way home from Falwell to go through Cuthbert. Going to Falwell first is a much better plan."

He still frowned, though what she said made a great deal of sense. He only hoped one of the last two would be their man. Preferably Tremaine.

She returned to gazing out the window while he tried once again to close his eyes and drift into a relaxing sleep, but he was unable to suppress his thoughts, thoughts of lords and fruitless quests -- and Louisa. Always, all thought returned to Louisa.

What would he do when he located the mysterious lord? His first objective, of course, was to persuade the man to sell him the house on Grosvenor Square. Harry was prepared to pay whatever it took to regain ownership of the house, even if he had to pay twice what it was worth.

But what else did Harry wish to accomplish when he finally came face to face with the evil man? A surge of hatred rippled through him. He would have to find out why the man had orchestrated his father's downfall. What could his father ever have done to generate such vile contempt? Harry would never be able to peacefully lay down his head until he knew the answer to that question.

Also, Harry was possessed of a strong conviction that the disappearance of his mother's portrait was intrinsically tied up with the mysterious lord. And he vowed to do everything in his power to learn the whereabouts of the portrait.

Despite his hopes that they would make Falwell by nightfall, Harry had not counted upon how early it got dark in these parts. Darkness forced them to stop for the night -- though it was barely past four in the afternoon -- in the village of Helporth. Had the terrain been less hilly with more reliable roads, he would have instructed John to continue. But it was far too dangerous for those unused to the region.

In Helporth, they disembarked from the carriage and stood still in front of the inn where they watched cool white mists rolling across the surrounding countryside like curls of smoke from a chimney. There was an eerie, unreal quality about it. Finally, Louisa set a gentle hand on his arm and urged him into the inn.

Surely, he thought impatiently, Louisa could not continue to feign fatigue and beg to go to her room for the night before the clock struck six.

Neither of them was hungry yet, though they had bespoken a private parlor at the Three Lambs Inn. In the room's darkness, he and Louisa perused the map of Cornwall.

"A pity it's grown so dark for I do believe we could have reached Falwell in another hour's time," she said, looking up at him with her blue eyes.

Fighting the urge to stroke the satiny skin of her face, he nodded. "There's something to be said, though, for arriving in the daylight."

Louisa turned away to watch the fire's licking flames. "If your offer for a game of piquet is still good, I believe I shall take you up on it.

He procured cards, and they commenced an amiable game, which was followed by another and another until they were finally hungry enough to eat.

Harry was growing sorely tired of eating at inns and sleeping on beds which were much smaller than what he was accustomed to. He was impatient to ride his mount and not sit in a cramped, stuffy carriage. He was consumed with curiosity about the vile man he was taking such great efforts to meet. Thinking on all this caused him to grow angry.

And as had become his custom, whenever he was angry, he took his anger out on Louisa.

"I think I shall be sorry to see our journey come to an end," she said softly, sipping her wine and gazing into his face with a dreamy expression.

He harrumped. "Not I! I'm so sick of Cornwall and of riding in carriages I pray I'll never again darken the misty peninsula as long as I live."

She looked offended. "Surely the journey's not been all bad?"

"Tell me, madam, one good thing that's occurred since we set off from London?"

It cut him to the quick to see the look of pain which flitted across her lovely face at his thoughtless words, but he knew it was better to hurt her now than to cause her a lifetime of pain.

"I shan't impede you, my lord," she said with dejection. "Once you find your lord, you have my blessings to ride off on your own precious mount back to London." She threw down her napkin and rose from the highly scrubbed table. "Now, if you'll excuse me, I believe I shall go to my bed."

Shoving the table as he got to his feet, he said,

"And I believe I shall go to the tavern."

* * *

Louisa would have been better off had she stayed in London. True, she would have had slimmer financial prospects, but at least her heart would not have been so badly bruised. How much better off she had been back in London than she was now.

Nothing could be more painful than having Harry's cherished presence slammed into her every waking minute. Being so close to him, yet knowing a love between them could never be. Wanting to touch him, too feel him close to her, yet knowing such intimacy could never happen. Worst of all was the painful knowledge that Harry detested her. What had she done to have merited such wrath? Surely she had not been mistaken weeks earlier in her thinking that he welcomed her company. He *did*. Then.

But not now.

She was torn apart. As painfully as she needed him, her need to be away from him was even greater. She lay in the soft feather bed, the peat fire smoking in the grate, her every thought of Harry. Already she mourned his loss.

Almost as much as she regretted having come on this journey with him.

* * *

The following morning they rode for ten miles when Harry decided he and Louisa would walk while the carriage went on to Falwell.

"I'm bloody tired of being cooped up in a blasted carriage," he said.

"Me too," Louisa said in a low voice as she fell in step beside him.

He was not sure how far they were from the

coast, but its feel and smell were strong here. His thoughts flitted to the day Louisa had plunged off the cliff and of how worried he had been that he'd lost her.

Fortunately, there was no coastal cliff to gobble her up here. Just a hilly, pleasing landscape, air tinged with salt water, and perennial breezes that swept Louisa's soft muslin gown to outline the gentle curves of her body.

He felt compelled to draw her hand into his as they walked along the footpath. Even with no words passing between them, he was oddly warmed by her presence as they trod up the forlorn hill.

When they reached the top of the hill, Harry's breath caught at what he beheld. On the next bluff there arose a mighty castle. Its turrets caught the light of the mid-day sun, the castle's solidness the antithesis of Tintagal's ruins. His chest tightened. This was it. Their quest had ended.

Chapter 20

Long after the innkeeper's wife had cleared away their dinner dishes at the Speckled Goose Inn that night, Louisa and Harry sat in the parlor discussing their plans for the following day.

"I cannot believe our good fortune," Louisa said happily. "To think tomorrow is actually the Public Day at Gorwick Castle."

"The home of Lord Tremaine," he added dryly.

"I know you're right. I shouldn't be getting my hopes up. After all, how many times have you been at Public Days and actually set eyes on the Lord of the Manor or – in this case – the Lord of the Castle?"

He looked at her incredulously. "I've never been to a Public Day in my life, unless you count Cartmore Hall."

"No, I don't expect you would have," she said, laughing. "How stupid of me."

"Except for pulling flowers from the edge of cliffs, I'll wager you've never done a stupid thing in your life."

The crimson began to roll up her face.

"I'm sorry if I embarrassed you," he said, placing his hand over hers.

A bubbling heat surged through her at his touch. "You know very well you have put me to the blush again."

"I seem to have a facility for doing that."

She smiled, glad that she could find humor in herself.

He grew pensive. "What if we don't see the Lord of the Castle tomorrow?"

"Then we'll just have to find a way to stay within the castle walls when the tour is over."

"I don't like the sound of that," he said. "It could be dangerous -- if Tremaine is the man who ruined my father."

"Since he's reclusive, I don't think the lord would recognize you. After all, you spent eight years out of the country."

"But he might recognize you."

"I told you there was no way he could have seen me that night."

"How can you be sure?"

"For one thing, I was in darkness. For another, he had to be sixty feet away from me."

"Had the man ever seen you, he would remember."

"How so?" she asked, puzzled.

"You are an exceptionally beautiful woman."

Sweet heaven above! Her cheeks were flaming again. She didn't know how to respond. To thank him would be to acknowledge the truth to his statement -- which would be the pinnacle of conceit. How did practiced flirts handle such a situation, she wondered, not that she wanted to resemble those empty-headed girls in any way. Her inexperience with men -- despite eight years as a married woman -- only brought home how inadequate she was for Harry. Not that he would have had her anyway.

He reached toward her and traced her nose

with a single finger. "Sorry I made you blush."

She tried to make light of the sensual gesture. "I daresay Cook could bring me to blush by reciting the grocer's list."

He laughed at that, then poured more wine.

Together they drank three bottles of wine, though Harry's glass count far exceeded hers, as did his capacity for drinking spirits. Louisa began to yawn, and the next thing he knew, she laid her head on the table, right next to the dripping candle, and went to sleep.

Harry carried her upstairs to their bedchamber, his insides turning to pure mush. Louisa had a habit of doing that to him.

Their room was dark when he placed her on the bed to light the taper. That done, he removed her pelisse. She would just have to sleep in her gown because he wasn't about to draw her wrath for such an action. He stood there a long while, drinking in her loveliness. He thought of going back to the tavern and drinking himself into oblivion, but for some inexplicable reason he could not leave Louisa.

He moved to the bed, stripping off his clothes until they heaped on the well-worn wooden floor. Then he climbed beside Louisa. She began to softly moan, then she called his name. *Harry*.

She called his name again.

Then with a disappointment deep and gnawing, he realized Louisa was asleep.

"Harry!" she said once more, urgency in her voice.

He placed his arm around her. That it was his name she called – and not that beast Godwin Phillips's – pleased him. His own comfort was far from his thoughts. He was consumed with the urge to take care of Louisa for the rest of her days. To protect her from men who would use her. Or abuse her. To let her know what it was to be cherished. To awaken the passion of true love he knew budded within her soul.

For in this passionate little bluestocking lay the promise of all his dreams. Louisa Phillips was the only woman who could ever replace his mother as the Countess Wycliff.

* * *

Edward stopped to change horses at Woking. Because of the fair weather, he had made excellent progress. He was going to push himself to make Salisbury by nightfall, and if he continued at this pace, he could be deep in Cornwall tomorrow. With his riding crop in one hand and his unraveled woolen neck scarf in the other, he jumped from the box and strode toward the tavern. A drink would do his parched throat good.

Then he heard it. A small voice had said his name. And the deuced thing about it was the voice sounded like Miss Sinclair's. "Mr. Coke."

There it was again! Couldn't be the young lady's. She was miles from here, safe and snug at Wycliff House, though it was no longer called that. Nevertheless, he decided to turn around to see who it was who was calling his name.

Had the king himself been standing there addressing him, he could not have been more taken aback. For the quite lovely Ellie Sinclair faced him, and she was dressed as a tiger! And from the direction she had come from, he realized she had been perched for the whole world to see on the back of his phaeton! That is, the whole world except him.

For a moment he scowled at her, completely seized with anger. *What could she possibly be thinking of to come all this way with no chaperon?* Whatever was he to do now? Two days could be lost in taking her back to London, and he had no assurances the foolish chit would even go.

What a fool he'd been to trust her to be complacent and stay behind. After listening to those radicals she surrounded herself with, how could he have been stupid enough to think the girl would do the conventional thing?

"You are angry," she said feebly, walking toward him in her masculine togs.

Where ever did she find them? From a distance she would be taken for a boy, but no one seeing that lovely face could have any doubt as to her gender. He wished for a fleeting second that she could be ugly. Then this would be much easier.

"Course I'm angry. You've cost me valuable time."

"How so, sir?"

Did the deuced girl have to gaze at him in such an innocent manner? Blast her! "Naturally, I'll have to take you back to London."

She huffed and stuck out her flattened chest. "I will not go."

Were she really a boy he would have been able to speak authoritatively to him, but he couldn't do so with Miss Sinclair. She was, after all, a lady. "Now see here, Miss Sinclair, you cannot travel with me."

"Why not?"

"Because you're a lady." He swallowed. "And I am a gentleman."

"My sister, sir, is a lady, and your cousin is a gentleman, and they are travelling together, and you yourself admitted there was no lewdness between them."

"But I never said it was appropriate. In fact, it would be extremely inappropriate if it weren't for the fact your sister's been a married lady."

She thought on all this for a moment, standing there in boys' clothing that was still too big for her. "There will be no impropriety if people *think* I'm a boy."

"But you're not a boy!" Seeing a man leave the tavern and not wishing to be overheard, Edward rushed toward Miss Sinclair and walked her back to his gig. "See here, Miss Sinclair, it ain't proper for you to be traveling with me," he said in a voice that was barely above a whisper.

She looked up at him, those blue eyes of hers flashing. "What is proper and what is improper is merely in the eye of the beholder. Do you not agree?"

"I agree," he said, rolling his eyes.

"You and I know there is no impropriety between us, do we not?"

"We know there is no impropriety," he said with the voice of one reciting a familiar passage in a favorite book.

"Then as long as others believe that I am a boy, there will be no impropriety! So it's all settled."

"What's settled?"

"I'll continue to act the part of you tiger all the way to Cornwall."

"Can't have you sitting behind on that rail," he uttered.

She shrugged. "Could I be your little brother, then?" she asked meekly, her voice like that of a much younger girl. She stuck out her chest. "See, I have bound my breasts so I look like a lad."

He turned away, an unfamiliar flush creeping into his cheeks. "I will not look at your breasts."

"Oh, you cannot see them," she said cheerfully.

"I should hope not!" he exclaimed, turning back to face her, a scowl on his face.

"Oh, Mr. Coke, I have put you to the blush!"

"You have not," he snapped.

She linked her arm through his. "Then it is all settled."

God in heaven, what have I ever done to be saddled with the likes of Miss Ellie Sinclair? he asked himself.

* * *

When Harry awoke Louisa with a cup of hot tea the following morning, she nailed him with an accusatory stare and said, "Confess, my lord, when I slept last night you brought a hammer into our chamber and pounded my head soundly with it."

He laughed. "I fear you consumed far too much wine."

She raised herself to a sitting position. "How did I get to bed?"

"I carried you up the stairs."

He thought he liked it better when she blushed. Her complacency disturbed him. This was not his Louisa.

His Louisa. He cherished the idea. To the very core of his soul, he cherished Louisa Phillips. She was undoubtedly the finest woman he had ever known.

Yet he knew Louisa was the only woman who could ever claim his heart. The only woman – indeed, the only person – whose life was more precious than his own.

$\mathcal{C}$hapter 21

At breakfast – which Louisa and Harry again took in their private parlor of the Speckled Goose Inn – Harry ate heartily, but Louisa had little appetite.

"Has my special elixir helped your head?" he asked softly.

She nodded. "The head's better. Would that I could say the same for the rest of me. Why did you allow me to drink so much, my lord?"

"I am not your master, Louisa."

She could have sworn he said those words with regret. The effects of the wine must be lingering, clouding her thinking.

When the innkeeper's wife brought another pot of hot tea, Harry questioned her. "I say, my wife and I are trying to decide if Lord Tremaine is the same man we once met in London. Tall, distinguished looking with a beard."

"That sounds like him," the woman said. "Only saw him once meself. At St. Stephen's Church the day they dedicated the new windows. Lord Tremaine paid for them himself. 'Twas the only time I know that he set foot in the church. The family pew sits empty as you please at the front of the church Sunday after Sunday."

Harry gave her a shilling and lavish

compliments over the comfort of their room.

Louisa could barely contain her excitement until the woman left the parlor. "Oh, Harry! Lord Tremaine has to be our man."

He nodded solemnly. "A good thing today is Public Day at the castle."

* * *

Since the weather was fair, they decided to walk to the castle, which perched on a cliff above the village of Falwell.

"I understand it dates to the twelfth century," Harry remarked as Louisa gazed up at the stone fortress.

A mighty fortress it must have been, guarding much of the Cornish coast through the Middle Ages. Its battlements had eroded over the centuries but were still plainly visible even from a half mile away. Bulky round turrets anchored each corner of the square castle grounds.

As Harry and Louisa wound their way through the cobbled streets of Falwell, Harry found himself wondering if there was a moat around the castle. Moats and castles had fascinated him as a youngster. He had more than once lamented that Cartmore Hall was not a castle.

The sun was high in the sky when they strolled up to the gate to Garwick Castle, which did have a moat, but which looked to have dried up centuries earlier.

They weren't sure where to go once they were within the castle yard, then they saw an old aproned woman with a throng of girls around her.

"Must be a school trip," Harry muttered.

They walked across the yard and stood waiting with the group of girls, whom Harry judged to be somewhere between ten and twelve years of age.

They only had to wait a few moments before the housekeeper opened the huge timber door and welcomed them into the castle, gratefully accepting their shillings.

She led them to the great hall first and gave accounts of the days when oxen were roasted in the massive fireplace. Despite his childhood fascination with castles, Harry found snippets about the *inside* of the castle exceedingly dull. When would they get to the interesting things like armor and buttresses? he found himself wondering.

He was rather amazed at Louisa's interest in the building, but he supposed women liked that sort of thing. He was a bit embarrassed at being the only man in the group.

Partly out of boredom, partly because he had not forgotten their reason for coming, he was careful to glance down every hallway and into every room, looking for signs of the lord of the castle.

Nearly an hour elapsed, and no luck yet. If only there were a painting of Lord Tremaine. That should be enough for Louisa to make her identification.

When they made their way to the second storey, his interest perked. Surely this was the floor where Tremaine resided. Harry continued to eagerly look down each hall and into each room, even if they were not on the tour. He sincerely hoped the housekeeper did not think he was scoping out the place with an eye to burglarizing it.

Then he realized the foolishness of his idea. The place practically crawled with big, bulky liveried servants. Why would a man need to keep so many strong men in his employ?

At eleven o'clock in the morning, it was far enough removed from mealtime to give the housekeeper liberty to show the group the castle's massive dining room.

"The table seats sixty," she said with pride as she led her group into the rose-colored room. She rather reminded Harry of a mother duck leading the way for a trail of ducklings. The room was carpeted, and the smooth walls had been covered with silk damask. Everything was the same soft shade of red. The housekeeper had called it rose. He called it red. Mindful to stand behind the girls so as not to obstruct their view when the housekeeper began her recitation, Harry strolled into the room and stood behind the students. Then he looked up at three huge crystal chandeliers suspended from the ceiling.

Next, his glance swung to a portrait that hung above the marble fireplace, and a chill sliced into him. His heart began to drum, and he swallowed hard. He began to break out in a sweat. He almost questioned his sanity. Was he actually standing in Garwick Castle, or was he standing in the dining room of Wycliff House in Grosvenor Square a decade earlier?

For the portrait was the missing portrait of his mother.

He felt as if her emerald eyes looked down on him. He loosened his cravat. He could almost hear her reassuring voice. Louisa guessed that something was wrong with him. She moved to his side and lay a gentle hand on his arm. "Are you unwell, Harry?"

He shook his head. "The bloody bastard has stolen my mother's portrait."

Louisa gasped, her glance shooting to the painting that dominated the room. "She's. . .beautiful," Louisa whispered.

* * *

That afternoon and evening, Harry drank with a vengeance. So much that Louisa worried about him.

She watched him as he sat beside her on the upholstered bench not five feet from the blazing hearth that lighted their parlor. His face took on a gold cast from the light of the fire. His brow was moist with perspiration, and his dark hair was tousled.

"It was almost like seeing her again," Harry said.

He wasn't really carrying on a conversation with her, Louisa knew. He was merely thinking aloud.

"You were very close to your mother," Louisa soothed.

"Everyone who knew her counted her a friend. She had that way about her. Everyone loved her."

"With such a disposition as well as beauty, I think she must have had an army of suitors – before she married your father, of course."

"Her suitors all came before my father. You can be assured once she wed him, she never looked at another man. She was completely devoted to him." His tone sobered. "You know she died but one month after my father died."

Louisa nodded sympathetically as he continued.

"She defended him when I berated him for losing everything."

"At the time I thought perhaps she would have been better off wedding the first man she had been engaged to."

Louisa's brows lowered.

Harry gave a little chuckle. "She actually ran off with my father. She had become engaged to a wealthy suitor – she called him George – but had not really been in love with him. Then she met my father and knew she belonged with him, not George."

Louisa asked, "Is there a possibility Lord Tremaine could be George?"

He shook his head. "They would have referred to him as Lord Tremaine."

"Perhaps he had not succeeded to the title until after your parents were married."

He thought on Louisa's comment for a moment, then hurled his glass into the fire.

The fire surged and sputtered, then died down to normal.

Harry turned to her. "You must be right."

They sat there in silence, Louisa watching light from the fire dance along the strong planes of his face.

His face grew solemn. "Killing him would give me great pleasure."

She curled her hand around his arm. "Don't talk like that. There are other ways of reaping vengeance upon him."

"Such as?"

"You could expose him for ruining your father."

"My dear Louisa, there are no laws against taking a man's money and possessions at a gentleman's club."

She thought some more. "We can steal back your mother's portrait."

He searched her face from beneath hooded brows. "You would do that for me?"

"It wouldn't really be stealing," she defended. "The painting belongs to you. Besides, he is a vile man. We don't want Lady Wycliff's portrait in his possession."

He lifted both of Louisa's hands and kissed them.

It was all she could do not to throw her arms about his neck.

She was drinking nothing stronger than warm milk tonight. No more morning-after headaches for her. She watched with worry as Harry continued to drink hour after hour. At midnight she finally persuaded him to come to bed. With one arm around him, she helped him climb the stairs to their room.

On his own, he staggered the short distance from the room's door to their bed and fell upon it. His eyes were shut and his breathing was deep but steady.

Louisa closed the door and walked to the bed where she pulled off his boots, then placed a single blanket over him.

A moment later, wearing her woolen night shift, she slid under the covers beside Harry. As she lay there, a feeling of comfort swept over her. Why couldn't she have been pledged to a man like Harry? How different her life would have been.

Her hand possessively stroked over the hardened planes of Harry's manly shoulders. She could see herself happily lying beside him for the rest of her nights, but such thoughts – such torturing pleasure – must not be invited. For Harry Blassingame, the Earl of Wycliff, was as far removed from her touch as the stars in the heavens.

With the Cornish winds howling outside their

casement, the smell of salt air flooding their chamber from the half-open window, and the warmth of Harry beside her, she fell into a contented sleep.

* * *

It was Louisa who brought tea and elixir to Harry the next morning. Harry was in the same position he had been in when he sprawled on the bed the night before.

"Can you not close the curtain?" he asked, refusing to lift his head from the bed. "The blasted sun's far too strong."

"As well it should be," Louisa answered. "It is almost noon."

"Our daylight grows short," he exclaimed, moving to sit up and force down the elixir Louisa offered. Then he laughed at himself. "I was thinking we were still on the road to finding our mysterious lord." He finished drinking and sat the glass on the table beside the bed. "Now, there's no longer a need to make tracks during daylight."

Louisa stood beside the bed and looked down at him. "Now, I think, we will need night, rather than day, to accomplish our mission."

He looked puzzled. "What mission would that be?"

"We're going to *reclaim* your mother's portrait."

His lips curved into a smile. "You are a positive vixen."

She laughed. "I know that's what all you aristocrats say about me."

He made room for her to come and sit beside him on the bed while he finished his tea.

It felt perfectly natural for her to be sitting here with a barefooted lord, on a bed, in the village of Falwell, carrying on a conversation about stealing a painting. Everything she did with Harry seemed perfectly natural. As if they were meant to be together. Which, of course, could never really be. Harry was an aristocrat, and she was a bluestocking, and the two did not get on. Add to that the fact Harry didn't really like her. He had made that perfectly clear when he had recovered from his grave illness.

"How would you propose to gain entrance into the castle at night? I expect the drawbridge will be up."

She bit at her lip. "I hadn't actually thought of that."

He looked down at his feet. "Pray, where are my boots?"

"At the foot of the bed."

"And who, may I ask, took them off?"

"I did."

He looked down at her with a devilish glint in his eyes. "Why did you not remove the rest of my garments while you were at it?"

"I had no desire to see you without clothes, my lord," Louisa said haughtily.

A cockiness swept across his face. "I don't believe you."

"Shall we continue our discussion on how we are to gain entrance to Garwick Castle if the drawbridge is drawn at night?" she asked, standing up and walking to the window, then turning back to face him. "I have determined the *reclaiming* must take place at night because of the immense size of the portrait. We could hardly escape detection in the light of day."

"That's true," he said, nodding. "Yet I believe we shall have to devise a way to get into the castle during the day and wait until after the Tremaine fiend has taken dinner, then we'll – I mean I – will have to, ah, *reclaim* the portrait."

"Why did you amend your statement, my lord?"

"I can't possibly let you be a party to the *reclamation*."

"Why, pray tell?" she demanded, her eyes narrowing, her voice hard.

"Because you're a female and because it may be dangerous."

She would see about that! "Tell me, my lord, how do you propose to get in? Public Day won't come again until next Thursday."

"I shall have to think on it."

Chapter 22

Once Harry had dressed and shaved, he met Louisa downstairs at the Speckled Goose Inn. This morning he declined breakfast but asked for rather strong tea. Since Louisa had already finished her meal, they just sat and talked in the privacy of their parlor.

"I have decided," Harry began, "not to steal into the castle at night but to go there in broad daylight and demand to talk with this Tremaine."

"He won't see you if you give him your real name."

"I have never been thwarted by resistance."

"But, Harry, you can't draw your sword and go barreling in there. Castle Garwick is not a ship and you have no fellow cutthroats to back you."

"Neither my men nor me were cutthroats."

"That is beside the point. You saw for yourself all those brutes he obviously keeps for protection. As large as you are, I daresay, they are larger."

Harry lowered his brows and took another sip from his mug of strong tea. "You have not changed my mind, you know."

"Promise me you won't do anything drastic until we talk it over."

"And what do you term *drastic*?"

"Forcing yourself into Lord Tremaine's

chambers when he has refused to see you."

Harry looked into his cup, his eyes inscrutable. "He'll see me."

She moved to get up. "Let's go."

With a firm hand on her arm, he held her back. "Forgive me if I don't take you this once, Louisa."

She sat back down and patted his arm. "I understand. It's a matter that truly doesn't concern me."

He stood.

"If you're not back in ninety minutes, I shall have the castle stormed," she warned.

He drank the remaining tea, kissed the top of her head and left.

For the first time since their journey had begun, Louisa picked up her pen and began to compose one of Mr. Lewis's essays.

* * *

It was surprisingly easy for Harry to get in to see Lord Tremaine. He merely presented his card – his real card – to the butler and said he needed to see Lord Tremaine on a matter of a personal nature.

Less than half an hour later he was face to face with the man he blamed for his parents' deaths.

Wearing a silken robe though the afternoon sun squinted in the room's small arch-shaped windows, Tremaine sat on a silk brocade sofa in the library. He looked much as Louisa had described him except that Harry had difficulty calling a man distinguished who lounged on sofas in silk robes. Harry could see that he was tall, even if he had not risen when Harry entered the chamber.

Tremaine looked up at Harry, a bland expression on his aging face. "I see that you have found me."

Harry refused to sit where Tremaine indicated. Planting his booted feet in front of Tremaine, he said, "You thought to get away with your cheating schemes?"

"But it wasn't I who cheated."

"It was you who bankrolled your pawn, Godwin Phillips, may he burn in hell."

Tremaine laughed. "It does me good to see so much hatred in you. Now you know how I felt toward your father when he stole Isobel from me."

"My father never did a hateful thing in his life. All he did was love my mother – as she loved him."

"She loved me once," Tremaine said.

Harry shook his head. "Never, George. She told me so."

Tremaine smashed the crystal goblet he was holding into the stone floor. "You lie."

"Had she loved you, she would have married you."

"She loved me until Robert--"

"She never loved you." The words gave Harry a perverse satisfaction.

Tremaine thrust his head into profile. "Believe what you like." Then he turned back to face Harry, devilment in his gray eyes. "While you're simmering in hatred for Godwin Phillips."

"I hate Phillips more for what he did to his young wife than for what he did to my father." He fisted his hands and walked closer to Tremaine. "It is you I hate for what happened to my father."

Tremaine laughed. "I have no fight with you. After all, you have much of Isobel in you."

"Then if you have no fight with me, allow me to buy the Grosvenor Square House back."

Tremaine thought for a moment. "How much are you willing to pay for it?"

"Twenty-five thousand pounds is more than a fair price."

Tremaine laughed. "Double that, and it's yours."

"The house and everything that was in it?"

"For fifty thousand pounds, yes."

"Good," Harry said. "You will have the money within the month." Then he did something that was repugnant to him. He bent forward and offered the vile man his hand.

They shook hands. A gentleman's agreement.

Then Harry said, "I'll just fetch my mother's portrait now," as he began to move from the room.

Tremaine rose. He was as tall as Harry. "You'll do no such thing."

Harry turned. "But we shook on it. *The house and all that was in it.*"

"I. ..I," Tremaine stammered, "I meant all that *is* in it."

"You know the portrait rightfully belongs to me."

"My young man, I have never done things in my life because they were right."

That was the last straw. Harry's fist flew into Tremaine's jaw.

Then Harry, with fists at the ready, was poised for the man. Instead, Tremaine's hands flew to his jaw, and he saw blood on his hand and screamed like a woman.

Footmen, who obviously were hired as sentries, scurried into the room with swords drawn.

Harry held up his arms. "I am unarmed, and I shall leave peacefully."

Tremaine made sure his footmen saw Harry all the way to the drawbridge.

* * *

Louisa was still sitting in the parlor writing by the light of a candle when Harry returned. When she saw him, her face alighted and she put down her pen. "Oh, Harry, thank goodness you're back! I was getting worried."

He cocked his head and peered at her with those glowering eyes of his. "No Harry Dearest?"

She could feel the blush climb up her cheeks like smoke rising in a chimney. He *had* heard her the day of his recovery.

"Why you. . .you utterly wretched, wicked, vile aristocrat!"

"Calm yourself, Louisa."

"Don't you dare call me Louisa!"

He placed both hands upon her shoulders and butted his forehead to hers. "I told you I refuse to call you by that man's name."

She brushed aside some of her anger. "You didn't get the painting, did you?"

He shook his head and lowered himself onto the padded bench nearest the fire. "He did agree to sell me back Wycliff House -- for twice what it's worth."

"But not the portrait?"

"Not the portrait," he said.

"Then we will just have to *reclaim* it."

"I – not we – Louisa. The man's quite deranged. I don't want you anywhere near that castle."

"You should know me well enough by now to know that you cannot dictate to me."

"If you want your money, you will do as I say."

"That's not fair. We found your man. You cannot renege on my money."

He lowered his brows and spoke in a low voice. "No, I can't, and I wouldn't."

"If I can think of a clever plan to reclaim the painting, then will you allow me to accompany you?"

"I'll think on it."

"I shall, too," she said happily.

* * *

Much to Edward's consternation, he rode all the way from Woking to the Cock and Stock Inn with Miss Sinclair – dressed as a lad – sitting beside him. To make matters worse, she would not stop talking about the Bentham chap. Edward would almost welcome mention of Miss Grimm right now.

He wasn't quite sure what he was going to do once they were inside the inn. It was dark, and they could go no farther, so he could put off his decision no longer. He could not very well procure a private room for such an ill-dressed *younger brother*. He could see no other way than to get a room together. Then, blast it all, he would have to give Miss Sinclair the bed while he slept on the bloody floor.

Before they alighted from the box, he drew Miss Sinclair's attention. "I want you to know that I have no desire whatsoever to rob you of your virtue, but I believe we must share a room tonight. I promise I will not touch you in any way, I will turn my back when you dress and undress, and I will sleep on the floor."

She sighed. "I am very glad you said that for you know I could not possibly stay at such a place alone in a room. That's one of the reasons I wanted to join you on this journey. I was frightened to stay any longer on Grosvenor

Square without Louisa, and you seemed to be the only person in London I could trust."

The lady's trust could be a very heavy burden, indeed. "There was your cook," he offered, his voice hoarse. It nearly put him to the blush to remember the fat old woman following them everywhere in Harry's gig because she was too large to fit in his phaeton.

She thought on this for a moment. "All in all, I trust women. It's the men who frighten me. Miss Grimm says--"

Edward held up his hands. "Pray, no more of Miss Grimm. Let us go procure a room."

They got down and began to walk to the inn.

"No, no," Edward exclaimed. "You had better stay here while I bespeak the room. I shouldn't want the innkeeper to see your face. I'll come back for you in a moment."

After he bespoke a room, they ate quickly in the private parlor. Edward was afraid Miss Sinclair's gender would be given away either by her voice or her dainty face, the fear of which caused him to lose his appetite.

He waited until no one was near the stairs then led her up in stealthy fashion.

As soon as he shut their chamber door behind him, she started fiddling with the bedding. "What, pray tell, are you doing?" he asked.

"What does it look like I'm doing, silly? I'm going to make you a pallet."

At least he wouldn't have to sleep on the wood floors. He sat on a wobbly chair and began to take off his boots. He really was beastly tired. Nothing quite as tiring as traveling. One wouldn't think the body would ache so much from just sitting all day. He looked up from his boots and saw that

Miss Sinclair had given him two blankets and kept but one for herself. "Look here," he protested, "I can't have you doing that. One blanket is all I need. I'll stay close to the fire."

"I insist," she said in the same tone his mum had used a thousand times. "After all, I have the mattress and you don't.

Now I shall blow out the candle and put on my night things. You are to turn around and close your eyes."

She watched as he stood and turned around and shut his eyes just before the light was snuffed. He stood there silently listening to the muffled sounds she made lifting one foot and the other in the process of getting disrobed. But instead of picturing her dressed in her boys' togs, he thought of the pretty little thing in a lace shift like Ruby would wear. Then he was mad at himself for thinking of Miss Sinclair at the same time he thought of his mistress.

But he still could not dispel the vision of Miss Sinclair, all creamy skin, lifting up her arms to him – wearing Ruby's white lace.

Then he listened as she climbed beneath the sheets. He pulled off his jacket, dropped his pants and fell exhausted onto the pallet Miss Sinclair had made for him beside the fire.

Just as he was drifting into deep slumber, the lady called him.

"Yes?" he answered.

"Have you ever been in love?"

Ruby didn't count. "No." Blast the girl. He was bone tired. He closed his eyes tightly, but he was not as sleepy as he had been. He found himself thinking about her question, then he became consumed with curiosity. "Miss Sinclair?" he whispered some minutes later.

"Yes?"

"Have you?"

"Been in love?"

"Yes," he said impatiently.

"No, I don't suppose so."

Her answer comforted him like warm milk at bed time. But he still could not go back to sleep. Another question kept tugging at him. Finally he whispered her name again.

"Yes?" she answered.

"Has any man ever offered for you?"

"That's why I came to London," she said.

His heart thudded. Had she come to London to fulfill an obligation to the man?

"I heard Papa discussing settlements for me with Squire Wheeler."

Now his heart raced. "And...what were your feelings toward Squire Wheeler?"

"Why, the man was the age of my father and had grown children my age. And he was completely bald."

Edward's hand raked through his hair to assure himself he was not going bald. "What did the demmed squire think?" Edward asked with outrage. "Trying to take the virtue of a young maiden. There ought to be laws against such." Now he was beginning to sound like Miss Grimm.

"I agree with you, Mr. Coke."

As Edward went off to sleep, his fists were clenched. He rather wanted to give that bald-headed squire a facer.

$\mathscr{C}$hapter 23

When Harry had gone to bed, Louisa had been sitting beside the candle writing one of her essays, and when he awoke, she was still writing, though she wore a different dress.

Her attention perked when she saw him stirring. "I have thought of a plan, my lord."

He reached for the tea she had set on the bedside table. "Allow me my tea first, if you please." He pulled the sheets up to cover his nakedness, took a welcome gulp, then asked that she turn around while he slipped on his pantaloons. Louisa's sense of propriety, thank God, did not extend to a revulsion over bare-chested men.

With his pants on and his eyes suitably open, he turned to her. "Have you been thinking of your plan all night?"

She put down her pen. "Of course not. I will have you know I slept rather well – *and* have nearly completed Mr. Lewis's newest essay."

"Shall I have the privilege of reading it before it is published?"

"If you like." The smug contentment in her voice belied her air of complacency. He knew she was most desirous that he read it.

"What is it about?"

"It's actually more ethical than political. It's on the extinction of honesty."

His brows lowered. "You may ruffle many feathers."

She shrugged. "I don't mind that – if the essay accomplishes some good."

"Or, to quote the great Jeremy Bentham, *for the good of all.*"

"You know, my lord, that I'm not a Benthamite purist," she said with indignation.

"I do know. You also respect the rights of the individual."

She gave him a condescending nod.

He finished his tea and stood up to finish getting dressed. Louisa, returning to her essay writing, seemed to take no notice of him. He was growing so comfortable in her company that he had a sense of what it would be like to share one's life with someone else, like one did with a wife.

A pity he would never find a wife whom he could care for as much as he cared for Louisa.

When he was finished he asked, "Pray, now you may tell me of your great idea for me to reclaim my mother's portrait."

"Us."

His lips compressed. "Me, my good woman," he said sternly, "not us."

"Then I will not tell you."

"Fine," he snapped.

Seeing that he was headed to the door, Louisa put down her pen and stood. "You could at least hear my plan."

He folded his arms across his chest and gazed down the bridge of his nose at her. "Tell me your plan."

"I cannot tell you when you're standing there

impatient to leave the room. Come, sit on the bed with me."

He strode across the room and sat on the bed beside her, their thighs parallel to each others'. He noticed that his extended a good eight inches beyond hers. She truly was not much larger than a child.

"Did you not tell me that anything could be had, provided one's pockets were deep enough?"

He nodded. "I did."

"So I thought you could purchase used clothing for you and I to disguise our station in life -- that is, if you can find someone large enough for you."

"The question is whether we can find some small enough for you. That is *if* I were going to allow you to participate -- which I'm not."

She scowled at him beneath lowered brows. "Once we are dressed appropriately, you bribe the greengrocer to hide us in his wagon when he enters Gorwich Castle. While he is conducting business to distract the cook, we sneak in. Then we wait until dark. You will then remove the portrait from its frame as I stand as lookout."

"And if we're caught?"

"Then I expect the vile Lord Tremaine would merely have you thrown out as he did yesterday."

Her plan really wasn't so objectionable, after all. And she was probably correct about Tremaine throwing them out on their ears.

Harry faced Louisa, devilment in his flashing eyes. "All right. It's a good plan." He got to his feet. "Now how do I go about finding the greengrocer?"

* * *

As much as he disliked the prospect of wearing well worn homespuns, Harry knew he would have to disguise himself from the small army of footmen who had removed him from the castle the day before. The disguise became reality when he actually found clothing to fit him. Well, not really fit him since he had to tie the waist with a rope to keep the pants from falling down. The village's huge blacksmith was the only man who was close to Harry's height. The man parted with his old clothing for a guinea. The condition of the clothes the blacksmith had outgrown was poor indeed. He must have worn them daily for a dozen years. Finding clothing for Louisa proved far easier. Any number of the stable lads were clamoring to part with their old clothing for a guinea. Only one of them, however, proved to be a close match in size to Louisa, and the poor lad possessed but one suit of clothing. Louisa promised she would bring it back as soon as she could, hopefully that evening.

She made rather a cute boy, Harry thought. Of course her breasts were a bit of a problem, but he was not comfortable discussing them with her, as much as he would like to. She would likely give him a facer.

Now suitably dressed, Harry had no problem persuading the greengrocer to carry a pair of extra companions into the castle yard -- and to keep quiet about it – for a couple of quid. The ruddy man's eyes rounded when he beheld the money. It was probably more than he earned in several months.

Harry was rather surprised at how easy it was to get within the castle walls. He and Louisa each carried a basket of vegetables down to the kitchen while the regular greengrocer spoke to the cook.

From the kitchen Harry and Louisa crept up

the servants' stairway and ducked into the silver closet. Since Tremaine was reported to be reclusive, surely there would be no upcoming function for which silver must be polished. Just to be safe, Harry and Louisa hid in one of the lower cupboards--which was no problem for Louisa, but which forced Harry to nearly fold himself into a box.

They had decided to stay there until they presumed the dinner hour passed. That's when they would enter the dining room and relieve Lord Tremaine of his ill-gotten portrait.

If the drawbridge was closed at night, they were prepared to spend the night under the dining room table and leave the castle when the drawbridge lifted at the first light of dawn.

The problem was the deuced cabinet was unbearably hot and far too little for him. He decided to take his chances just *standing* in the silver closet. After all, anything could be had for a price. He would merely pay whomever discovered him to keep quiet.

Then Harry remembered the fear he had seen on the London solicitor's face when he had declined Harry's generous offer. Tremaine instilled that kind of fear in people. The butler -- or whoever found them -- would be no different, Harry realized with disappointment.

If he couldn't bribe the bloody butler or whatever servant might catch him, he would just have to tie up the servant and gag him with the rope that held up his pants. Harry had no idea how he would then hold up his pants in such an event.

"I can't stand this another minute," Harry whispered to Louisa.

"I know," she whispered. "I can barely breathe."

"I expect I'm taking all the air."

Unable to sit in the cupboard another minute, Harry got out. It felt deuced good to stretch his legs and fill his lungs with the plentiful supply of air.

Louisa followed him.

"What will we do if one of the servants comes in here?" she asked.

"We shall have to see if my pockets are deep enough."

A pity there was no window in the silver room. How would they know when night fell? Though it was only morning, the meager chamber was as dark as midnight. And to think, they would be confined here for another ten hours.

Taking Louisa's hand, he slid along the back wall to a sitting position, and she rested beside him. Once again he was filled with a protectiveness toward the slim woman who sat so close to him in the darkness. He cursed himself for allowing her to come. If something should happen to her. . .it was far too painful to contemplate. He only knew he would give his own worthless life to protect hers.

They sat in the dark stillness for an hour, neither of them needing words to bind them, for they were closer to one another than those bound by flowery phrases -- or by a vicar's ceremony.

"Harry?" she whispered finally.

Nothing she could have said would have been more welcome. He hated it when she reverted to calling him *my lord*. *Harry and Louisa* suited them and their peculiar relationship. "Yes?" he answered softly.

"I suppose when you regain Wycliff House

you'll want to start a family."

How had she known? Since the day he had reclaimed Cartmore Hall, his goal had been to find a fine woman who could bear him children, thereby fulfilling the Wycliff legacy. Until he met Louisa he had never thought to find a woman who owned his heart as his mother's heart was secured by his father. "That's been the whole point," he said.

She was silent a moment. "You want to reestablish the family that once meant so much to you," she said with an irrepressible sadness in her voice.

"You know me too well," he said curtly.

Silence hung between them. They could hear the shuffling of servants' feet outside their tiny chamber, and despite himself, each time footsteps drew near, his heart stampeded. Not for himself. Fear had always been a stranger to him, but a numbing fear for Louisa consumed him. "Perhaps you should get back in the cupboard. We can leave the door open, and I'll swiftly shut in the event our presence is detected."

"No!" she shrieked. "I believe I'd rather die with you than go on without you."

Her words swamped him in a flurry of passionate emotions. His arm slipped around her slim shoulders and his lips hungrily moved to hers.

She lifted her face to his and eagerly received his kiss.

Then he drew away from her. "Forgive me, madam."

She was silent, and he feared he had greatly offended her. "Would that I could see my watch," he said in a feeble attempt to change the direction of her thoughts. "How will we know when supper is over?"

"I expect we'll hear the sound of plates being carried back to the kitchen.

Another great period of silence fell. Poor Louisa, he thought, was just learning to trust a man for the first time in her life, and he had forced himself on her. How vile he was! Then he remembered the sweet taste of her lips – lips that had eagerly sought his. He remembered, too, the pleasure her words had given him when she had said she would rather die with him. Such thought had the power to give him hope that the proper little bluestocking did not find him so repulsive after all. He must do nothing more to repel her. She was far too precious to lose to his own carnal needs.

After the passage of more than an hour, she spoke again. "I had not realized how hungry I'd be."

He found her hand in the darkness and squeezed it. "You'll eat to your heart's content as soon as we get the painting." His stomach plummeted. What if they were caught? He had no assurances Tremaine would not prefer to mete his own punishment. Harry could not risk Louisa's safety. Suddenly, his mother's portrait seemed not worth the huge risk.

He rose to his feet. "I have lost my eagerness to reclaim my mother's portrait. If I pay Tremaine handsomely enough, perhaps he will allow me to have it copied."

"Listen," Louisa whispered, "'tis the sound of dishes."

The clatter of stacked plates tapping into one another drew closer, then faded away toward the basement. Tremaine had finished eating.

Louisa came to stand beside him. "We can get it now, Harry. You've come so far, I can't let you leave empty handed."

"It could be dangerous."

"You have no confidence in my plan," she said with disappointment.

He could envision a pout on her little rosebud mouth. He hated like the devil to squelch her confidence. "It was an excellent plan, but I seem to be too great a coward to pull it off."

"You're lying to protect me," she said. "There's not a cowardly bone in your body."

"You don't know me as well as you think."

"But I do, Harry," she said in a soft voice. Then she laid a gentle hand on his arm. "Please, Harry, let's get your mother's portrait. I assure you we'll go undetected."

She sounded so confident, his fears for her were swept away. "Very well. Shall we go for it, Mr. Lewis?"

"You remember where the dining room is?" she whispered.

"On the next floor. I believe we should take the servants' stairs."

He crowded in front of her so he could be the first out the door. He crept into the cold stone hallway and turned back to motion for her to come. Then he rounded the stairway, placing his foot on the first step. As soon as he did so, he heard two laughing maids on the landing above.

He and Louisa scurried back to the silver closet, with their ears to the door. They waited until the women had passed, then left the sanctuary of the closet once more.

This time they made it all the way up the

stairs. They saw and heard no one.

"Which way's the dining room from here, do you think?" he asked when they arrived at the central hallway.

"I believe it's on the other end of this hall," Louisa said, "but how can we avoid being seen by those footmen at the end of the corridor?"

"We can sneak into the first room, and from there I can climb out the window and make it over to the window of the dining room."

"Just because the dining room has been modernized with large windows doesn't mean the other rooms have. Do you remember how high and how small castle windows normally are?"

"You have a point there," he said.

"Not to mention we're on the second floor. You know how to climb horizontally?"

"You have another good point."

"It's a very good thing I came along with you."

They stood there at the base of another flight of back stairs with no idea how they were going to get into the dining room. After some length and a dozen faulty scenarios, he exclaimed, "I have an idea."

"What?"

"I'm afraid we'll have to use you as a distraction. You will need to try to creep along the main rooms of this level of the castle and creep up the main staircase, then distract the footmen who are on the other end of this hall."

"How can I distract them?"

"Certainly not with feminine wiles," he muttered. "Not dressed like that."

"I know! Pretending to be a boy, I'll say I'm looking for my Papa, who had business at the castle. I'll say I was playing with the baby kittens, and I fear he must have left me."

"How do you know there are baby kittens?"

"I don't." She smiled. "But they don't, either."

"There's one major problem," he said hesitantly.

"What, pray tell?"

"Your. . .your breasts." He coughed.

She looked down at her chest. If one looked closely, two smooth humps the size of small apples could be seen. "You do have a point there."

"More like two," he mumbled. "Sorry, I couldn't help myself."

She glared at him. "I suppose it's back to the silver closet. There were many rags in that room I could use to flatten my bosom by binding it."

To his consternation, his heart raced as they went down the same flight of stairs they had just climbed.

In the silver closet, Louisa took the longest rags, presented her back to Harry, shed her boy's shirt, and asked him to wrap several layers of rags tightly around her chest, tying them in the back.

It was bloody difficult not to think about her breasts, and the devil take it, he could not repress the desire to see them, to feel them. But, of course, he must.

When they were finished, it was back to the second floor. He stood near the servants' stairs while Louisa stole through the main corridor where she was supposed to distract the footmen.

Just around the corner from the two liveried servants at the other end of the hall, Harry waited and worried for the next ten minutes. It was with relief he heard Louisa's child-like voice speaking with the sentries.

With that as a distraction, Harry dropped to his belly and crawled like a snake, slithering into the first chamber. Fortunately it was the lady's study, which was a good thing, since there was no lady of the castle. He got to his feet and walked across the room, then dove to the floor again to crawl a few more feet down the hall to the dining room. Louisa's voice carried as she talked to the footmen, whom Harry felt would not be as likely to notice a dot on the ground as they would to notice a brute of man like himself strolling down the hall.

All was well, and he got safely to the red dining room, breathing a sigh of relief. He remembered the housekeeper calling it the *rose* room. The room's candles were no longer lit, but the room was not in total darkness because its large windows gave out onto the lantern-lit castle yard below.

He looked up reverently at the portrait of his mother, a lump in his throat. God, but it looked so much like her he could almost smell her lavender water and hear the soft whisper of her loving voice. He stood for a moment gazing at her elegance. The darkness of her hair contrasted against her smooth, milky flesh and ivory silken gown. It was as if her serene presence filled the room, lifting away his fears.

Then he scooted a chair over to the fireplace so he could stand on it to lift down the gilded frame of his mother's painting. It was deuced heavy, but he managed to hold on to it until it stood on the floor. Then he set about removing the canvas from the frame.

Just then the room became filled with bright candlelight.

He turned to see a dozen or so footmen, some bearing candelabra, others, swords. They flanked Tremaine, who had a sadistic grin on his face.

And Louisa was there, too, a gag over her mouth, a knife held to her throat.

$\mathcal{C}$hapter 24

Harry had stood in the face of danger any number of times but had never before experienced a fear as numbing as that which now gripped him at the sight of Louisa with a rapier poised to slit her lovely throat. He suppressed his first instinct, which was to hurl his fist into the man holding the knife to Louisa. Louisa's safety had to be his first concern.

His gaze flicked to her. She stood proudly, even regally, at the side of the towering sentry. No one save Harry, who had come to know her so thoroughly, would ever detect the worry on her sweet face.

"It seems I have outsmarted, you, Wycliff," Tremaine said. "Tell me, where did you hide all afternoon?"

Harry, the tip of a sword nipping at his chest, refused to answer.

"Never matter," Tremaine said with a wave of a bejeweled hand. "We have known you were here all day, but as I knew this room was your destination, we waited."

"I beg that you remove the rapier from the lad's throat," Harry said, watching Louisa as his fear mounted.

Tremaine threw back his head and laughed

heartily. "Come now, Wycliff, surely you don't take me for an idiot. I know your traveling companion is none other than Godwin Phillips's lovely young widow."

Harry's pulse accelerated and his mouth dropped open. "Whatever makes you think such a thing?" Harry asked, trying to sound incredulous. Anything to throw them off Louisa's scent.

"I have spies in Falwell who inform me of the activities of *Mr. and Mrs. Smith*, but it was not until you spoke of Godwin Phillips's widow yesterday that I actually knew." Tremaine's eyes were faraway. "I know the signs of a man deeply in love."

Harry realized in a flash of a second the truth in the words of the demented man. Harry knew he was, indeed, in love with Louisa.

And he had to get her out of here.

"Let us go now, Tremaine, and you'll have your fifty thousand pounds -- as well as my gentleman's pledge to never reveal your vileness. I only beg that you'll allow me to have my mother's portrait copied."

A ruthless look came over Tremaine's face. "I am sorry I will not be able to oblige you. You see, Mrs. Phillips knows too much about me and my activities. I told that fool husband of hers not to tell his wife anything, but I see he did not keep his word, which should not come as a surprise to me."

"He told her nothing," Harry countered. "Let her go. Your fight is with me, not her."

"Actually, my fight is now with both of you, though I don't think fight is the right word." Tremaine stood back and stroked his beard, glancing first at Harry then at Louisa. "You see, fight implies two somewhat equal sides, some reciprocation. But you and Mrs. Phillips will not be at liberty to strike back." He looked at the dozen huge footmen. "I have not decided quite how I am going to get rid of the pair of you. It's most difficult to dispose of an earl, even if the good people of Falwell think of you merely as *Mr. Smith.*"

"Please," Harry said, "let her go."

"I cannot do that. What I think I can do, however is lock you both away in the turret until I decide what to do with you."

Tremaine began to stroll from the room, then turned back. "Take heart, Wycliff, ever the one to encourage love, I shall let you and Mrs. Phillips die together."

* * *

At least there was a window in the turret room they were locked within, Louisa thought encouragingly. Of course, it was barred as securely as the bar slotting across the heavily timbered door.

Harry had used every bit of strength he possessed to try to dislodge the bars on the windows. Not that it would have done much good. The drop from the turret window had to be more than a hundred feet.

With the aid of moonlight, Louisa could see Harry, sitting on the stone floor. Unused to rough homespun, he had removed the shirt. She could no more remove her eyes from his magnificent body than she cold cease to draw breath. Her gaze trailed from his solid shoulders, down the taut muscles of his manly chest to his narrow waist, where a trail of dark hair disappeared beneath the rope-tied waist of the blacksmith's former pants.

She swallowed hard. "Harry?"

"No more Lord Wycliff?" he asked in a teasing voice.

"No more Lord Wycliff," she said with a sigh. "I have decided to forgive you for the life which you formerly led."

"That is welcome news indeed." He did not sound sincere. "Why, pray tell, do I warrant such approval?"

Her words came fast and with urgency. "Because we're going to die, and I can't go to my death without telling you how close I've become to you and how much I've come to care about you. That's why." She swallowed hard, thankful that Harry could not witness her humiliation.

He crossed the small room in two strides, fell to one knee in front of her and took her hand. "My dearest Louisa, I shall die a most happy man."

Then he drew her into his arms and held her close for a very long while. She could scarcely believe that he continued to whisper *my dearest love* and *my angel* into her ear as he lay a trail of kisses from her ear down to the top of her breast. Could he truly love her as she loved him? "Blast it all, Louisa, will you allow me to remove that ridiculous binding?"

She cradled his face in both her hands and solemnly nodded. After he had unwound the rags and tossed them to the cold stone floor, he took her hands and kissed them. "I am not worthy of your affection. That's why I've behaved so abominably to you at times. You're far too good for me."

She stroked the strong planes of his cheek with one hand. "Don't say that, dearest Harry. I am glad that if we have to die, we will do so together for I don't believe I could live without you."

"I think I've known since that day I first saw you that my life would be rather meaningless without you."

She came to him with both arms open, and their lips met in a hungry, wet kiss. She loved the feel of him, the taste of him, the smell. . .everything about Harry Blassingame, the Seventh Earl of Wycliff. Even if he was an aristocrat.

"I love you with all my villainous heart, my dearest love," he whispered, burying his face into her neck.

She moved closer and kissed him lightly on his mouth. "We will be together for eternity, my love."

He kissed her quickly then straightened. "Damn it all, Louisa, love, I don't want to die. Not now that I have you. Don't you see, we've got to live. I want to marry you. I want you to bear my children." He reached over and kissed her tenderly. "I want to grow old with a beautiful bluestocking at my side."

"Oh, my dearest Harry, that's the nicest thing anyone has ever said to me."

"I wanted to say it before now, but I didn't think you could stand me."

"What about when I called you *dearest Harry* when you regained consciousness after your illness?"

"I thought it was an angel who had spoken," he said teasingly. "I didn't think we'd suit because you are so fine and I'm so wicked."

"You are not wicked."

"Never mind discussions of the past. It's the future that's important now."

"But you've already examined every way you

could think of to get out of here, and you pronounced the turret impossible to escape from."

He raised a finger to his chin and drummed. "There must be a way."

"Do you think Lord Tremaine meant it when he said he'd let us die here? Think you he plans to starve us to death?"

"We shall have to see."

* * *

Not just because they were starved from not having had dinner the night before, Louisa and Harry were delighted that a heavily armed pair of menservants opened the door to the turret prison the following morning, dropped off two bowls of porridge and a slab of stale bread, then closed and locked the door.

They ate greedily, even though the porridge was cold and the bread hard.

"So we are not to be starved to death," Harry said when they finished. "That is good."

"That will give you more time to devise a plan of escape. I dare not try for my plan to get us *in* here proved to be quite disastrous."

"I will think on it," he said with authority.

Louisa leaned against the wall of their tiny room and watched her beloved Harry as he thought. She had come to love everything about him.

Finally, he said he had a plan but that it would be difficult. "Do you suppose they mean to feed us only once a day?"

She shrugged.

He came toward her and set his hands on her shoulder, kissing her gently. "It may take some time."

No more meals were served that day.

"I will assume that we will receive the meal -- I will call it that for lack of a better word -- each morning at about the same time. Do you agree?" Harry asked.

"I suppose so."

"What time would you say they came yesterday morning?"

"I have no idea," she answered. "It was still dark."

He nodded.

Harry stayed awake. He could not allow himself to go to sleep. He lay beside her, drunk with contentment and vowing to get out of here so he could live a long life with his dearest love.

When it was half past four in the morning by his watch, he left Louisa's side and attempted to climb the stone wall, but he succeeded in nothing but awakening Louisa.

"Ah, it's good that you're awake," he said. "I'm afraid I shall have to put my weight on your back."

She shot him a puzzled look. "You have to what?"

"Come here, my love."

"Now, if you will," he said when she crossed the floor, "put yourself in a dog position so I can climb on your back. I'll try to put weight on it but for a second."

She obliged him.

He looked up, then used her back rather as a springboard. One foot on her back, the other propelling his movement upward. He leaped in the air, grabbed for the long disused lantern suspended from the ceiling and caught hold of it on his first try. "Thank you, madam. Your services are no longer needed." God, but his hands stung from holding the forged iron.

She looked up at him. "What are you doing?"

"I am suspending myself above the doorway. When I hear the striking of the men's boots outside the door, I shall tuck these long legs of mine under me, then pounce on the men when they open the door. If you are able, I will need you to relieve them of their weapons, but take care not to get hurt."

She smiled up at him. "A brilliant plan, my most intelligent lord."

"I'm blasted heavy to hold."

"I suspect you are."

They waited ten minutes. His arms were killing him. They were so sore he doubted he would be able to strike a good blow when the jailers did come.

The ten minutes stretched into twenty. If it weren't for Louisa, he would have given up by now and accepted that they would never get out.

He really didn't think he could last much longer. He thought about jumping down and waiting until he heard them before launching himself from Louisa's back again. But he remembered that yesterday the men were upon them as soon as he'd heard the sound of their steps.

He had to keep holding on. God, but it was hard. The most difficult thing he had ever done. It was a wonder his arms hadn't grown ten feet long.

Then he heard the click of the jailers' heels.

He tucked his legs under himself, then stretched them out parallel to the ground, which made them higher than they would be tucked beneath them.

He heard the voice of one of the jailers. "Don't know how long the master plans to keep 'em here."

He heard the sounds of keys rattling. *Oh, God, please hurry.*

Then the door squeaked open, then open wider. The jailer with the food scanned the room for a sign of Harry.

Harry jumped on top the other jailer, the one with the drawn sword.

$\mathcal{C}$hapter 25

Edward was bloody tired of Cornwall. For three days now they had gone to nearly two dozen remote villages, surveying every livery stable in Cornwall for Harry's coach. Though they had not come upon it, they had come across a number of stable hands who vividly remembered the *grand coach and four*. It was not often one came through these parts. Harry's trail pointed steadily west.

Edward had also learned that Harry and Mrs. Phillips were traveling as Mr. and Mrs. Smith. Such a piece of information might or might not come in handy.

He shot a stealthy glance at Miss Sinclair. At least Harry had the pleasure of traveling with a lady. A woman who dressed as a woman, breasts and all. And he would wager Harry had not had to sleep on any wooden floors, either. If he knew Harry as he thought he knew Harry, his cousin had gotten beneath Mrs. Phillips's skirts by now.

He glanced at Miss Sinclair and sighed. None of his friends would believe he could travel for days on end with a young woman, share a bedchamber with her, and not get beneath her skirts. Or in Miss Sinclair's case, beneath her pants.

But when he came to think on it, he realized he would never discuss this trip with Miss Sinclair to anyone. Do her unpardonable harm. And he couldn't have that.

For the past half hour Miss Sinclair had expounded on the finer points of Jeremy Bentham's series of talks. Glad of it he was. For in her retelling, he thought he actually understood what the deuced man had been saying. Not that he really cared, but he might be called upon to discuss it with Miss Sinclair, and he really did not like to sound like a bloody moron.

She stopped talking, and things got quiet. Too quiet by far. He had grown accustomed to Miss Sinclair's prattling. Finally, she started up again. "I was wondering, Mr. Coke. . ."

"Yes?"

"Well, I was wondering if you would like to share the bed tonight." Before he could respond, she explained herself. "You have proven yourself as a true gentleman, and I am sure it must be difficult for you to ride all day when your body must ache from sleeping on a floor the night before."

His mind streaked ahead to tonight. Unfortunately, he responded below the waist. It really would not do to share a bed with Miss Sinclair. After all, she unbound those breasts at night. . .and one morning when he woke before her he saw that she slept in a thin linen lawn under which he clearly saw the outline of her nipples.

He was not a strong enough man to resist such a temptation. And, besides, he had no desire to nurse for the rest of the journey the black eye Miss Sinclair was sure to deliver him. "I don't mind the floor at all," he lied. His debauching ways would be the end of him yet.

"Oh," she said meekly. She almost sounded disappointed.

They rode for another great while with her saying no more to him. He excessively disliked a quiet Miss Sinclair. And he also feared he had upset her.

Therefore it was with relief he heard her call him. "Mr. Coke?"

"Yes," he said, smiling because she did not appear to sound angry.

"You must tell me of your other brave deeds."

"Other?"

"Racing through the whole of West England in singlehanded pursuit of evil-doers is a most brave thing, to be sure."

"Now, Miss Sinclair, we do not know that your sister and Harry have come upon evil-doers."

"But if they have, you are bravely prepared to deal with them."

He stuck out his chest with self importance "That I am most assuredly, Miss Sinclair."

They rode but a short distance more when she asked, "Have you ever fought a duel, Mr. Coke?"

How he wished he could tell her an elaborate tale about dueling with swords on Primrose Hill over a lady's honor, but, alas, he could not lie to Miss Sinclair. "I have not had that pleasure," he said sadly. That did not come out at all as he had wanted it to.

"See what I mean! You are so brave that to you a duel is a pleasure."

She really was an awfully clever girl. "Rest assured," he said, "that I am well prepared if a duel should present itself."

"You are trained in swords?"

No nodded cockily. "And with pistols."

Filled with wonder, her face lifted to his. Quite a taking thing she was, too.

Enough talk about him. The girl would take him for a braggart, and he couldn't have that.

He looked at the sky and saw the sun had dropped lower. They would be lucky to reach Falwell before dark.

* * *

Taken completely by surprise, the armed guard crashed to the ground. Harry quickly relieved the man of his weapon, put his boot on the fallen man's stomach, and probed his chest with the sword's tip. In the meantime, the man carrying the food had dropped it in his haste to draw his weapon, but Louisa had been too fast for him. She quickly drew his sword from its sheath and held it to his chin.

She was not at all sure if the food-bearer's look of complete surprise was due to the dangerous situation he found himself in or to the discovery that the lad had breasts. For the man could not remove his eyes from the humps beneath her boy's shirt.

"Back him into a corner, my love," Harry ordered. Waving the sword swiftly at him, the man, his eyes huge and his arms raised, backed up until his shoulder bumped into the cold stone. At the same time, Harry backed up his man until the two guards were shoulder-to-shoulder against the wall.

"Pray that you do not learn of my legendary skill with a sword," Harry said to the men. "Louisa, my dear, find your bindings, if you will, and tie the men's hands behind their backs."

She did as instructed and still had more strips

of cloth left. For good measure, she thoroughly gagged each man.

"Good job, my love," Harry commended.

She and Harry backed out of the cell. The keys had been left in the lock. They locked the door and took the keys with them.

It was still dark, so hopefully many in the house would still be sleeping. They would have better luck exiting by the main door at this hour. It was too early for the butler and footmen to be about. At the back door they were sure to run into the scullery maids.

Under the blanket of darkness, they moved quietly through the castle, going first down the main staircase, then across the great hall, then through the vestibule.

She worried that the castle's main door, a huge timbered affair hinged with heavy forged iron, would be locked, but it was not. They passed right through it into the castle yard.

That is when Louisa was most thankful for the dark, for a number of men were about in the castle yard, including the man churning down the drawbridge.

Harry's arm shot out to stop her progress forward. "We'll wait here in the dark until he finishes and is gone," Harry whispered.

The bruising hulk of a man soon finished, then strolled across the castle yard away from Harry and Louisa.

Louisa's glance darted to the drawbridge some fifteen yards away. If no one were around she and Harry could run and easily be off the castle grounds in a matter of seconds. Then they could run like the wind until they reached Falwell.

They looked in all directions until they were

sure no one was near. The need for haste increased, for with every second the sun rose higher and the light grew brighter.

"Now!" Harry whispered.

The two of them stole slowly across the bricks between them and the drawbridge, careful to stay close to the building. Once their feet touched the wood of the drawbridge, they took off running, praying that no one saw them.

They both ran as hard and as fast as they could, peering over their shoulders to assure themselves they were not being followed. Harry, of course, was faster than she, but once they had clear vision of the castle behind them, he stopped and waited for her.

Arm in arm, the ill-dressed couple walked to the Speckled Goose Inn, where all the guests still slept. The only sounds heard were those coming from the kitchen. They tiptoed up the stairway, entered their bedchamber, and changed into clothing appropriate to their station.

When he went to the local magistrate, it would be as one peer charging another. "I'm warning you now," he said to Louisa, "our days of sharing a room as Mr. and Mrs. Smith are over. Very soon, we shall share a chamber as Lord and Lady Wycliff – if you'll do me the very great honor of consenting to become my wife."

"Of course I shall have to become your wife. I *am* a reformer, and you must own, you do need reforming."

The magistrate already knew what a nasty piece of work Lord Tremaine was, and Harry brought him a statement of charges that would stand up in a court of their peers – rather what the magistrate had been hoping for.

Once Harry had given his statement, he told Louisa he wished to be on the road before Tremaine's evil henchman came after them. One quick meal in the private parlor, and they would be off.

Louisa was disappointed to see two seated men -- or were they boys? -- facing the fire, their backs to them. She was disappointed because she had thought of it as *their* private parlor since there were no other persons of Quality staying at the inn. Harry led her to the table farthest away from the fire so they could enjoy privacy.

She and Harry held hands as they waited for the serving maid. Feeling thoroughly content, she smiled up at Harry. "I believe Mrs. Winston may have been a most intelligent observer, after all."

He smiled back.

The serving maid re-entered the room to bring the pair at the front their ale. Louisa could have sworn she heard a familiar voice. "Does not that lad sound much like my sister?"

Harry cocked his head and listened. "By God, that's Edward! Know his voice anywhere."

$\mathcal{C}$hapter 26

Frozen to her seat, Louisa watched as Harry leapt to his feet and crossed the room. "Edward Coke, what are you doing here? You're supposed to be keeping an eye on Miss Sinclair in London."

First Edward turned around to meet his gaze. Then the boy turned. And he was Ellie!

Edward stood, kicking his chair back as he did so. "I will have you know I have come here with my future wife."

Now Ellie stood. "Your what, Mr. Coke?"

Edward turned to Ellie. "I am not so dishonorable a gentleman to travel all the way to Cornwall with a young lady and not offer marriage."

"Then you will marry me solely for the sake of propriety?"

"Told you I was an honorable man, Miss Sinclair."

Her hands thrust to her hips, Ellie glared at him. "You can forget your *noble* offer, sir! I would not marry you were you the last man in England."

"But. . ." he stammered, throwing a questioning glance at his cousin as Ellie stomped off to sit down with her sister.

"Oh, Louisa, I am so glad you are unhurt. Has your quest been successful?"

"How did you know of the quest?"

"That. . ." Ellie elevated her brows haughtily, "that horrid man told me."

"Mr. Coke?"

Ellie nodded. Then the two women turned to see the cousins talking animatedly.

"You mean you actually had Aunt Isobel's portrait in your hands?" Edward asked.

"Yes," Harry said, clapping a hand on his cousin's back. "Have you eaten yet?"

"No, and I could eat an ox."

"Then we must order two," Harry said, walking toward the table shared by the two women. "Let's all sit together and eat. It's very good to see you, Edward."

They did not eat two oxen, but they did go through enough food to feed half the village of Falwell. And throughout the dinner, Harry narrated the events of the last two days.

Most impressed over his cousin's cunning in extricating himself from the turret room, Edward hastened to brag on what good time he had made coming from London, despite being slowed down with a lady.

"You were not slowed down by me. I *wasn't* a lady!" Dropping her mouth, Ellie amended her statement. "That is, I behaved as a boy the duration of the journey." Then, pouting, she said, "I mean. . ." then faltered.

Harry laughed and squeezed Louisa's hand.

Edward watched smugly, then whispered to Harry. "Knew you'd succeed with the bluestocking."

"The bluestocking, my dear Edward, is the next Countess of Wycliff."

Edward had been in the process of swallowing

a swig of ale. At this announcement, he spit it out. "The hell you say! You cannot be serious."

"Never been more serious or more in love in my life."

"Do you agree to this match?" Ellie asked Louisa.

Louisa nodded happily. "Oh, yes."

This time Ellie spit out her ale.

All was silent the next few minutes, then Ellie spoke, "I beg you will allow me to ride home in your carriage, Lord Wycliff. The thought of returning with the *noble* Mr. Coke is quite repugnant to me."

"I am sure you'll be far more comfortable in my carriage than in Edward's curricle."

Louisa patted Ellie's hand. "Yes, my pet, and you will have to tell me all about Mr. Bentham's talks."

"Lucky Harry," Edward lamented, rolling his eyes. "Timing your journey so it just happened to coincide with the silly Bentham man's talks. I believe you'd fight wild tigers rather than sit in the room with all those bloody bluestockings."

Her heart shattered, Louisa looked from Edward to Harry. And with a sickening realization knew that Edward did not speak in jest.

Harry's face went white as Edward spoke.

From the look on his cousin's face, Edward knew he had said something wrong. "Why. . .if the two of you are to be married and knowing your feelings about honesty in marriage, I assumed Mrs. Phillips knew your true feelings toward the reformers." Edward swallowed hard. "I can see now that she does not."

Louisa rose, pulling her sister with her. "Mr. Coke, I beg that you take me back to London. I

cannot ride home with your. . .your odious
cousin!"

"And I *will* ride home with your odious cousin,"
Ellie asserted. "Riding with a liar is preferable
than riding with an insincere snake."

Edward's shoulders slumped. "I seem to be
putting my well shod boots into my mouth rather
thoroughly."

"I beg a word with you, Louisa," Harry
implored.

She turned to him, her eyes hollow, her voice
hard. "You can say nothing to me, my lord, for I
shall never believe you again."

"But, Louisa--"

She turned her back to him and stormed from
the parlor. The groom had brought the gig, and
Louisa hitched herself up into it without
assistance from Edward. He got in on the other
side, took up his crop and drove the horse from
the inn yard.

As he had coming, Edward made excellent --
even better -- time returning to London. For the
first several hours, Louisa choked back tears.
From the beginning, Harry had been lying to her.
He possessed none of the qualities she had
credited him with. She had only been a pawn in
his game of reclaiming the family riches. Had he
even meant it when he told her he loved her, or
had it been a sham?

Every tree, every blade of glass they passed
reminded her of the journey over this same land
with Harry by her side.

She and Edward had to spend but three nights
at inns -- where they secured separate rooms.
Sharing a room with a man would only have

reminded her of all the nights she and Harry had slept together.

She should have trusted her original instincts. There was no such thing as a trustworthy man.

On the second day, she began to ask Edward about his and Ellie's trip.

"It would have been bloody boring, indeed, miles and miles of bleak scenery, if you ask me. Thank goodness for Miss Sinclair's lively recounting of the Bentham man's talks. First time I ever understood him was through El-- er, I mean, through Miss Sinclair's intelligent comments. You should be proud of your sister. Got a head on those pretty shoulders. Never thought I'd ever be interested in a smart woman, but now I don't think I'd want one who wasn't."

Pretty shoulders? Could Edward Coke be smitten over Ellie? Was that *really* why he stepped forth with an offer to marry Ellie?

"Tell me, Mr. Coke," Louisa began coyly, "was it difficult procuring a room for the lad Ellie pretended to be?"

He coughed, and she wasn't certain, but she thought he blushed. "Actually, I didn't like to think of her alone in a strange inn. She's such a tiny, helpless little thing, you know. And she wasn't keen on it, either. Never saw a gal with fears as great as hers. A good thing she trusted me. . .then." His face fell.

"Sir, I believe you are in love with my sister."

"In love with your sister?" he said incredulously. "I admit we have grown close, and I am truly fond of her, but love?" He whipped at the horse. "Never gave it a thought."

"A pity because I believe my sister is very fond of you."

"She told you so?" he asked.

Louisa would swear there was hope in his question. "Not exactly, but I know my sister quite well."

"You are, after all, almost a ringer for her."

She smiled.

He waited for ten minutes before he decided to continue the conversation. "If it wouldn't be too much trouble for you, I would be obliged if you could. . ."

"Ask Ellie what her feelings are toward you?"

He shrugged. "I would hate her to have any hard feelings toward me. After all, we did share a bedchamber together -- quite innocently, I assure you. I slept on the floor."

"Then I was much kinder to Lord Wycliff."

He blushed.

She giggled. "It was all quite chaste. Your cousin was a gentleman. A pity he's a liar. And a pirate."

"Former pirate. You're the only other person he's ever told about the source of his wealth."

"A pity I cannot be gratified that he was only partially dishonest to me."

* * *

When Louisa reached the Grosvenor Square House, Harry was waiting for her on the pavement. "I have to talk to you, Louisa," he said.

Refusing to make eye contact with him, she brushed past him as if he were invisible. She walked up the two steps, opened the door herself, then called back to him. "My butler will tell you I am not in, my lord."

Then she slammed the door on him.

Ellie ran down the stairs, threw her arms around Louisa's neck, then burst into tears.

Tears springing to her own eyes, Louisa held her close. "I know. You have fallen in love with Edward Coke, have you not?"

"Yes I have," Ellie said through sobs. "And it's not at all pleasant as I thought it would be."

Louisa held Ellie with straightened arms and wiped a tear. "That, my pet, is because you acted very foolish."

"How?"

"By getting mad at Mr. Coke when he offered for you."

"But he didn't offer for me. He only said what he said because he was obliged to!"

"Come, my pet, he was obliged to offer for someone dressed as a boy?"

"What are you trying to say?"

"That whether he was consciously aware of it or not, Edward Coke is in love with you."

"Did he tell you that?"

"That is not what matters, pet. Your feelings are all I care about. If you truly love someone, you must put aside foolish pride. Are you willing to do that?"

Ellie burst out crying again. "He's all I could think of with every churn of Lord Wycliff's carriage wheels. Every village and every rock seemed to bring back memories of our journey together. I've never in my life enjoyed myself so excessively."

Louisa held her close. "I know, my pet."

"What should I do?"

"Mr. Coke made the first move when he offered for you. Since I've always promoted honesty above everything and never believed in feminine coyness, I believe you should make the next move and tell Mr. Coke your true feelings."

She handed Ellie a handkerchief.

Ellie dried her tears. "I don't know how I shall do that, but I must."

$\mathcal{C}$hapter 27

During the following week, Harry called every day at the Grosvenor Square house, but the butler's grim reply was always the same. *Mrs. Phillips is not in.* After that week, he did not call any more.

When it was clear to Louisa that Harry would not call again, Louisa convinced herself that his remonstrances were merely to assuage his conscience. While he would resume the usual practices of men of fashion, she felt she had nothing to return to. The pain in her heart was irreparable. She lost interest in her Tuesday meetings with the bluestockings. She did not feel like writing essays. She spent a great deal of time dwelling on the month she and Harry had spent together in Cornwall. Every glance, every conversation that had passed between them continued to invade her thoughts. And the intimacy they had shared invaded her dreams.

Ellie, too, was glum and full of remorse over her refusal of Mr. Coke. Like Louisa, she spent hours on end reliving in her mind those few glorious days she had spent with the most wonderful man on earth. She had decided that Louisa was right. She was the one who needed to make the first step toward repairing the damage, but she did not know how, nor did she know if such a move would meet with any success at all. It wasn't as if Mr. Coke were beating her door down, as Lord Wycliff was doing for Louisa.

Ellie had rather resigned herself to the fact that she and Louisa would live a most sedentary life together. No more gentlemen of quality paying morning calls. No reason whatsoever to dress fashionably for no one who mattered would ever see them. So it was that she and Louisa were sitting in the drawing room sewing one afternoon when Williams informed them that he had shown Mr. Coke into the morning room.

Looking at Louisa, he said, "Your denial to Lord Wycliff did not extend to his companion, did it?"

Smiling, Louisa assured him that Mr. Coke was most welcome. Then, turning to Ellie, she said, "It appears you will have your chance with Mr. Coke. It is hoped you will not destroy it -- for you may never get another." Inwardly, Louisa ached with her own regrets. Perhaps she *had* been too unwavering with Harry. But she knew her chance was long gone. Harry had already lost interest in her.

Ellie leaped to her feet, her hands on her cheeks. "I cannot go to him like this. Just look at what a horrid sight I am!"

Louisa laughed. "You are not, my pet. You always look lovely." She took Ellie's hand. "Remember, Mr. Coke made his offer to you when you were dressed like a lad. I think he loves you however you look."

"Pshaw!" Ellie protested.

"Trust me." Louisa squeezed her hand. "Mr. Coke will find you beautiful."

* * *

Edward had never been so nervous in his life. It had taken him a week to gather the courage to come see Miss Sinclair, then another week to think of an excuse for his visit.

When Miss Sinclair walked into the morning room, the air nearly swished from his lungs, fairly robbing him of breath. Demmed but she was a deuced fine looking girl. Or was eighteen considered a woman? Her looks were so extraordinary, she even made a fine looking lad. At the thought of her dressed as a lad, sitting up beside him on the box hour upon hour, he grew melancholy. Never before in his life had he wished to turn back the clock. Until now.

His throat grew dry. His pulse accelerated. "How very good it is to see you again, Miss Sinclair."

As graceful as a swan gliding across a pond, Miss Sinclair strolled to him and offered him her hand.

He took it in both of his hands and bent to kiss it. When he came back up, his face was flaming. He could not even remember what excuse he had come up with to explain his presence. Fortunately, she did not ask for one. "How very good it is to see you again, Mr. Coke," Ellie said, her eyes alive and dancing. "Won't you please sit down."

He sat on one of the twin settees that faced each other in the middle of the room, and Miss Sinclair sat on the other one.

"I see the fine weather we enjoyed on our journey to Cornwall has continued," she commented.

"Yes. Very fine indeed." Then he had no idea what he was going to say next.

"You have enjoyed good health?" she asked.

"Excellent. You?"

She sighed. "Physically, quite excellent." Then she took a deep breath and continued. "I find myself reminiscing with unexpected fondness over the journey you and I took together." She could not meet him in the eye.

A smiled flashed across his face. "It is the same with me! I find I think most fondly of the journey."

"Not just the journey," she said coyly. "The degree of closeness we gained -- you and I -- during the journey. I have found that I enjoyed that excessively."

"'Twas the same with me! I'd give my next quarterly to do it again."

"A pity I was so beastly proud when you felt compelled to offer for me, for I believe I should very much have enjoyed being married to you." She had not been able to look him in the eye when she spoke.

He leaped to his feet, bounded across the patterned carpet, and dropped to one knee in front of her. He took her hands in his. "It's the same with me, Ellie." He looked up into her smiling face.

"Oh, Edward, I am so very happy to hear you say that. Would it be too presumptuous of me to ask you to procure a special license so we could be wed quickly? I find myself wanting to be with you every minute of the day."

He rose up and joined her on the settee. "I will have it today."

Then he took her in his arms and kissed her soundly.

* * *

The following week, they married one morning

at St. George's Hanover Square. Louisa and Harry stood up with them. It was the first time Louisa and Harry had seen one another since the day she returned to London.

After the ceremony, he said, "I beg that you will allow me to escort you back to the house."

To protest would only be to make things difficult for everyone.

She allowed him to hand her up to his carriage. They rode in silence for the first block. "You might be interested to know," he began, "That I alerted the House of Lords about Tremaine's murder attempt."

"Had the magistrate confronted the vile man?"

"We did together, just as soon as I saw you off with Edward."

Her hand flew to her heart, and she directed a frightened gaze at him.

"You'll be pleased to know Tremaine is now being incarcerated. I don't know if I'll ever regain Wycliff House, but doing so is no longer as important as it once was to me."

Her pulse quickened. What, then, was important to him? "What of your mother's portrait?"

He smiled. "I have it."

"Lord Tremaine gave it to you?" she asked incredulously.

His eyes danced with mischief. "Let's just say I convinced the magistrate it was my property, and I actually filed a theft complaint against Tremaine."

"But, Harry, the man will find a way to kill you!"

He lifted a brow. "You care?"

She sat up ramrod straight. "Not at all."

"Then don't worry your pretty head. Tremaine is terminally ill. The doctors don't give him another month."

Her eyes narrowed. "Good!"

They grew silent again. Then Harry said, "Your anger toward me for my lack of sincerity in your causes was well placed. It made me start thinking, trying to analyze what my own positions were on the causes you promulgate."

"And?"

"And I realized that you really had won me over despite my initial reluctance. I admit that I had no intentions of taking my seat in the House of Lords, and I especially had no intentions of embracing your radical politics.

"But the more I thought on it, the more I realized how right you have been all along. I came to know that I was obligated to work toward all those reforms you and I had discussed. The extension of the franchise. Restrictions on child labor. Penal reform. Compulsory education. All the things I had initially laughed at behind your back."

"You are not lying to me to *get beneath my skirts*," she asked, looking up to him with smiling eyes.

He stopped. Right there in the middle of Piccadilly Road. "I will never lie to you again."

"Would that I could believe you," she uttered.

Traffic grew snarled behind them, and harsh voices shouted at him.

All of which he seemed oblivious to.

"I have taken my seat in Parliament," he announced. "That I am a Whig, I thought, would make you happy."

Her heart was bursting with joy and love. "I

can think of no better wedding present," she said. When he did not respond for moment, she began to tremble. Had she horridly embarrassed herself with her forwardness?

She watched as Harry set down his riding crop, turned to her, took her into his arms and kissed her slowly and passionately.

Neither of them minded -- nor even seemed to hear -- the angry shouts from behind them on Piccadilly Road. "Perhaps Miss Grimm has been right all along," he said. "I do aim to get beneath your skirts -- after you're Lady Wycliff, that is."

THE END

Author's Biography

A former journalist who, in her own words, has "a fascination with dead Englishwomen," Cheryl Bolen is the award-winning author of more than a dozen historical romance novels set in Regency England, including *Marriage of Inconvenience, My Lord Wicked*, and *A Duke Deceived*. Her books have received numerous awards, such as the 2011 International Digital Award for Best Historical Novel and the 2006 Holt Medallion for Best Historical. She was also a 2006 finalist in the Daphne du Maurier for Best Historical Mystery. Her works have been translated into eleven languages and have been Amazon.com bestsellers. Bolen has contributed to *Writers Digest* and *Romance Writers Report* as well as to the Regency era–themed newsletters *The Regency Plume, The Regency Reader*, and *The Quizzing Glass*. The mother of two grown sons, she lives with her professor husband in Texas.

Printed in Great Britain
by Amazon.co.uk, Ltd.,
Marston Gate.